"Moral Divorce"
and Other Stories
by Jacinto Octavio Picón

Portrait of Jacinto Octavio Picón in the Ateneo de Madrid. Artist: Emilio Sala Francés. Photo by Robert M. Fedorchek. Courtesy, Ateneo de Madrid.

"Moral Divorce" and Other Stories
by Jacinto Octavio Picón

Translated from the Spanish by
Robert M. Fedorchek

In Collaboration with
Pedro S. Rivas Díaz

Introduction by
Gonzalo Sobejano

Lewisburg
Bucknell University Press
London and Toronto: Associated University Presses

© 1995 by Robert M. Fedorchek

All rights reserved. Authorization to photocopy items for internal or personal use, or the internal or personal use of specific clients, is granted by the copyright owner, provided that a base fee of $10.00, plus eight cents per page, per copy is paid directly to the Copyright Clearance Center, 222 Rosewood Drive, Danvers, Massachusetts 01923. [0-8387-5299-3/95 $10.00+8¢ pp, pc.]

Associated University Presses
440 Forsgate Drive
Cranbury, NJ 08512

Associated University Presses
25 Sicilian Avenue
London WC1A 2QH, England

Associated University Presses
P.O. Box 338, Port Credit
Mississauga, Ontario
Canada L5G 4L8

The paper used in this publication meets the requirements of the American National Standard for Permanence of Paper for Printed Library Materials Z39.48-1984.

Library of Congress Cataloging-in-Publication Data

Picón, Jacinto Octavio, 1852–1923.
  "Moral divorce" and other stories / by Jacinto Octavio Picón ; translated from the Spanish by Robert M. Fedorchek, in collaboration with Pedro S. Rivas Díaz ; introduction by Gonzalo Sobejano.
    p.   cm.
  Includes bibliographical references.
  ISBN 0-8387-5299-3 (alk. paper)
  1. Picón, Jacinto Octavio, 1852–1923—Translations into English.
I. Fedorchek, Robert M., 1938–   . II. Rivas Díaz, Pedro S.
III. Title.
PQ6629.I3A6   1995
863'.5—dc20   94-28807
                                                               CIP

PRINTED IN THE UNITED STATES OF AMERICA

This translation is for Don Juan Manuel Ortiz Picón,
grandson of Don Jacinto Octavio Picón.

Contents

Translator's Foreword	9
Acknowledgments	15
Introduction	
Gonzalo Sobejano	17
The Irreverent Nun	29
Keep Holy the Sabbath Day	39
The Last Confession	43
A Matter of Conscience	48
The Lady and the Storms	63
An Act of Revenge	72
The Wreaths	81
Moral Divorce	88
Disillusion	96
The Overdressed Woman	133
The Prudent Woman	141
Sacrifice	151
Love Cure	158
Elvira-Nicolasa	165
The Threat	173
A Wise Man	179
Pepita	186
Eve	193
The Partner	197
Duty	203
The Portrait	211
Notes	218
Select Bibliography	220

Translator's Foreword

An examination of the nineteenth-century Spanish short story looks, at first glance, like a reduced mirror image of an examination of the nineteenth-century Spanish novel. With the exception of Gustavo Adolfo Bécquer, virtually all of the *cuentistas* are *novelistas* whose short prose fiction generally exhibits the same characteristics—of theme, style, and form—as their long fiction. But not all of these novelists achieved prominence as short story writers. According to Mariano Baquero Goyanes, in a study published nearly a half century ago, Clarín did, Armando Palacio Valdés did, and Emilia Pardo Bazán did.[1] Today we can safely say that, despite an occasional—and even, in some cases, memorable—story, Benito Pérez Galdós did not. And today how many readers are there, except for scholars and academics, of the short stories of Antonio de Trueba, Felipe Trigo, José Ortega Munilla, José Echegaray, and Eugenio Sellés? Although Fernán Caballero, Luis Coloma, José María de Pereda, Juan Valera, and Vicente Blasco Ibáñez would be included in any anthology of the nineteenth-century Spanish short story, they would be overshadowed by a number of the stories of Pedro Antonio de Alarcón, some of whose tales ("The Nun" ["La comendadora"] and "The Fortune" ["La buenaventura"] and "The French Sympathizer" ["El afrancesado"]) have become classics.

What, then, of Jacinto Octavio Picón, whose novels are undergoing reevaluation? In 1976 Gonzalo Sobejano published a much cited edition of Picón's *Sweet and Tasty* [*Dulce y sabrosa*][2] and praised, in passing, his short prose fiction; in 1986 Noël M. Valis published an insightful analysis of Picón's novels and praised, in passing, his short stories.[3] Clearly the latter merit reconsideration. Not as readily available as the stories of Clarín, Palacio Valdés, and Pardo Bazán[4]—no modern editions have been published—the stories of Jacinto Octavio Picón deserve to be examined again to determine why they appear so modern, why they speak to our age, why, in brief, they seem—in outlook—timeless.

The Revolution of 1868 toppled Isabel II from the Spanish throne and ushered in freedom of thought and conscience that gave rise to the much debated "religious question." Alarcón, Clarín, Galdós, Palacio Valdés, Pardo Bazán, Pereda, Picón, and Valera all wrote novels that probe religion's underbelly. And religion is Catholicism, a force so rooted in Spain's history and culture, from the Reconquest to the Inquisition to the Discovery and exploitation of the New World, that it is as much a part of Spanish artistic life as it is of Spanish spiritual life.

Some of Picón's novels (*The Enemy* [*El enemigo*], *Lázaro*, and *Sweet and Tasty*) were considered rabidly anticlerical, particularly by ecclesiastics concerned with protecting vested interests, but he was exposing abuses and criticizing messengers, not the message— and he does the same in his stories. "The Irreverent Nun" questions the meaning of charity as a convent contends with native sons who have been wounded fighting the forces of Napoleon during the War of Independence. The sisters open their doors in response to a threat, not from any spontaneous outpouring of compassion that would reflect love of God and His creatures; and the one nun who does rally her efforts to aid the maimed, bloody victims of the French meets with an unexpected fate. "Keep Holy the Sabbath Day" does, on the other hand, represent compassion as well as generosity of spirit. Don Cándido is a village priest who understands the hard work of stonecutters; what he does not understand initially is the need to work on the Lord's day, and when he does understand, he realizes that he must open up more than his pocketbook to help a breadwinner support his family. This is a good minister, a humble minister who lives the message. "The Last Confession" depicts the severity of an uncompromising messenger, a confessor who sees evil in a home situation that does not conform to his rigid notion of family structure. His malevolence alienates and embitters a young woman who refuses to allow a pure love to be sullied.

One of the constants in Picón's novels[5] and short stories is his espousal of greater freedom—personal and sexual—for women. In a number of his tales they are variously deceived and duped by men, but when these wronged women are courageous enough to fight back they run into the well-fortified wall of society's disapproval or risk ostracism. Not only do they incur the wrath of men, they invite, as well, the censure of other women whose ingrained submissiveness cannot cope with the independent identity of their protesting sisters. In "Moral Divorce" Rosa Castilla, a married woman, learns that her husband is a swindler, but what can she do with her outrage in the light of his denials? Can she live with a fraud? Since (legal) divorce, which Picón supports, is impossible, Rosa takes a stand that flies in the face of convention, a stand that, while it earns her reproach, allows her to hold her head high. In "Disillusion" Soledad argues for sexual equality and suffers the consequences of being a woman of mettle, as her independence of thought and spiritual (as well as physical) courage raise formidable barriers for insecure men. Enriqueta, "The Overdressed Woman," is cheated out of her rightful inheritance before she can marry and has little recourse— other than a convent or prostitution—except to become a kept woman; in a conversation with the narrator she makes the pointed observation that free love, which Picón also supports, is censured while adultery, the hypocrisy of the age, is winked at. In "The Prudent Woman" Manolita bemoans the lot of women because they are unable to learn about a future husband's moral makeup *before* marriage, and the simple, obvious reason is that they do not enjoy the same freedom of movement as men. And in "Sacrifice" María del Amparo learns that some calculating men discard a woman as a possible marriage partner if she does not represent financial gain. All these female protagonists are heroines if we think of heroines as women of courage and bravery, and all are liberationists if we think of liberationists as women (and men) who promote equality of the sexes. In this, Picón was a modernist, like Pardo Bazán, several of whose stories ("The Torn Lace" ["El encaje roto"] and "The Faithful Fiancée" ["La novia fiel"]) echo those of a man who proclaimed the moral superiority of women.[6]

Stories of conscience, of psychological inquiry, abound in Picón: the road to justice ("A Matter of Conscience"), the affront that provokes revenge ("An Act of Revenge"), the anguish of early widowhood ("The Wreaths"), the unexpected discovery ("A Wise Man"), the coquette ("The Lady and the Storms"), the dreamer and realist who complement one another ("Love Cure"), the past-his-prime Don Juan duped by a young girl ("Pepita"), the nature of gratitude ("The Portrait"), a mother's love ("Duty"), a philanderer ("The Partner"), illicit love ("Eve"), and the country girl

("Elvira-Nicolasa") who is corrupted in the big city. And there is yet one more kind of story of conscience to be found in Picón—stories that look at society and find it wanting. Many of his tales originally appeared in Madrid's *El liberal,* and in the preface to *Stories from My Day* [*Cuentos de mi tiempo*] he explains that the newspaper's political orientation prompted him to fight "like an army private"[7] for the ideas in which he believed and the causes that he espoused. In "The Threat," for example, he takes up the cudgels on behalf of an oppressed proletariat; what happens to Gasparón on a factory floor is bad enough, but callous treatment at the hands of insensitive owners push his fellow workers toward extremes to remedy a blatant wrong. But Gasparón refuses to be a party to violence and labels it a coward's act, a coward's solution; he determines a different course of action and converts his tragedy into society's open wound. The dual themes of injustice and repression become an indictment.

A bibliophile and a Francophile (his mother was French); a native of Madrid who loved Paris; a member of the Royal Spanish Academy (of the Spanish language) and the (San Fernando) Royal Academy of Fine Arts (he published a volume of art criticism entitled the *Life and Works of Don Diego Velázquez*); a novelist, short story writer, and journalist; a liberal (in politics, religion, social philosophy); a Spaniard steeped in his own literature (from Cervantes to Galdós) but knowledgeable about others; an aesthete whose appreciation of French cooking prompted Emilia Pardo Bazán (probably tongue-in-cheek) to provide a recipe for a "Jacinto Octavio Omelette" in her *Modern Spanish Cuisine*[8]; a friend of literary greats of his time (Clarín, Galdós, Palacio Valdés, Pardo Bazán, Valera, etc.); and a loving father whose son's premature death at the age of forty nearly drove him to despair, Jacinto Octavio Picón deserves to be read anew, for in his stories he deals with timeless and universal themes—freedom, justice, equality, compassion, suffering, love, and hope.

* * *

Original Spanish story titles appear at the top of each story.

Translator's Foreword

Words and passages marked with an asterisk (*) in the text are explained in the Notes at the end.

NOTES

1. Mariano Baquero Goyanes, *El cuento español del siglo XIX* (Madrid: CSIC, 1949), p. 177.
2. Gonzalo Sobejano, Introduction to *Dulce y sabrosa* by Jacinto Octavio Picón (Madrid: Cátedra, 1976), pp. 34–35.
3. Noël M. Valis, *The Novels of Jacinto Octavio Picón* (Lewisburg, PA: Bucknell University Press, 1986), pp. 191 and 199.
4. Clarín, *Treinta relatos*, ed. Carolyn Richmond (Madrid: Espasa-Calpe, 1983) and *El señor y lo demás, son cuentos*, ed. Gonzalo Sobejano (Madrid: Espasa-Calpe, 1988); Palacio Valdés, *Aguas fuertes* (Madrid: Fax, 1947), *Papeles del doctor Angélico* (Madrid: Fax, 1946), *Seducción* (Madrid: Fax, 1946), *Tiempos felices* (Madrid: Fax, 1947) and *El pájaro en la nieve y otros cuentos*, ed. Carmen Bravo-Villasante (Madrid: Mondadori España, 1990); Pardo Bazán, *Cuentos completos*, 4 vols., ed. Juan Paredes Núñez (La Coruña: Fundación Pedro Barrié de la Maza, 1990).
5. Sobejano, pp. 17 and 27–33; Valis, pp. 115–40.
6. But Picón opposed admitting Emilia Pardo Bazán into the (then all-male) Royal Spanish Academy. Cited by Valis, p. 202.
7. *Cuentos de mi tiempo* (Madrid: Imprenta de Fortanet, 1895), p. xiv.
8. Sobejano, p. 18.

Acknowledgments

We are greatly indebted to Don Juan Manuel Ortiz Picón for his gracious permission to publish this English translation of his grandfather's short stories; we thank Don Fernando Lázaro Carreter, director of the Royal Spanish Academy, and Professor Millán Arroyo Simón of the Universidad Complutense de Madrid; we also thank Nancy van Vlissingen of Fairfield University's Nyselius Library, Ashley B. P. Hanson of Connecticut College's Charles E. Shain Library, Michael A. Micinilio of Fairfield University's Media Center, and Theresa L. Fedorchek and Milton Anderson. And we are grateful to Alejandro Sanz of the Ateneo de Madrid, who gave gracious permission to photograph Emilio Sala's portrait of Don Jacinto Octavio Picón.

The original Spanish texts used for this translation are listed in the select bibliography.

RMF
PSRD
GS

Introduction

GONZALO SOBEJANO

Among Spanish novelists of the second half of the nineteenth century, there were, "the same as in sown wheat fields," tall stalks and not so tall stalks, in addition to the weeds that do not take root and leave no trace. The simile is not mine, but Jacinto Octavio Picón's, a not-so-tall stalk that along with others "constitutes wealth."[1]

If Picón did not reach the level of greatness of Juan Valera or Benito Pérez Galdós, his elder masters, nor that of Leopoldo Alas or Emilia Pardo Bazán, the most innovative novelists of his age group (born in the early 1850s), he nevertheless represents considerable wealth along with such other fiction writers of the period as José Ortega Munilla (father of the philosopher Ortega y Gasset), Armando Palacio Valdés, Luis Coloma, Vicente Blasco Ibáñez or Felipe Trigo.

Moreover, judgments vary according to the times and to readers. In 1975 Mario Vargas Llosa could write that Leopoldo Alas's *La regenta* was the best Spanish novel of the nineteenth century and today it is considered, along with *Don Quijote* and *Fortunata and Jacinta*, one of the three pinnacles of the genre, while, to cite but one example among many, in 1922 a certain respected critic who was reviewing the development of this genre included Alarcón, Picón, Alas and Coloma, in a section of "minor novelists," devoting a separate section to Palacio Valdés and Blasco Ibáñez, two authors who were read a great deal in the 1920s (especially in the United States) and who today are almost forgotten.

Without engaging in speculation on the fickleness of fortune, I will only say that in Jacinto Octavio Picón's prose fiction (eight novels and six books of short stories and novelettes) certain qualities stand out that, I believe, preserve his appeal and dignity:

liberalism in all spheres of human activity and a defense of true love through a varied and careful examination of the lot of women in the bourgeoisie—his style characterized by a harmonious balance between story and scene, exposition and description, and an almost Impressionist realism based on a finely detailed perception of forms and tones.

Picón's first non-journalistic works were an extensive study of caricature (1877), an example of his competence as an art critic (which, as time went by, would bear fruit in a beautiful book on Velázquez), and several short stories of moral import, written in a sentimental vein or with an air of the fantastic. His works then began to appear at intervals, the novels between 1882 and 1914, and the books of short stories from 1892 to 1916.

Of Picón's eight novels the most successful and the most characteristic are the second, *Love's Stepchild* [*La hijastra del amor*], 1884, and the last four, *The Honorable Woman* [*La honrada*], 1890; *Sweet and Tasty* [*Dulce y sabrosa*], 1891; *Juanita Tenorio*, 1910; and *Sacramento*, 1914; all have female protagonists and all are set in Picón's native Madrid, which the author always evokes in a genial, lively style. Each of these five novels presents a narrative study of love from the woman's point of view: Clara, "love's stepchild"; Plácida, "the honorable woman" to the utmost extent; Cristeta, the "sweet and tasty" fruit of an ostensibly off-limits orchard; Juanita, a female "Don Juan" in spite of herself; Consuelo, the honorable woman beyond reproach, and her daughter Sacramento, the unhappily married woman who becomes emancipated to a certain extent.

This sampler of women is divided into two groups: the seduced (Clara, Cristeta and Juanita) and the unhappily married (Plácida, Consuelo and Sacramento). The danger for the seduced is taking up prostitution without ever getting married, and their hope is finding a man capable of giving affection and worthy of receiving it, someone they can choose freely. The danger for the unhappily married consists of perpetually suffering unfaithfulness, which debases the home, and not responding in kind because of public honor and personal integrity observed to the point of martyrdom; and their hope can only be pinned on adultery (another form of free choice), which is accepted with sorrow or entered into as a conscious decision, and a justified one, seeing that divorce is not possible.

All these women have one thing in common: an ideal of love that combines generosity and affection without scorning pleasure. None of them, when she is attracted to a man, affects a prudish modesty or the delaying tactics of easily frightened moral virtue. On the contrary, they submit in good faith and somewhat quickly to the man who pursues them. Their mistake is not exactly in submitting but rather in doing so while trusting in a man's love and, above all, believing themselves in love with that man when in actuality—and they are not long in recognizing it as such—they were in love with love. And they were in love with love because they imagined that, yes, it was a pleasurable exaltation of the senses, but they were hoping that it would also be a convergence of spirits, a sharing of ideas and feelings and tastes, company in happiness as well as grief, mutual respect, endless dialogue, lasting harmony, genuine compassion, affection, in short, or generosity between two people. But it is no such thing: it is merely desire that vanishes in a short time, or it is even less—vanity or selfishness disguised as desire. (And as the reader will soon see, women with this view of love will appear in such stories as "Moral Divorce" and "Disillusion.")

This may seem like trivial "romanticism," the commonplace subject matter of a newspaper serial, but although in some of these novels, especially in *Love's Stepchild*, the fantastic and melodramatic elements play an obvious role (as in several of the novels of a Balzac or a Galdós), the consistency with which Picón undertakes these narrative studies on the man/woman relationship in the bourgeoisie and the variations with which he tempers this unique theme show that he is writing to give artistic form to a reforming cause: the freedom of women and their equality in relation to men, if not yet in the workplace or in politics, certainly in other respects and principally in love and marriage. (And the reader will also see this theme in short stories like "The Prudent Woman" and "Sacrifice.")

Picón is urging that women be educated and given responsibility, and that they not be exploited by Money, the State and the Church. He is saying that if they do not raise a family, they can lead purposeful lives on their own; that if they lose their virginity outside of marriage, they should not be condemned to prostitution; that if they have the misfortune of entering into legitimate unions with contemptible men, they should be able, with the very same legitimacy, to dissolve those unions and attempt others; and that they should not allow themselves to be subjugated by repressive forces that want to keep them in ignorance and that brandish concepts like virginity, prostitution and adultery to reduce them to the status of an object that is weakened, worn down and ruined. In this sense Picón is profeminist (a supporter of gaining greater freedom for women), as opposed to the nonfeminism of Galdós, a certain occasional antifeminism in Leopoldo Alas, and the theoretical and practical feminism of Emilia Pardo Bazán.

The seduced women who are protagonists of Picón's novels neither can (because of laws and customs) nor wish (because of prejudice, fear and obstacles created by those laws and customs or because of their own pride) to tie themselves down in marriage. In *Love's Stepchild*, Clara, seduced by one man, kept by another, and drawn finally to the free love of a third by whom she becomes pregnant, lets herself die when faced with the terror of giving birth to a child who could be ashamed of her. Cristeta, in *Sweet and Tasty*, seduced and almost purchased by a declining and not at all romantic Don Juan, has a less ill-fated history, a less pressing financial situation, and, above all, a more resolute character than Clara. Thanks to these circumstances, she stops after the first stumble and straightens out by virtue of her willpower and her ingenuity (winning back her man by pretending to be married to another), in this way transforming the seducer into her life's companion while it is possible, and, naturally, outside of the marriage bond. In *Juanita Tenorio* the "seducer" is an actant and personified in two characters (the cold calculator and the weak admirer), there is a "buyer" responsible for Juanita's prostitution, and a final possible "savior" for whom she can only be a companion and nurse. If the misfortune of the seduced women, stated in very simple terms, is "not being able" to marry, or, stated in less simple terms, "not being able to want" to marry, the sentence passed on the women in *The Honorable Woman* and *Sacramento* is a bad marriage, being unhappily married, because for the latter "the law provides no recourse, our fellow creatures no forbearance, and religion no real compassion."[2]

The female protagonists of the above five novels, both the victims of seduction and the victims of a bad marriage, stand out for their goodness, honesty, and sincerity—for their purity, I would say, in the best sense of the word. These qualities testify to the admiration that the author professed for women, in body and soul.

But in a number of short stories and novelettes, as well as in certain female figures that play secondary roles in his novels, the reader will find greater variety in the representation of the ways that women live and conduct themselves. And, in the first place, I would like to point out that "Disillusion," the longest of the tales selected and translated by Robert M. Fedorchek, is the story of a woman who prefigures the Sacramento of the eponymous novel published seven years later—though as a fictitious character, she strikes me as incomparably better drawn than the latter. Soledad, the heroine, is neither a seduced nor an unhappily married woman. She is the most truly free of the women in Picón's gallery. Attracted to the man who is courting her, a man who is very inferior to her morally and intellectually, she does not confuse her love of love and her attraction to him. Before committing herself, she puts Luis to the test passively and actively. The passive or indirect test consists of discovering that this suitor, supposedly in love with her, reproaches her for having looked after a sick neighbor woman who had contracted a contagious disease (the reason for his reproach being that said neighbor, abandoned by everybody during her illness, is a prostitute). The active test is asking him, if he loves her, to forsake his profitable moneylending business, which Luis refuses to do. The disillusion becomes more and more apparent through the conversations between the sincere Soledad and her conventional-minded friend, but it culminates in the scene in which Soledad, condemning herself to spinsterhood (she is not pretty and Luis is her first suitor), defines marriage as "an intimate union, based on mutual esteem . . . the same thoughts, the same feelings . . . each side having the best possible opinion of the other, and thinking that nothing can be done by one that won't be approved and defended by the other." Soledad is the most noble, intelligent and independent female character created by Picón, and so wise that she experiences "moral divorce" (title story of this book) before matrimonial ties.

Three of Jacinto Octavio Picón's best collections of short stories stand out owing to their predominant motifs. *Stories from*

My Day [*Cuentos de mi tiempo*] (1895) contains tales inspired basically by a social morality. This becomes apparent in "Keep Holy the Sabbath Day" (a village priest does "servile" work on a Sunday to help a sick stonecutter who cannot do without the day's wage) and in "The Threat" (a labor dispute is solved through an eye-opening act of revenge instead of a strike). Stories like these are related to the novels of religious thesis, *Lázaro* (1882) and *The Enemy* [*El enemigo*] (1887), while in others of this collection one finds female figures invested with a certain exemplary nature. It is a positive exemplary nature in "Elvira-Nicolasa" (Elvira the courtesan, on visiting her home town and going back to the past, momentarily recovers the virtue of the Nicolasa that she once was) and in "The Portrait" (a woman, ashamed, relates to another the ingratitude of her husband toward the friend who bequeathed his fortune to them and whose portrait lies discarded in the attic); and it is a negative exemplary nature in "Eve," the adulteress who puts on and keeps on appearances.

Women [*Mujeres*] (1911), the second of the three collections, contains female profiles that depict generosity and greed. The young woman in "The Last Confession" is generous—she understands the pure love that her widowed and impoverished mother has for a man who also loves her, a relationship condemned by the girl's confessor as scandalous; and also generous is the woman in "Sacrifice" who, inured to deception, later finds the revival of love in the kiss that a dying soldier asks of her. "Pepita" personifies, on the other hand, the type of selfish and somewhat perverse young woman who, through histrionics and distortion, inveigles a man on the verge of widowhood. And in a number of the most successful tales in this collection the dominant theme is psychological curiosity: "Moral Divorce" is the story of a married woman's incompatibility with the husband who cruelly exploited and ruined a friend (Rosa is reminiscent of Plácida in *The Honorable Woman* and foreshadows the protagonists of "Disillusion" and *Sacramento*). Another exercise in intellectual inquiry is "The Lady and the Storms," narrative entertainment about a bold, mischief-making coquette; and in "Love Cure" a deluded, inhibited man and a candid woman—albeit with extravagant tastes—offset each other's imbalances when they come together.

Lastly, in the book that takes its title from the first story, *Disillusion* [*Desencanto*] (1925), the most pronounced feature is its moralizing sense.

The present anthology, so ably compiled by Robert M. Fedorchek, provides the reader with additional examples that illuminate further the character and fate of women in stories like "The Irreverent Nun" and "A Matter of Conscience," in both of which charity exercised for the good of others rises in contrast to a barren spirituality; "An Act of Revenge," about inexorable fury unleashed by jealousy; "The Wreaths," a sensitive depiction of a consolable widow; "The Overdressed Woman," about a woman similar to Juanita Tenorio in her just wrath toward her corrupters; "The Prudent Woman," whose protagonist, like Soledad in "Disillusion," in the nick of time escapes marriage to a despicable individual; "A Wise Man," a variation on the traditional theme of the old man and the young girl; "The Partner," in which a man urges his wife to yield to the desires of his business partner, harassing her until she accepts the challenge of the surrender with vindictive wrath; and "Duty," about a long-suffering wife who kills her husband when he is in the act of walking off with the money that she had scrimped and saved to exempt their son (and only child) from the draft.

Jacinto Octavio Picón never abandoned his adherence to realism, understood as a fictitious conception of a keenly observed present-day world, and although in theory he placed beauty in the foreground and didacticism in the background by proposing entertainment as the aim of *Sweet and Tasty* and even *Juanita Tenorio*, his novels and many of his short stories are studies of women and love.

In his monograph on Velázquez, Picón defined the art of his favorite painter by a series of qualities which could be viewed as aesthetic attributes of our author: a sketch done not only with lines, but with color, distance and atmosphere; credibility in the overall impression; and the gift of seeing what is natural conform to the tone and perspective of subject matter. And he added that "sincerity in the expression of feeling, simplicity of execution, and precision in the relationship of values through the study of light and air" would characterize Velázquez and "*modernism*, in the loftiest sense of the word."[3]

With *modernism* in the strictest sense of the word, that is, with the modernism propagated at the turn of the century by Rubén Darío (who visited, read, and praised the author of *Sweet and Tasty*), Picón's fiction has a certain affinity in that a sharp sensory vibrancy, a new sensual fragrance frequently flows from his best writings. But the circumspect author embraces neither the amorality, nor the anarcho-aristocracy, nor the "art for art's sake" of the modernists. His liberalism, his unswerving defense of the dignity of women, his personal modesty, and the compassionate tone of his vision of the world and life shield him from those excesses.

Notes

1. "Literary Vermin" ["Sabandijas literarias"], in *Juan Vulgar*, 2d ed. (Madrid: Fernando Fé, 1885), pp. 299–300.
2. Jacinto Octavio Picón, *Sacramento* (Madrid: V. Prieto, 1914), p. 73.
3. Jacinto Octavio Picón, *Life and Works of Don Diego Velázquez* [*Vida y obras de don Diego Velázquez*], 2nd ed. (Madrid: Renacimiento, n.d. [1925]), p. 257.

Bust of Jacinto Octavio Picón in the Madrid home of Juan Manuel Ortiz Picón. Artist: Mariano Benlliure. Photo by Robert M. Fedorchek. Courtesy, Juan Manuel Ortiz Picón.

Oval of Jacinto Octavio Picón that accompanies Henri Peseux-Richard's article on the Spanish writer in the *Revue Hispanique*, Vol. 30, 1914. Photo by Michael A. Micinilio. Courtesy, Charles E. Shain Library, Connecticut College.

"Moral Divorce"
and Other Stories
by Jacinto Octavio Picón

La monja impía

The Irreverent Nun

I

In the time of the War of Independence* there existed in Castile a religious order of women so neglected by God and man that for many miles around people called them "the needy nuns."

They lived, far from any inhabited place, in a large, ramshackle house converted into a convent that had glassless windows fronted by wobbly grilles and a roof full of leaks and unsafe tiles. Only patience and disdain for life could take up residence in such an inconvenient building. To make matters worse, the ground in the garden was unproductive and sandy, the chapel dark and damp, and the well water unpalatable and unsanitary. The ornaments, vestments, and liturgical vessels that the order owned for the divine service were so ancient that the humblest village priest would have rejected them.

To such an extent, in short, had the Lord forgotten his brides and in such want did they live, that in the course of a certain pastoral visit the bishop of the diocese almost had to pass the convent by because it had neither a room to lodge him decorously nor milk with which to make him chocolate. His Excellency rested for a brief period in the shade of the garden's walls and then continued on his way, praising such evangelical poverty . . . and vowing that never again would he be caught near the place.

In spite of being so poor, these nuns were the owners of a statue of the Virgin, made of solid silver, that weighed more than seventy-five pounds and that in their eyes was worth a fortune.

As sculpture it was an abomination, but they imagined it superior to a piece by Berruguete* or Alonso Cano,* admiring as marvels of execution the ugly face, the rough cloak, and the crude, badly shaped hands. So exquisite did the sisters consider the image that for some time they even hoped that it might become miraculous in addition to being beautiful. Spurred on by their own desire, they did all that nunnish devotion could do to see a dream come true, but to no avail.

Once, when the prioress took ill, the nuns brought the statue down from its niche with great difficulty. Then, amid candlelight and canticles, they bore it in procession to the patient's cell and devoutly applied it to her wasted legs, which was where the disease had taken hold. The prioress died that very night.

On another occasion, with the water from their well becoming more bitter by the day, they decided to sweeten it with the Virgin's help, and, tying the statue securely with lengths of rope, lowered it into the well and left it submerged for hours. Afterward, divided in groups that took turns, the entire community pulled on the rope and out came Our Lady. The most hopeful nuns pounced on her to wet their lips in the water that she was dripping only to suffer a jarring disillusion: it continued to taste just as bitter, as if they had not done a thing.

The nuns finally became convinced that no miracles could be expected and that the Virgin paid as little attention to them as did her Divine Son. Considering, however, that the statue, in spite of everything, was made of silver, that it weighed a full seventy-five pounds, and that it could occur to any cruel soul to break into the convent to steal it, they decided to give it a coat of lime that would hide the silver. No sooner said than done. With the same brush and the same solution that they used to whitewash walls, the nuns painted and repainted the statue a half dozen times until it looked just like a plaster of paris figure; and when they were finished, they put the Virgin back in her niche.

II

The clamor of war reached even that remote area, and towns sounded the alarm. Monks from a nearby monastery organized a resistance group, while young men from the region, mainly drovers and herders, formed a guerrilla party. In the neighboring city, women and children made lint and old men made cartridges; fine sheets were converted into bandages, and hunting pellets became rifle bullets.

Finally it was learned that the "Frogs" had entered the province and that they would not be long in showing up where they were least expected.

"The needy nuns" also decided to win favor in the eyes of God and serve their native land. The first thing they agreed to do was pray in twos, around the clock, to petition the Lord to keep the soldiers of the intruder king from coming close to their convent; the second was to decide that if the invaders drew near, all of them would boldly file out to the vestibule door, led by the prioress and singing Salve Reginas, prepared to let themselves be killed before consenting to the desecration of their nunnery. And lastly, not trusting the whitewash that hid the precious metal, and knowing that the French were greedy and ungodly, they resolved to bring the Virgin down from her niche and bury her in a corner of the garden.

Day after day went by and nobody turned up in the surrounding hill country, until one afternoon when you could hear the distant boom of cannon shots and heavy rifle fire. Then the most daring nuns went up to the pigeon house, which had been converted into a bell tower, and off in the distance, at the furthest reach of the horizon, they saw clouds of smoke. The wind brought the smell of gunpowder and in the rays of the setting sun they made out shimmery, moving lines that must have been rows of bayonets on which the light played.

The next day the din of the hard-fought battle was heard closer up, and troop movements could be followed not only from the pigeon house but from the very windows of the convent. One sister declared that she saw the French flee, and the prioress, taking her word for it, ordered them to light every candle in the house and sing a hymn of thanks to the Lord.

III

After midnight the nuns began to hear swearwords, curses, and oaths uttered next to the walls of the convent. The portress went down to the vestibule and opened the huge entry door; by the light of the moon she saw the most pathetic sight that human eyes could take in.

On the small plain that stretched out on either side of the entrance to the holy retreat, three carts full of wounded men had come to a stop, and underneath each there was a little pool of blood. From the mobile heaps of mutilated men rose a continuous clamor of moans, groans, wails, imprecations, and howls.

"Sister," said one of the carters, the one whom the others seemed to acknowledge as their leader, "these wounded men need help."

"Men cannot enter this house."

"Well, these will! And you had better let them in soon, or we'll set the convent on fire! Besides, they're not really men any more. Don't you see how much blood they're losing?"

The nuns bent their rule and, with the help of the carters, brought in the wounded and made them as comfortable as they could. The critical ones were put in cells, while others were taken to the vestibule and refectory, and some were even laid on the flagstones of the cloisters, corridors, and passageways. But there was neither a doctor nor a pharmacy at the convent—no means whatsoever to alleviate the pain of the poor devils, many of whom, in their torment, were screaming bloody murder and blasphemies that shocked the nuns. The only real thing accomplished by taking the men there was that, if they were to die, they would die indoors and not out in the open.

The prioress wanted the carters to notify the mayor of the next town so that he could send a doctor and medical supplies, but the one who served as their leader refused to do so, claiming that at daybreak he and his comrades had to join the battalion to which they belonged. And without another word, he set off with his followers, his animals, and his carts.

Then, confused and distressed, the poor woman summoned the sisters whom she considered the most quick-witted and sought their views on what course of action she ought to take in such a difficult situation. One said that the best thing was to light a huge blaze so that, attributing the brightness to a fire at the convent, people from the surrounding area would come to their aid. Another proposed that the bravest of them mount the donkey that they kept in the stable for bringing provisions from the city and go there to notify the authorities. A third advised that they get on their knees in the chapel and sing Salve Reginas until God inspired them with the right solution.

Unexpectedly Sister Gervasia came forward.

She was young and pretty and had an intelligent expression. One look at her was enough to spot the kind of bright, lively, cheerful nun who is usually found in convents and who ends up running away, dying from sadness, or committing suicide.

"Mother," she said, facing the prioress, "if I'm allowed to do what I'd like to, most of the wounded will be saved."

"What do you propose?"

"The Virgin has refused to perform miracles here because this wretched convent is unworthy of her, and because we're great big sinners. But my heart tells me that if I take her to the city, if I can get someone to let me place her on an altar in the cathedral and there, under those beautiful vaults, in that rich, luxurious temple, so worthy of her, if right there I pray a Salve Regina to her in the name of the order, just one Salve . . . well, I'm certain that we'll get out of this all right. Perhaps she'll even perform the miracle that she has denied us other times."

"All this talk about a miracle when she refused even to sweeten the well water for us!"

"That had to be because we don't deserve it, but these men have received sword wounds and have been cut to shreds by bullets fighting in defense of their God and their country."

The discussion was very heated.

Several nuns declared that rather than permit Our Lady to leave the premises they preferred to allow all those men to die without relief; others feared that God would punish them for their lack of compassion; and some were buoyed up with hope by the possibility of the miracle. Meanwhile the wounded men, tormented by pain, were shouting such profanities, curses, and blasphemies that all the nuns were scandalized.

"Do you hear how they're howling and swearing?" Sister Gervasia then asked. "Do you hear how they're losing their souls through our fault? And the trouble is that not only will *they* go straight to hell, but *we* will too for not having helped them in a Christian manner, for letting them use that foul language, and for not acting on the idea that the Virgin herself has suggested to me."

The discussion continued for a time, but Sister Gervasia's argument was so persuasive that in the end she got what she wanted, after taking a solemn oath that she would return with the Virgin as soon as possible.

A half hour later the holy image was disinterred, placed in a pannier, and loaded on the donkey's back. Sister Gervasia grasped the creature by the halter and, at a good pace, the two took the road to the city with her in the lead. The wounded men and the nuns remained behind, the former howling with pain and the latter consumed with curiosity because not one of them could guess what their companion had in mind.

IV

After six hours of anguished waiting had elapsed, the more impatient nuns, who were watching from the top of the pigeon house, saw a covered wagon enveloped in a cloud of dust. It was heading toward the convent, pulled by two powerful mules, and inside it there were four men plus the driver, and one woman, whom they recognized immediately by the white wimple that the wind was blowing around her head.

The wagon pulled up at the main door in less than a quarter of an hour. Sister Gervasia got down, and the four men did the same; the coachman, without waiting to be told, lowered a box from the driver's seat. It was as big as a medium-sized chest.

"Sister, who are these people?" the prioress asked.

"These two," replied Sister Gervasia, pointing to the two best-dressed men, "are surgeons, and the other two and the one who was driving are their assistants. In that big box called a medicine chest they have instruments and implements for healing, waters, ointments, poultices, and all the cures needed by those who are suffering."

"That's all well and good, but what about the Virgin? And the donkey?"

"The donkey's eating his fill of fodder at the inn's stable and Our Lady is on an altar in the cathedral, in the middle of a forest of luxurious spiral candles the likes of which she's never seen here, and in the keeping of a canon who is a close friend of my family. We can set our minds at ease. I didn't bring them back with me now to save time, because the statue weighs a great deal and the poor animal moves at a snail's pace."

"A very ill-advised decision!"

"Don't worry. One of the doctors has to go back in the wagon the day after tomorrow, early in the morning, to get more of the medicines that are needed. I'll go with him and we'll return in the afternoon with the drugs, Our Lady, and the donkey."

During the two days that the Virgin spent "away from home," in the words of the prioress, the nuns were very upset. Finally, on the third day, Sister Gervasia left early in the morning with the doctor, according to plan, and returned as she had indicated, bringing the statue and donkey with her.

The animal went to the stable to rest, and later, under cover of darkness, which made it safer, the nuns reburied the Virgin in the same corner of the garden from which they had very reluctantly removed her. It seemed impossible to them that she was once again in their possession. They were so pleased that they sang a solemn Salve Regina to give thanks.

Forty-eight wounded men had been brought to the convent. Seven of them died—and it was no wonder, what with the loss of blood and broken bones—and were given a Christian burial. The remaining forty-one recovered. Those whose convalescence still required considerable care were taken to the city raving about the admirable charity of "the needy nuns." Those who healed completely took up arms again because there was a plague of Frenchmen in Spain.

And thus did calm once more reign in the convent, which to many nuns seemed more dreary and dismal than before.

V

Several years later, when the war was over, one of those wounded men made a substantial donation to the order, thanks to which the convent was restored. The roofs were refurbished, the grilles were made secure, panes were installed in the windows, and the chapel was decorated luxuriously. A gardener and errand boy were even taken on.

At that point, because the nuns considered their house worthy of Our Lady and believed in addition that it was unlikely that anyone would risk stealing her while two men were continuously present, they decided to proceed to her exhumation amid litanies, Salve Reginas, and other devotions. But as it turned out, the statue emerged from its burial site in a deplorable state. Its hollows and cavities were filled with dirt, stones had scratched it everywhere, and the coat of whitewash with which the silver had been hidden was so soiled that the Blessed Virgin looked as if she were wearing a filthy cloak. For all these reasons it was decided that a skillful craftsman should strip and polish the statue to draw out the brilliance of the precious metal so that afterward the Virgin could be placed, in a solemn ceremony, on the main altar of the chapel, for which a magnificent retable had been built.

So the craftsman came and the nuns showed him the statue. No sooner did he begin to work than he dropped his cleaning cloth and laughed openly and heartily, making a noise that had never before resounded in that holy enclosure.

In a corner of the chapel Sister Gervasia was shaking like a leaf.

"Why are you laughing so hard, my friend?" the prioress asked.

"Didn't you say the Virgin was made of silver?"

"Yes, and she is. We know what we have in our possession."

"You do, huh? Well, this sculpture, which as a work of art couldn't be worse, is—with all due respect—worthless, because it's made of lead. And it's bad lead at that, the common, cheap variety used for eaves and glass casings."

The man was telling the truth. The nuns came up close and he continued removing plaster from the statue until a sizable section lay exposed to view. It was clearly not white, shiny, gleaming silver but dull, dirty, blackish lead.

The prioress, astonished and thunderstruck, kept shouting: "It was made of silver, it was made of silver!"

"I believe you, and it must have been worth a fortune, but now ... unless you want to take and melt it down and use it for drainpipes on the roofs..." And he added: "There's been a switch here, without a doubt. A well-disguised theft."

On hearing this, the prioress looked at the nuns, the nuns looked at the prioress, and then, gripped instantaneously by the same suspicion, they all turned, their eyes flashing with anger, toward the spot where a trembling Sister Gervasia had a wild look on her face.

What happened then was terrible. First there were shouts, questions, and insults; afterward, reproaches, pinches, and shoves; and finally each sister conceived of a different punishment. One wanted her condemned to a regimen of bread and water until she confessed; another wanted to give her only dried cod and moldy cheese for eight days, with nothing to drink; a third wanted to thrash her with candles; the fieriest one suggested that she be buried alive in the same pit where the statue had lain hidden.

The prioress was now beginning to fear that if her authority was ignored something terrible might happen there, and she alone would be responsible for it. And Sister Gervasia, making a desperate attempt to screw up her courage, started to push and punch until she managed to distance herself from the other nuns.

"Yes," she said at once in a firm, spirited voice that overcame the commotion. "Yes, I sold the silver Virgin in the city and had a lead one made in its place. With the money from the sale, I paid the doctors that I brought, I hired the wagon in which they came, and I purchased the medicines that were needed. I deserve punishment? Then let certain mothers come to inflict it on me, the mothers of those men who came in here half dead and left sufficiently recovered to continue fighting. And think twice about trying to hurt me because someone'll be sorry."

Having said this, she quickly unfastened from her waist the long rosary with beads the size of walnuts, twisted it like a whip, and assumed such a menacing attitude that not a single nun risked moving toward her or uttering a word.

VI

Given the uniqueness of the case and the extraordinary nature of the offense, the prioress informed the bishop.

Sister Gervasia was brought before an ecclesiastic review board and expelled from the order.

She was sentenced to leave the convent with her head covered by a black veil, discalced, and carrying a snuffed candle in her hand. And she went out into the countryside by the very same door that had been opened to admit the wounded men.

One of her relatives in the city took her in and showed her hospitality. At the end of two years a hardworking, honest young man fell in love with her, and, since she returned his love, she got married.

As in children's stories, they were happy, raised a family, and lived for many years.

All of which caused the prioress to exclaim when she learned about it: "Good Heavens! We were right when we said that that unfortunate creature hadn't come into this world to serve God!"

Santificar las fiestas

Keep Holy the Sabbath Day

On Monday, 9 May 1892, Don Cándido took possession of his parish in Santa Cruz de Lugarejo and immediately went about setting up house with the rickety old furniture he had brought on a cart from the small town where he had lived until then, a town where he had been a refuge for the needy and a model for the virtuous. For more than forty-eight hours nobody realized that a new priest was in residence.

Several days later the few people who saw and talked to him spread the word that he seemed like a good person. And those who reached this favorable judgment so quickly were not mistaken, for Don Cándido was a saint. Because of his height, face, and bearing he brought to mind the description that Cervantes gave us of his immortal hidalgo. Don Cándido was also "close on fifty, of a robust constitution, on the thin side with a gaunt face, an early riser," and, if not fond of hunting, like Don Quijote, indefatigable in searching for and alleviating sorrow.

He was a man of superior moral qualities, a man of sincere piety, pleasant manner, humble speech, and quiet charity; and a man so compassionate and tolerant of everything that, although the respect he commanded was great, the affectionate trust that he inspired was even greater. His education could not have been very extensive. The books that he owned fit into a single small case, and the one with the most worn binding and most well-thumbed pages was the New Testament. Neither the Fathers of the Church nor the sublime mystics delighted him as much as those simple verses that offer, to the person who knows how to read them, a vast array of thoughts stated in sober language.

Every day, right after his midday meal, Don Cándido would lean against the window sill in his room and reread and meditate on a few chapters by St. Mark or St. Matthew. He would then set the book down and, sunning himself and smoking cigarettes, spend a while watching stonecutters at work in an adjacent, fenced-in lot that had been converted into an outdoor shop.

A number of months back, an arch in the church's chapel had collapsed, and when a certain pious lady bequeathed funds to rebuild it, an architect from the neighboring city came from time to time to inspect the new work. The space next to Don Cándido's room soon filled with white limestone blocks that made a striking contrast with the plush green grass, and little by little the pieces became keystones, voussoirs, skewbacks, and sections of archivolt.

From morning until evening, except for one hour at midday, multiple monotonous sounds rent the air continuously as mallets and martelines struck the limestone. The sun lit the whole work site, heightening the vivid, rectangular shadows created by the straw lean-tos under which the cutters sought shelter. And every now and then, from that jarring concert of clanging iron, splitting stone, and echoing blows, there arose the loud and mournful singing of a song partially drowned out by the din of the work, like a sigh amid the sorrows of life.

During the last four days of Don Cándido's first week in Santa Cruz de Lugarejo, he looked out of his window without fail to watch the stonecutters, and if someone had observed him closely, he could have suspected, from the emotion that showed on his face, that the hard, exhausting labor struck a compassionate, sympathetic chord in the priest.

On Sunday, the first one that he was spending at his new parish, Don Cándido left the house very early, said Mass, took a long walk, and ate later than usual. Just before he finished, when the housekeeper removed the tablecloth and brought him matches and the tobacco jar, he heard the work begin. At first the noise was isolated and faint, then it grew loud and incessant as the cutters chipped and shaped limestone in the adjacent lot.

"Even on Sunday," Don Cándido muttered in sadness and surprise. And, leaning out of the window, he shouted at the nearest worker: "Hey, my friend, tell the foreman or overseer or whatever he is to do me the favor of coming up here for a minute."

Keep Holy the Sabbath Day

A few moments later the master stonecutter was in the priest's dining room. Don Cándido treated him to some fresh cheese and an old wine, and gave him a cigarette as thick as a thumb. Then, very unwillingly and going against his own grain, he reprimanded him with the little, and timid, asperity that his kindness allowed, saying: "Have you no religion, no sense of shame? Working on Sunday!"

The stonecutter, annoyed by the reprimand but inhibited by the hospitality, replied humbly: "What are we to do, Father? We get paid by the pieces we turn out and we're saving time because wages are low and food's expensive and when you least expect it, another child comes along. That big blond fella," he added, going to the window and pointing him out, "has five kids. The guy next to him has three. The lame one across from them supports his parents. Everybody needs the money. Believe me, Father, there are no feast days on an empty stomach and in a cold house."

Don Cándido looked baffled; finally, making an effort to appear angry, he replied: "That's beside the point. No one should work on Sunday. How many of you are there?"

"Twelve."

"How much does each one make? All together: what will the wages amount to?"

The stonecutter counted on his fingers and answered: "One hundred and five *reales*."

Don Cándido went to his bedroom, opened a credenza, removed from a drawer a small green silk moneybag with steel rings, counted out one hundred and five *reales*, and handed them to the foreman with these words: "Here: each one of you say an Our Father and go and rest. Don't profane the Lord's day!"

Five minutes later the work site was deserted.

* * *

The following Sunday, when Don Cándido went up to have breakfast after saying Mass, he heard, to his astonishment, the stonecutters back at work. Frowning, he muttered: "Today too?"

The scene that ensued was a repeat of the previous Sunday. He summoned the foreman, reprimanded him more sternly, went to his bedroom, and gave him money to clear out the work site. The workers left in a happy mood, some heading for home, most for the tavern. The green moneybag was empty, and the priest, leaning out of the window, spent a while contemplating those pieces of stone; and the way he looked at them they must have held a hidden and mysterious charm for him.

During the following week the work accelerated to such an extent that the adjacent lot was nearly emptied. The church's new arch was on the verge of completion.

Nonetheless, on the third Sunday the dull, metallic knock-knock of a tool striking stone began even earlier, though the noise was considerably fainter; undoubtedly very few workers were on the job.

Don Cándido ran to the window and saw that there was but one man busily fashioning and completing a piece in the shape of a voussoir; he worked in such haste and with such zeal that he neither rested nor looked up.

Don Cándido went down and, approaching the worker, asked him curtly: "Are you like Jews who don't observe Sunday? Why are you working?"

"Father," the stonecutter replied, "yesterday everything was completed. Tomorrow, Monday, at daybreak, delivery will be made. Only this voussoir isn't finished, and it's my fault because I was out sick two days this week. And I have to finish it today, before sunset, to collect my wages, because yesterday they refused to pay me and won't until I finish."

After saying this, he looked down, bent over, and resumed chipping.

"And if you don't finish?"

"The hassle is the least of it. The bad part is that I don't get paid, and the money is needed at home."

Don Cándido became pensive. Only he could divulge all the mental calculations that he made; he must have remembered that the green moneybag was empty, and maybe he said to himself that true charity does not consist of giving money, but of giving of one's self. Perhaps very private memories came to mind. In any event, he looked at the stonecutter with compassion and said to him in a low voice, as if confiding a secret: "My father and brothers were stonecutters. As a boy, I also learned the trade. I'll help you!"

And rolling up his sleeves, he picked up a chisel, grasped a mallet, and began to chip the stone.

La última confesión

The Last Confession

She herself told me the story.

"To understand and appreciate what I suffered," she began, "we have to go a long way back.

"Mama was an orphan, and people say a very pretty one, when she got married at the age of twenty.

"A relative who had acted as her guardian surrendered to her husband—the man who was my father—the capital goods that made up her inheritance: in excess of forty thousand *duros* in government bonds.

"Ten months later I was born. Eighteen months later my father didn't return home to eat one afternoon; night came and went and he still didn't turn up. They tried to find out if he had had some sort of accident and drew a blank. Friends, neighbors, servants, and the authorities chased around Madrid in vain. At first it was believed that he had been the victim of a crime; then, that he had committed suicide; finally, the governor, at I don't know whose request, cleared up the mystery. By questioning people at the stock exchange he discovered that my father had sold off everything that he had—rather, everything that belonged to Mama—and that after staying in Le Havre for a few days, he had set sail for the United States, taking along a woman with whom he had been having an affair that began long before he married. Overnight, at the age of twenty-three and with a baby girl, Mama had no alternative but to live off relatives' charity or find work. And what work would she have been able to do, a young lady raised, if not in luxury, in the ignorant idleness of middle-class women?

"She sold all items of value—furniture, paintings, lace, jewels—and dismissed the servants. She was determined to look for the cheapest possible room, but didn't know how she would pay even for that in the long run, because when my father disappeared from Madrid he left only a handful of money in the house.

"This can be told in no time, but attention has to be paid to what it means.

"The day after Mama told the doorman and his wife that she would be leaving, the landlord, informed of what was happening, came in person to see her. He was thirty years old, with a nice figure, and in mourning for a sister with whom he had lived since the death of their parents. I was told about this scene between him and my mother by a onetime maid who became very talkative with age. Mama was crying softly, seated on a low sewing stool, because the secondhand dealers had taken everything of any value, and the landlord was standing, hat in hand, without daring to utter a word for fear of offending her with what he had on his mind. 'Madam,' he said finally, 'I implore you to stay here until you find a place where you're free of worry, until you've resolved your difficulty—even if you don't pay for quite some time; you'll pay whenever you can.' She thanked him only by the way she looked up at him through her tears, and he left that emptied room with greater signs of respect than if he were withdrawing from the royal chamber.

"I know that a few days later Mama took a small interior room in a very unassuming building in an unfrequented district. I don't remember the move, but my earliest recollections of childhood are associated with that man, with Don Luis. I've always seen him at our side; it's impossible to imagine what he's meant to us. What happened between him and my mother? Was he in love with her before our misfortune? I haven't the slightest doubt about it. Was it fear of destitution that made my mother predisposed to compromise herself with an illicit relationship and accept it? Was gratitude then imperceptibly transformed into love? Or could it be that past suffering and derived benefits were no more than propitious circumstances for the awakening of love? What's indisputable is that they came to love one another, and do love one another, with such heartfelt tenderness that her beauty isn't enough to explain his worship, nor is his goodness enough to explain her devotion. The inescapable conclusion is that there exists between them, one spirit to another, an attraction that I'm unable to put into words, but whose nature and core surely are divine.

"Mama doesn't see anybody, she doesn't visit anybody, and she seldom goes out; she's content only at his side. She's like a nun whose cloister is her home and whose God is the man she loves. As for him, I can't conceive of one human being giving to another greater proof of loving respect. Several times I've caught glimpses of passion in his eyes, and at all times I see in his behavior toward my mother signs of the purest affection. When he met her, he was rich; afterwards he lost everything, and now he works for her. One day I overheard him say to her: 'Now that I have to work and battle for all of you to have everything that you need is when I understand how much I love you.'

"Until I started school I had no perception of our irregular living arrangement. The little girls who were my classmates opened my eyes to it, but my spirit as a child was already a captive of that man's goodness.

"Owing to one of those useless acts of hypocrisy with which one creates the illusion that she's hiding what everybody knows, I had been accustomed to calling him godfather.

"Their first child, a boy, died within months; the second one, whom I love with all my heart, was born when I was pretty grown-up. When he began to talk, I taught him to say "Papa"; and all on my own, pretending at first that I was making a mistake and getting confused by repeating the word to the little one, I also called Luis father. I'll never forget the indescribable glance that he exchanged with my mother the first time that he noticed it, believing what he heard because my brother wasn't present.

"The recovery of her well-being and tranquillity, and the atmosphere of self-denial that existed at home were not, however, enough to make my poor mother happy. The mean, petty consequences of their illicit union humiliated her cruelly, and gossip, impoliteness, or a simple snub would cut her to the quick. Since she didn't want to see anybody, her withdrawal from the world was complete. Although she had always been religious without a trace of fanaticism, she began to be devout in an exaggerated way. That was when her longtime confessor died—a little old man who had known her as a child and who was well aware of how much she had suffered.

"Undoubtedly to avoid unbosoming herself to a strange priest, Mama went several months without fulfilling her religious obligations, but because she had no qualms where I was concerned, one day she instructed a very dependable maid to take me to confession the following morning.

"We arrived at the church very early. The good woman knelt to pray in a chapel and, fortunately, didn't learn immediately what took place. I asked the acolyte which priest I could go to and he pointed to one who was almost finished hearing an elderly woman's confession. When I saw her leave, I approached the confessional.

"He looked no more than forty and was a skinny man with a sharp face, prominent cheekbones, and thin, colorless lips. He had black, limp hair which was stuck along his sunken temples, a somewhat sallow complexion, and bright, ebony eyes like small jet beads. When his eyelids were drooping he inspired pity; when he looked straight at you he inspired fear.

"As I knelt he asked me: 'Do you wish to confess on your own or do you want me to question you in the order of the commandments?'

"I replied that I preferred the latter, and he began. When he came to the fourth commandment and asked me if I loved and respected my parents, as a good daughter should, I answered.... I don't remember exactly what I answered—because I was accustomed to confessing to the little old priest—or what contradiction I stumbled over. I guess I said, first, that I only had a mother, and then that my father was far away, but that I loved and respected both of them with all my heart. I don't know for sure; I've never been able to remember, but my unchecked naïveté must have aroused his curiosity. He began to ask me questions, which I answered unsuspectingly, and he realized on the spot that Mama wasn't married to the man she was living with and that I called him father even though he really wasn't my father.

"Then he fell silent, and through the lattice window I saw his hard, bright eyes riveted on me like black swordpoints. All of a sudden he said in a low voice and in a very harsh tone: 'Impossible, impossible, this is an abomination. I can't absolve you! You have to talk to your mother. Tell that poor wretch that all of you are living in mortal sin; if it's necessary, tell him too—let them separate forevermore! Turn against him, especially against him—

turn against the two of them! And if you accomplish nothing, leave home. If you have relatives, live with them; if not, with whomever is willing to help you. Become a servant for a Christian family or enter a religious order, but get out of that house soon, and let those two transgressors separate because all of you are mocking the Lord.'

"Listening to him stunned me, as if I had been beaten on the head. I don't know what pained me more—what he said to me or how he said it. Trembling, and not from fear, I answered him slowly, coldly, feigning a calmness that I didn't feel: 'Father, I can no sooner say such things to my mother than I can to the man whom I look upon as my true father, nor do I care about being damned provided they don't weep for a single moment through any fault of mine.' 'Well, I won't give you absolution!' 'Then let God's will be done!' I responded, getting to my feet.

"He also stood, and staring at me—not through the lattice window, but through the wide opening that served as the entrance to the confessional—he asked: 'How old are you?' 'Nineteen.' 'And you're certain that that good man has always treated you the same way . . . always like a little girl?'

"Then I felt blood rush to my face as if some sort of filthy flare-up had set it ablaze. I lowered my eyes, turned around, and walked away. I touched the shoulder of the maid who accompanied me, we left the church, and I breathed the outside air eagerly. I didn't say a word to my parents; they'll go to their graves without knowing about it. But I swore to myself that never again would I tolerate an intermediary between God and my conscience, nor will I confide my troubles to someone who cannot understand them because he's hardened his heart in dealing with the world."

Caso de conciencia

A Matter of Conscience

I

Don Diego Fermosella was an honest, wealthy, Madrilenian gentleman whose annual income exceeded fifteen thousand *duros*. He lived a life of luxury, was a widower, and had two daughters—one twenty-four and the other twenty.

Teresa, the older one, was religious in the extreme. She thought only about avoiding sin and gaining eternal salvation, believing that she would achieve the latter through virtuous conduct and continual prayer.

She made a show of disdaining fashion and finery and dressed humbly. She paid little attention to personal hygiene, was unconcerned about eating badly, and didn't care a whit that other women, including her sister, enjoyed a reputation for elegance, were bright, and found favor with men. With respect to love, whether from inherent coldness or from complete submission to the precepts that glorify chastity, she would not tolerate the notion that an earthly, worldly passion could distract her from loftier thoughts. She rose before dawn, heard early Mass in a nearby chapel, and then, shut up in her room, would spend the morning immersed in pious literature. The servants used to say that frequently she would seem to be ecstatic and enraptured, like paintings of certain saints much favored by the Lord. At noon she would lunch alone in order to have greater independence in the observance of fasts and abstinences, which she kept rigorously, and in the afternoon she received a number of priests and brothers from a confraternity. She gave little to charity but very frequently donated vestments, flowers for the altar, and candle wax to her parish church.

Teresa never missed a Forty Hours Devotion, no matter how far away the church was and at nightfall she would return home to eat with her father and sister. Their conversations often became acrimonious because she almost never thought along the same lines as Don Diego and Luisa. After the meal she would read in *The Christian Year* the lives of all the saints who were to be commemorated the following day; then it was back to prayer and meditation and ecstasies until she went to bed, which she did without ever having her sleep disturbed by housework, sewing, annoyances, or even those vague amorous longings that dwell in a woman's heart.

Luisa's tastes and habits were just the opposite, and she led a very different life. She would rise at nine and inquire what they were to be served for lunch to ensure that there was always a dish to her father's liking; then, after their meal together, she would read him a paper while he drank coffee. She never let him leave the house without tying his tie for him, satisfying herself that his shirt was properly ironed, and making sure that he was bundled up. Luisa did all of this despite living very comfortably, which goes to show that if she had been poor she would have been even more industrious and hardworking. Afterward she would dress elegantly and wait for a girlfriend, with whom she had set a time the evening before, to come for her to take a carriage ride. Her favorite entertainment was the theater, but if her father, because he was in a bad humor or was suffering from the ailments of old age, didn't want to go out in the evening, she willingly stayed home and played écarté with him or entertained him at the piano. When this occurred, Don Diego would become drowsy around midnight, and Luisa, after seeing him to bed, would then retire to her own room where she devoted several hours to writing to some friend who was away or reading contemporary novels of manners. Although Luisa deplored coarse books for their vulgarity, she wasn't shocked on seeing facts of life treated with a certain decorous candor—what she objected to was lewdness and hypocrisy.

Both sisters were pretty, but in different ways. Teresa was dark-haired, small, and plump; Luisa was blond, trim, and slender. Neither had a boyfriend—the first because love and sin were one and the same in her eyes; the second because she hadn't found a man who knew how to appreciate everything that she was capable of feeling.

One evening Don Diego returned home earlier than usual, complaining of great pain on both his sides and abnormal heaviness of the head. The following day the doctor had to be called, and four days later he died of pneumonia.

During his final moments the two sisters had a violent altercation. Teresa tried to have extreme unction administered to their sick father while he still enjoyed full use of his faculties; Luisa would not consent to it until she was persuaded that he could not comprehend what they were doing for him.

"You want him to lose his soul!" Teresa said very angrily.

"What I want is for him to die in peace," Luisa replied forcefully.

Finally, when the dying Don Diego had irretrievably lost consciousness, she allowed a priest to come and administer to him *sub conditione.**

After their father's death Teresa prayed a great deal and on her own gave money for numerous Masses, but outside of this her grief was controlled and resigned. At the conclusion of the nine days of mourning, she did not miss a novena, a triduum, a rosary, hymns to the Virgin or any other church function that she thought she could attend. Luisa renounced entertainment, finery, and carriage rides, and distributed in alms a considerable portion of the money that she had earmarked for dresses and accessories; and together with her sister she tried to put Don Diego's affairs and business matters in order so that both would know soon what to expect with regard to the assets that constituted their inheritance.

II

One afternoon Luisa was engaged in this sad yet necessary task when the maid came to tell her that Don Agustín, a close and longtime friend of her father, wished to see her.

Don Agustín, a sensible, discreet, and dignified old man, came in and said to Luisa: "It is imperative that you call your sister. What I have to tell you is serious, and both of you should hear it."

A Matter of Conscience

Teresa came and sat next to Luisa. Don Agustín began to speak: "You girls are good, bright, and familiar with the ways of the world. You know, above all, that reality asserts itself in the fortunes of life and that the clearer and more out in the open things are, the better. So, without beating around the bush, I'm going to tell you the reason for my visit. Your father died in his sixties. He became a widower as a young man. You were still very small. Immediately after your mother's passing, he made his will, a copy of which I have and shall turn over to you. Naturally you two are his heirs. Now—so far so good.

"But I've told you that he became a widower as a very young man. Not many years afterward he met the woman..." (at this point an expression of surprise showed on the faces of both sisters) "an unmarried woman, thirty years old—a good, caring woman worthy of being loved. In a word, your father had relations with her, intimate relations.... Do you understand?"

"Good Heavens!" Teresa exclaimed, covering her face with her hands.

Luisa asked: "And you say that the woman was worthy of being loved?"

"I have no doubt whatsoever."

"Well, then why didn't he marry her?"

"Because of you. He told me a thousand times that he didn't want you to have a stepmother."

"He was right!" Teresa interrupted harshly.

"For that at least we have to thank him," Luisa added.

"Let me continue," Don Agustín said, "because here comes the critical part: the result of that love affair was a baby girl."

"Good God!" Teresa blurted out.

"It's not a pleasant piece of news, but go on," Luisa said.

"A baby girl who today is a young woman, nineteen years old, and as beautiful as either of you."

"How shameful!"

"The poor girl!"

"This girl's mother died a year ago. Do you remember several nights last winter when your father took to going to bed at an ungodly hour, almost at daybreak? Well, that's when the poor woman died. Since that time, your sister... because that's what she is...."

"Yes, that girl..."

"You're right, she is our sister. Do continue."

"... your sister has lived with an aunt on her mother's side."

"She's our relative too?"

"Not her," Luisa interjected very calmly.

"Please don't interrupt me because we'll never finish. Diego faithfully and punctually gave her a sum of money every month, enough for them to live modestly. The girl's a gem, but your father made no other will except the one drawn up immediately after the death of your mother."

"Well, so what?" Teresa inquired.

"Hush!"

"In a word, she has no one now to look after her and is literally down-and-out. And I've come to tell you all this so you can talk it over and decide whatever you think best."

"Just what do you want us to decide?"

"Well, it's quite clear. Whether we go on as *two* sisters or become *three*."

"If it had been up to me I would have waited a while before breaking this news to you, but the fact is that the aunt with whom she lives is poor and concerned. Now she suspects that she'll get left with the girl at her own expense and ... she doesn't want that. She called me ... and now you know all of it. Speaking plainly: it turns out that you have a sister who's as poor as a church mouse, and I've come to tell you so you can determine whatever you think best. Oh! Let me add that, under the circumstances, she cannot *legally* demand one *peseta* from you, nor trouble you for anything, but I would think...."

Teresa stood, as if indicating that the meeting had come to an end. Luisa, sensing that she was going to have an unpleasant scene with her sister, said in the nicest way that she knew how: "We'll talk it over. Please come back to see us tomorrow."

After Don Agustín's departure, Teresa leaned backward against a small piece of furniture and looked very anxiously at Luisa, who remained seated in a pensive posture. For several minutes neither wished to be the first to speak. Finally, Teresa said: "This is horrible. What do you think?"

"It's not a happy turn of events, because when all is said and done, it's somebody we don't know, but—"

"But what?"

"Teresa, what do you want me to say? It's one of two things:

either that unfortunate girl is our sister or she isn't and, given the facts of the matter, I believe she is. You can bet that Don Agustín knows what he's talking about! And what more confirmation is needed than certain incidents that come to mind? Now I understand why I would sometimes see Papa with a torn pocket or an unraveled buttonhole and then find them sewn without knowing who had worked the miracle. Now I understand that insistence of his on going out at night even though the weather might have been bad. Now I understand what the key was for, a huge key that I saw one night in his wardrobe."

"Yes. He would go off on us because he had another daughter—a daughter born of adultery!"

"No, not of adultery."

"For me it's the same thing."

"That's not what we have to discuss."

"I suppose you want to bring her home and cause a scandal."

"In the first place, I don't see the scandal part, and as for the other . . . right now, today, no. We neither can nor should bring into our home—just like that, all of a sudden—a woman whose moral makeup is totally unknown to us."

"Oh! But later on we can?"

"I don't know nor can I know now. All I do know is that if she's Papa's daughter we cannot allow her to starve to death. After all, she's a woman who might bear our name."

"Dishonoring it!"

"We don't know that. If she's a good person one way or another, she is also, whether you like it or not, our sister."

"Well, that's not my concern. I don't know for sure."

"We're not going to get anywhere like this. Tell me frankly what you think."

"Well. . . Don Agustín has come to us with the story—now we know and that's that. From now on he doesn't have to be concerned about anything."

"And us?"

"We don't either."

"Is it possible that you think like this?"

"Then what do you want? To bring her—and God only knows what kind of woman she is—here to this house? And you give her half of what's yours and I give her half of what's mine . . . and we all live together? Come on, don't be a fool. Our father,

I'm ashamed to say, forgot something that he shouldn't have . . . he had a child. Imagine what a treasure the mother must have been! And now we're supposed to welcome this 'sister' with open arms. Who would conceive of such a thing? If you want to give her a little money . . . fine."

"And what if she doesn't ask for any?"

"Then so much the better."

"You've already been told that she has no *right*—do you understand?—no *right* to claim anything. It's a matter of conscience."

"Of conscience? Well, Papa. . . . We're going to do what he didn't?"

"Maybe Papa didn't do anything because it would have required a new document, and you know that the elderly are loathe to change a last will. But Papa used to visit her. You've heard that he never stopped attending to her needs."

"What a mess we've had dumped in our laps!"

"I've already said that it's not a happy turn of events, but we're not talking about a dog or a piece of furniture either."

"All right, all right. I'll talk to Father Graciana and we'll see. I don't dare decide anything. It's a real matter of conscience."

"You don't say? Well, for that very reason I don't need to be advised by anybody. You'll decide whatever you want. As for me, I know what I have to do."

"I can see it now. Life imitating art. You'll visit her—and God only knows what kind of woman we're talking about—throw yourself in her arms, and the two of you will shower kisses on each other. A regular spectacle."

"Look, I have no desire to quarrel with you. Think it over and decide whatever suits you. I'll do the same, and we'll make an end of it, as people used to say."

Teresa left the sitting room and slammed the door without answering her sister. Overwrought, irascible, and almost talking to herself, she rushed to shut herself up in her room, but long before the hour when she was accustomed to doing so, she summoned her maid and went off to church. She returned late, and Luisa had to wait until evening before they ate. During the meal they hardly spoke, and when they had finished, Teresa said: "Come to my room."

They entered, she closed the door, and, facing her sister and attaching great importance to her words, spoke: "I knew that what you were thinking was absurd. I told Father Graciana the whole story. You know who Father Graciana is."

"And what did he say?"

"That the first thing we have to do is be absolutely convinced the woman in question is our father's daughter."

"That's sound advice."

"Then, ascertain if her mother was unmarried or not, because he says that this would change things considerably."

"That's not as clear to me. Why?"

"Because if the mother was unmarried and we're of a mind to do so, we can help the girl."

"What if the mother was married? But there's no need to discuss this point. Don Agustín stated unequivocally that the mother was unmarried and that she went to her grave unmarried."

"If she had been married we wouldn't be obligated to do a thing . . . not lift a finger!"

"Some charity."

"Well, that's what Father Graciana said!"

"Well, I don't care if the bishop himself says it!* What fault was it of hers? But I repeat: this discussion is futile because the mother wasn't married. What else?"

"He says that when we make sure of it—without seeing her or talking to her—we should help her so that she won't go astray, and we should look for a devout, respectable woman with whom she can live. The thing is not to neglect her and, most important of all, to go about it without telling everybody our private business—in other words, without causing a scandal, so nobody will know that Papa . . . in short, to preserve Papa's good name."

"And nothing else?"

"He says that the best thing . . . but this would be expensive. . . that the best thing would be to provide her with a dowry to become a nun."

"And what do you think of all that?"

"I like it—very much."

"Well, I don't—not at all."

"Do you presume to know more than Father Graciana?"

"No. And I've already told you three times that I don't want us to quarrel. But the idea of helping like that, 'going to her aid,' strikes me as humiliating. If I were in her place I'd rather scrub floors. And being my father's daughter, most likely the same thing will occur to her. With regard to looking for a woman she can live with, that's reducing her to servant status. Let's be honest about it. And as for becoming a nun—if it's not her idea, if she doesn't have a vocation, I frankly think it's a preposterous suggestion. Let's put an end to this: what do you want us to do?"

"What I've been advised by someone who knows more than we do: let Don Agustín make payment to her in whatever amount we decide—I thought of ten *duros* a month. And let him hint at her entering the convent to see how she reacts, and if the idea doesn't go over, we keep a stiff upper lip and continue to give her ten *duros* a month. It's charity."

"Charity! God forbid! I'm going to say it for the hundredth time: she is or she is not our sister. If it's the former, forget about charity—it's called duty, justice, however you want to conceive of it; if it's the latter, there's no reason for us to become angels of mercy nor to assume an obligation that isn't ours. Let's not skirt the issue. Is she our sister? Yes. Does she have the right to ask for anything? No. What do we do? Disregard her completely? Give her a handout? Treat her like a sister? This is the question."

"I see that you're not afraid of scandal. You'd be capable of tracking her down and bringing her here to live and of letting even the servants find out that Papa did what he shouldn't have done."

"What, again? Listen to reason, Teresa. Nowadays we girls aren't brought up in complete ignorance of certain things—that's not possible. What with visitors, gossip, servants, the theater, we see and hear more than enough. Look, you know that we're of good character and that we don't ignore our religious obligations, but we also know full well that babies aren't delivered by the stork. Bear in mind that when this happened Papa had to be pretty young. Afterwards wasn't he good and affectionate with us to a fault all his life? Did he neglect us? Did he ruin us? Of course not. He loved or had relations with a woman who couldn't have been bad because she didn't influence him to our detriment. And now it turns out that we have a sister. For the last time, what shall we do?"

"I've already told you—ten *duros* a month, and that's that!"

"Would you take them if you were in her shoes?"

Teresa was silent, unable to find words to answer. Luisa finally said: "With that quick temper of yours you'd refuse the offer."

"Look, Luisa, don't bother me any more. We'll never agree. You want the whole world to know. What a scandal it would be! The worst part of all, according to Father Graciana. Well, I'm finished talking. Next month Don Agustín will take her, on my behalf, five *duros*; you do whatever you like, but don't cause a scandal or bring her here for any reason, because I won't tolerate it."

After speaking out so forcefully, Teresa turned her back on her sister and withdrew to her room.*

The same evening that this conversation took place Luisa sent for Don Agustín and held a long meeting with him.

III

The following morning she went out early, accompanied by her trusted maid, and took a coach, giving the coachman a street name and number. Twenty minutes later she was alighting alone from the hack in front of a house located in a new district, remote from the center of Madrid. She entered a hall and spoke to the portress.

"Third floor, rear apartment on the left," was the woman's response.

Luisa pulled on the bell cord and several moments later the door opened; standing there was a young woman, twenty, on the small side, dark-haired, and plumpish with a stunning resemblance to Teresa, but prettier.* When she saw her, Luisa was momentarily astonished, taken aback, thinking: "Well, I'll be! The ways of the Lord are unfathomable. The very picture of the other one!"

The young woman was dressed unpretentiously, like Luisa, who was also wearing an outfit of extraordinary simplicity. The following dialogue started up between them:

"Would you be kind enough to tell me if your name is Juana?"

"At your service."

"Do you know who I am?"

Juana, silent for a moment, stared at her questioner, and then, opening the door all the way, said at once: "Please come in."

They entered a small, modestly furnished room and sat, face

to face, in armchairs. Luisa glanced around, and the first thing she took in was a photograph of her father on a console table.

Juana said: "Yes, I know who you are because. . . . Oh, I wanted so much to meet you and your sister! I asked Papa again and again and finally, two years ago, he let me go with a friend of mine to a top gallery at the Royal Theater. Between acts he came up but before he did I had already spotted you. You were with him in a box. From that high up I didn't see you very well, so shortly before the opera ended I went down with my friend to one of the vestibule doors, and there, at the exit, I saw you perfectly. That's why I know you and your sister too. This was over two years ago and I haven't seen you since then. No, wait! Once I did, in the street, in passing."

"Can you guess why I've come?"

"Frankly . . . I can't. I know you're my sisters and I also know that I have no right to demand a thing from you. Therefore, I need to exercise patience. You can do a great deal for me . . . or nothing, because I don't believe that you want to cause me harm."

"None. On the contrary. The reason I've come is that you are our sister and, now that our father is dead, we can't allow you to be in need of anything. But the fact is that Teresa and I aren't in. . . . I don't like to lie . . . we aren't completely in agreement about what we should do concerning you. In view of this, it's essential, *for now*, that you be patient, because later everything will be worked out."

"Do you mind if I say something?"

"Be as frank as I am."

"Well, up to now I haven't bothered you for a thing."

"So I see you're a little bit haughty, like us, but please understand that it's not necessary yet for pride to come into play. Listen. Teresa has a very strange character, but she's a good person and I'm certain that I'll convince her and then the situation will be different. For now don't be ashamed. The truth: how much was my father giving you a month?"

"Why do you want to know?"

"Tell me."

"Forty *duros*."

"Fine. Well, my sister and I will give you the same amount each month."

"That's only partially true."

"What do you mean?"

"I mean I know that this is all your own doing. Haven't you just told me that your sister isn't in agreement with you?"

"Our difference of opinions isn't about this. Look, I can't tell you everything today, but don't respond to my good intentions with—"

"Pride? Not at all. Whatever you give me to live on cannot humiliate me because we're sisters."

As she spoke Juana didn't take her eyes off Luisa who replied: "Don't think that I doubt it. Therefore, from one sister to another, will you accept the forty *duros*? And I promise you that—"

"Stop. If what the two of you are offering me is a monthly sum so that I'll leave you alone, remember that I've neither asked for anything nor want anything. I'll get along one way or another. If you're speaking for yourself and hope to persuade Teresa to look upon me eventually without aversion, then . . . that's a lot, too much. I don't need it all. What I want is that whatever you do give me not be a way of taking a weight off your mind, but something you're giving to your sister."

"Do you have any complaints about the way I've approached you or about what I've said to you?"

"None at all."

"Then don't go ruining everything because of misplaced distrust or sensitivity." Luisa then removed two banknotes from a small pocketbook. "Here are forty *duros*. And now . . . the rest is up to me. Time works miracles and my sister isn't a bad sort. I'll arrange everything. Oh! I won't send you the money next month, I'll bring it myself. And if you have no objection, I'll come before then to see you. I want us to know each other— everything depends on it."

Luisa stood, signaling an end to the visit. Juana, easily given to tears, said without being able or wanting to mask her emotions: "What a good person you must be! I'll take whatever you wish to offer me and in whatever way you wish to give it to me. No shame, no embarrassment, no humiliation. It's charity? Then as charity!"

And taking hold of one of Luisa's hands, she kissed it twice before her sister could withdraw it.

When they were at the door to the stairway saying good-bye, Juana said: "I'll never forget what you've just done."

"Well, the best is yet to come."
"Good-bye, Luisa."
"Good-bye, Juana."

IV

Ten months have passed.
Scene of the conversation: the doorway of the church.
Time: the close of a beautiful evening.
Participants: Luisa and Father Graciana, a tall, slender man of fifty with a highly intelligent expression, distinguished air, and polished manners; he prefers rich cloaks and wears them with singular elegance.

"No, no, there's no reason to be shocked, Father. I'm not proposing a crime to you. It's like any other business deal. It doesn't even require deliberation."

"The things that occur to a woman—the devil himself wouldn't think of them."

"The devil doesn't contribute to charity."

"All right, then. You know me, so speak freely."

"You're head of the board that's been charged with building, managing, etc., etc., the Holy Name Hospital, are you not?"

"I am."

"Well, a certain charitable person . . . Mrs. So-and-so . . . the name is beside the point, is giving you through me five thousand *duros* to further the work of the hospital."

"Very good."

"Not so fast. With one condition. Those five thousand *duros* will be handed over to you by me the day that you convince my sister Teresa that Juana should live with us and that she should be treated exactly the way I am treated. As soon as Teresa says to me, 'Tomorrow you can bring her,' that pious person who speaks through me will give you the twenty-five thousand *pesetas*. Is the arrangement acceptable?"

"But, my child, do you think we're discussing a scene from a novel?"

"I don't think anything. I'm proposing and you're deciding. Just imagine what five thousand *duros* represent. Lots of sheets and blankets and cups of broth for those unfortunate patients—and all in exchange for an act of justice."

"With a touch of scandal, because it will become known that your father...."

"That's our affair."

"Wouldn't it be better to convince that pious person to give the five thousand *duros* now, and then as time goes on, let me, prudently and slyly, try to persuade your sister?"

"Impossible. The pious person will not budge and does not trust anyone."

"Do you take me for a fool?"

"Why?"

"Because *you* are the pious person!"

"All right, I am. So what? Will the five thousand *duros* cease being five thousand *duros*?"

Father Graciana was pensive for a moment, pretending to look at the silver buckles that he sported on his shoes. Luisa, determined not to give in, kept silent. At length the priest said: "You'll hand over that amount in person to the building committee."

"When?"

"Soon. The first day that I talk to Teresa."

"No. The day after Juana comes to live with us."

"You're rather distrustful."

"Is it agreed?"

"Agreed. All means are good when they serve to aid the poor!"

"Then I won't keep you any longer. As we've said: you'll talk to Teresa and she, of course, will talk to me and the day after Juana comes to our home I'll give you the money."

Father Graciana smiled kindly and said: "Good works would profit immensely if we could count on numerous people who are as intelligent as you are!"

"Thank you for the compliment, Father, but do you think it's a bad thing to attempt to avoid a woman's ruin? And as for spending twenty-five thousand *pesetas* on broth for the poor, well.... Anyway, good-bye, Father, and I hope you can follow through on what we've agreed to."

* * *

Fifteen days later almost every newspaper in Madrid published the following news item: "A pious lady, unwilling to reveal her name, yesterday handed over to the illustrious head of the Building Committee of Holy Name Hospital the sum of twenty-five thousand *pesetas* as a donation to assist that charitable institution in carrying out its mission. Acts of generosity like this one require no commentary."

La dama de las tormentas

The Lady and the Storms

One night I was walking across the stage of some theater or another with a friend of mine when I noticed that he had stopped a few steps behind me, looking upward with intense curiosity.

"What are you looking at?" I asked.

"Is that the thunder run?"

"Yes."

I had to give him a complete description of the device.

"Do you see," I said, "those four planks, joined lengthwise at the edges, that form a kind of narrow, long case, very narrow, and so long that it extends almost from the gridiron to the pit? Well, the interior of that case is lined with big, irregular and protruding wooden pegs that are securely fastened. At the top, next to the upper section of the scenery prop, there's a container with heavy, uneven stones of different sizes. When the drama or comedy calls for a thunderstorm, the person who has the role of the invisible Jupiter dumps the contents of the container in the opening of the case, and the stones fall through the inside, making a horrible racket as they bump into the staggered pegs and tumble down to the pit where the depth causes the noise to decrease. It becomes so fearsome and dreadful that it imitates with amazing fidelity a real thunderstorm, when echoes rumble from mountain to mountain, reverberating in hollows."

"You don't know how anxious I was to see one of these contraptions."

"Why?"

"I don't mind telling you the reason for my curiosity."

We had dinner together and afterwards he told me the following story.

"A young, attractive, and very wealthy widow, whom I'll call Clarisa to be discreet, once invited a number of us, members of her regular social set, to spend a few days at a mountain retreat that she owned near Madrid. We all met at the train station at the agreed-upon hour. There were five of us: a general in the reserves, a painter who took first prize in the competition of 1860, a stockbroker who handled Salamanca's* account, a politician who had conspired with Olózaga,* and me, the youngest man in the group—rather, the only young one. Shortly afterwards, dressed with elegant simplicity, Clarisa arrived in the company of her aunt and two maids; we got on a parlor car that was reserved for us and the train departed.

"To keep it short, I won't go into details about the estate, at the entrance to which we were met by the manager, guards, servants, and workers. Suffice it to say that the house is magnificent. In front of the main entrance there's an imposing French-style garden, and in the back, orchards and farmyards. The wild aspect of the countryside contrasts with the endless number of comforts that the house offers; I won't describe to you the severe luxury, so ingeniously modest, with which it's appointed. The important point for my story is that there's a charming little theater there, built in the time of Carlos IV by an actress, Godoy's* mistress, who never lost her fondness for the stage and delighted in continuing to act for the amusement of her quasi-royal lover and a handful of friends. In any case, the house has a theater, and Clarisa, whose fondness for drama borders on the insane, had renovated it, spending a great deal, so that on a small scale it's as complete as the best in Madrid. On the stage, which was rebuilt just a few years ago, six or eight sets can be hung; and it has trapdoors and its own thunder run. It really does have everything, because *Don Alvaro** and *The Goth's Dagger** have both been put on there, and you'll recall that the former ends with a dreadful storm and the latter begins with one. I've forgotten to tell you, and you need to know to grasp clearly everything that follows, that the rooms assigned to guests are on the second floor, and Clarisa's are on the first, near the theater and with windows and doors that open on the garden.

"A few hours after arriving I realized that my situation there was going to be impossible. As it turned out, the general, the stockbroker, the painter, and the politician spent the mornings hunting; after the midday lunch they talked a while with Clarisa and then accompanied her on a short walk, but at four o'clock they would begin their game of ombre and you could forget about them until the dinner hour. And as soon as they had their coffee and lighted their cigars, they went back to their game because our gracious hostess let them do whatever they wished. Clarisa's aunt doesn't merit special attention; she was also a great one for ombre, and when she didn't play she would fall asleep.

"Since I don't hunt and dislike playing cards, the result of all this was that I ended up talking to the enchanting Clarisa for hours on end: from the time that she went out to the garden in the morning until lunch, that is, while those four gentlemen chased after rabbits and partridges, and from the time that they began their ombre until shortly before dinner, when she withdrew to her room to freshen up and dress. Can you conceive of a more difficult situation for a man?

"Clarisa was thirty, the age at which a woman is most pleasantly dangerous for a man, *and* for herself. She was of medium height, but very slim, and very fair-haired; she was quick and quite witty, and used rather spirited, colorful language with that insouciance of the refined Madrid girl who can hold her own in risqué conversation; she was sly and mischievous, subtle in discussion; and she was fond of being complimented and very fond of bewildering and disconcerting the person she was talking to. But all these traits were checked, moderated, and, I'll even venture to say, seemingly dignified by that aura of modesty and wisdom which suits a respectable widow so well.

"The word coquette won't do when applied to a woman like Clarisa. Her lightheartedness would turn into solemnity when you least expected it; then you'd think she was taking you seriously and she'd answer ironically. She was an enigma or, rather, an abyss that beckoned, but one into which you couldn't throw yourself because its edges were lined in some places by prickly thorns that prevented you from getting close, and in others by delicate flowers whose perfumes confused the senses. I'm timid. Can you understand how much I suffered as a result? Could I, by abusing her hospitality, get Clarisa to fall for me? At first I thought that this would have been taking advantage of the circumstances, but at the same time it occurred to me that not to say a word or do anything that would show my admiration for her beauty was a sign of ignorance, of bad taste, and even of scorn.

"Despite my timidity I was also mortified by the absence of a rival to beat out, because I would be exposing myself to being victorious for want of another suitor and aided more by the lovely woman's boredom than my own efforts. In the end, I could not tolerate looking like a fool, and it was the height of foolishness to live next to a desirable woman and not try to become her lover when she didn't have one. All this reflection, stimulated by Clarisa's continual, disquieting presence, filled my mind with doubts. You can laugh at everything philosophers have written about whether intelligence is an organic, objective faculty, as some say, or whether it is a physiological product which is consumed at the instant that it is produced, as others maintain; and you can laugh at the systems thought up to explain the union of the body with the soul. All these considerations are trifles and absurdities compared with the problem that those circumstances had created for me, a problem I was supposed to solve. Because the truth is that as long as a man is alone and in a bad temper, he can devote himself, like Prince Hamlet, to determining whether it's important 'to be or not to be,' but when he spends eight or ten hours a day face to face with a woman like her, the real problem is 'to dare or not to dare.'

"Several days had gone by since our departure from Madrid. The weather was so gorgeous that Clarisa decided that we wouldn't return until it rained or turned cold. Meanwhile, she watched me, apparently not surprised or angry that I wasn't making eyes at her, but she did show signs of unquestionable pleasure whenever I stayed back and talked to her instead of going hunting or sitting down to play cards; and no sooner did my words reveal the slightest hint of a tribute to her charms than she would smile in a mysterious way that left me intimidated and bewildered. At such moments the look on her face seemed to attract me, but her mouth would curl disdainfully. What's to be done when the eyes say *Come* and the lips say *Keep still?*

"The excellent food, the country air, the exercise, and, above all, the constant proximity of beauty in its most desirable form provoked in me a physical and moral state that was impossible to define and even more impossible to endure. At the same time that I felt capable of undertaking great ventures, I was fearful of attempting them, and I had no doubt that Clarisa saw right through me. Fortunately nature came to my rescue. Like dramatists, it speeds up events whenever it sees fit.

"One oppressively hot afternoon, the painter, the politician, the general, and the stockbroker decided to take a nap instead of playing cards, and each one went up to his room. Clarisa and I stayed in the garden under a small bower that had jasmine and clematis vines climbing through the latticework with such a profusion of flowers that here and there the green stems looked as though they were covered with snow. The lady was wearing a very lightweight dress, and thanks to the sheerness of the fabric her beautiful body was outlined without compromising decency, although enough could be seen to appreciate the harmony of lines that constitutes such eloquent testimony to the Creator's goodness. The low collar, which had neither ribbons nor bows, and the short sleeves allowed glimpses of whiteness that were more pleasing to the eye than those of the bower's flowers. And one more detail: she sported a big, fanciful straw hat with long ribbons that enveloped her face in a mysterious half-light and enhanced the sparkle of her eyes. I was looking at her and trying to appear natural and at ease, but from time to time I felt that, even without my wanting them to, my glances became stares, sometimes with the stupidity of fascination, sometimes with the boldness of desire.

"Clarisa, understanding that something had to give, got up all of a sudden and said: 'Finish your coffee and let's go to the parterre. I want to pick the flowers for the table myself.'

"She started walking and I followed her to the garden where she began to cut roses. She handed each one to me and I carefully placed them inside her big straw hat, which she had taken off and given to me to hold by the ribbons for use as a small basket.

"We were engaged in this poetic operation when a current of air began to blow and quickly turned into a gust. The branches of the trees whipped back and forth, the sky swiftly filled with leaden clouds as huge drops began to fall, and thunder boomed. Clarisa, looking at me panic-stricken, shouted: 'Back to the house! Back to the house!'

"The wind intensified in its fury. You could hear the creaking of the pines that were bent by the storm; chickens were scurrying to the coop to take shelter; pigeons were flying in flocks toward roofs; and all of a sudden there was a flash of lightning and the rumble of a second thunderclap, more formidable and awesome than the first.

"Clarisa then ran off like a blue streak. When I caught up with her and made her take my arm, she said: 'You have no idea how much this terrifies me.... I can't put it into words.... I get so that I don't know what I'm doing.'

"When we were close to the house the flashes of lightning were so frequent that the sky looked as though it was on fire and the thunderclaps scared the daylights out of us. Clarisa held onto me half convulsed with terror. We went in the house through a service door. She not only didn't let go of me, but clung to my arm all the more tightly, and had me cross the hall, the billiard room, and the drawing room until, all of a sudden, as if we had flown on a magic carpet, I found myself alone with her in a boudoir, with a view, through one of the doors, of the curtains in her bedroom. The thunder and lightning seemed to announce the end of the world. Then, in a supplicating voice, she said: 'For the love of God, don't leave me alone! Not alone! Not alone! And close those windows—shutters and all!'

"I did as she asked and closed the big windows that overlooked the garden; a draft slammed the door shut too and we ended up in total darkness. Fortunately the streak from a flash of lightning let me catch a glimpse of Clarisa, who had thrown herself on a sofa, covering her face. I approached her, groping in the dark; without warning my feet got tangled up on cushions that were strewn on the floor and I fell headlong, landing on my knees. I extended my hands. One came across something fine and silky that yielded easily to a squeeze; it was Clarisa's hair. The other one felt the soft smoothness of an arm.... The storm lasted all afternoon with the crash of thunder lingering until nightfall. The claps receded with a racket comparable only to the kind made by numerous pieces of artillery rolling along poorly paved stone streets.

"'We can open up now,' Clarisa said.

"The sun had set, the clouds were being dispersed by the wind, and stars were beginning to shine in the firmament. Something that looked divine also shone in Clarisa's eyes—perhaps it was the reflection of my happiness. She wouldn't let me leave by the door that led to the salons, but indicated another one, a side door adjacent to the maids' quarters. Nobody learned how I got up to my room. On finding myself alone I experienced a certain release, the effect no doubt of the recent inner turmoil and of the highly charged air of electricity that I had just breathed. But neither Florambel the knight on taking leave of Groselinda, nor Leandro on parting from the beautiful Cupídea, nor the renowned Amadís, having just enjoyed the favors of Oriana, could consider themselves as fortunate.*

"One hour later Clarisa appeared in the dining room looking prettier than ever. Perfume-laden air entered the windows that gave onto the garden and it was a magnificent night; the storm had not left a trace on either the sky or the lady's face.

"What surprised me the most was Clarisa's calmness, her absolutely imperturbable composure. She treated the other guests warmly and joked with them, but for me there was no glance, no touch as we brushed together to sit at the table, no utterance, no allusion whatsoever that might imply acknowledgment of what had passed between us. Comments were made about the storm and she said dryly: 'I had an awful time.'

"I was stunned and looked at her in disbelief. Then she fixed her eyes on me with such icy indifference that I thought I had had a dream. After the meal I tried three or four times to approach her and she skillfully dodged my attempts. For the sake of pretense and precaution it was too much. Of necessity it had to be anger. Then it occurred to me that perhaps I had committed an unspeakable outrage, an odious mixture of cunning and violence, by taking advantage of the poor woman's terror, and that she, fearful of a scandal, was keeping silent, unwilling to forgive. But how was I going to become convinced of this when there still resounded in my ears those tender words that, in spite of being spoken in a quiet, controlled voice, had made a much greater impression on me than the fantastic roar of the storm? Finally, I wondered if maybe the atmospheric disturbance had brought about a nervous state in Clarisa that suspended the rule of will, a condition that first subjected her to an upheaval of the senses and then deprived her of memory.

"For a moment I entertained the idea of inventing a pretext and leaving the following morning, but, realizing that the suddenness of my departure might give rise to suspicion, I chose not to go but rather to change my routine. I would no longer remain at her side while the others went off with shotguns on their shoulders, and I would stop staying with her when they began to play cards; what I would do was set out with the hunters in the morning and go off for a walk in the afternoon. And this I did—for four days, trying to play, for Clarisa's benefit, the role of the ashamed, embarrassed man who's avoiding the fury of the affronted woman.

"I was taken aback to see that her anger grew. When she was certain that nobody could observe her, she would quickly fix eyes on me that blazed with fury. I imagined that she was looking for chances to approach me, but I worked wonders of cowardly proficiency to avoid that. Finally, on the fifth day, as I was going downstairs at lunchtime, hoping to find her in the company of the other guests, I met her in the hall pretending to inspect the plants that adorned the base of the staircase. She looked around cautiously and, barely moving her lips, said to me: 'At five-thirty this afternoon, through the same door as the other time.'

"I thought that the terrible moment of shame and expiation had arrived for me! Of course I had no alternative but to go.

"During lunch Clarisa encouraged the hunters to skip their afternoon card game and take advantage of the mild weather to go to the oak grove, where there were rabbits. Then, saying that she needed to discuss bills with her business manager, she retired to her rooms. I don't know if it was discretion or indifference, but it didn't occur to anybody to ask what I would do. I went up to my room and waited. A little after three I heard the hunters leave; at five-thirty sharp I went down to the garden.

"It was a magnificent afternoon, and in the clear blue sky not a single cloud could be made out. I walked around the house and found the door ajar. When I entered, I crossed the very same rooms that I had gone through on my way out the day of the storm, and I reached her boudoir. It really took me by surprise to see that it was almost in darkness, with one of the two windows completely closed and the other one more than half-closed, leaving an opening of no more than a few inches between the slats of the shutter. Thanks to the light that filtered through them I saw Clarisa sitting in an enormous armchair, reading.

"'I have the room like this,' she said on seeing me, 'because the sun comes streaming in until it sets, and it's very hot.'

"The precaution startled me because it was a balmy day, but

mindful of something more important, I knelt at the lady's feet and, taking one of her hands, began to protest my respect, my regret for what had happened, and, above all, my love. I tried to give my words that mixture of sincerity and fervor that usually produces excellent results—sometimes because people believe us and other times because they pretend to believe us. I soon realized that Clarisa wasn't looking at me angrily, nor was she wrinkling her pretty brow; she wasn't even taking her hand out of mine. . . .

"For more than a quarter of an hour I was waxing eloquent and she was watching me in indulgent silence, when unexpectedly, without being preceded by a flash of lightning, there was a fairly long and fairly loud thunderclap, noisy, but not of the intimidating variety. I involuntarily let go of Clarisa's hand, and as I did, she quickly got up and closed the half-open slats of the window. When the room was in total darkness she said, in a fainthearted voice that struck me as somewhat sardonic: 'A storm, a storm!'

"I held her close and managed to prevent her from being overcome by terror, and then for a long time I whispered words of passionate tenderness in her ear, words that made her tremble not from fear but love. We said good-bye to each other the same time as the day of the big storm.

"As I was crossing the stretch of garden that I had to cover to go up to my room, I noticed that the sky was completely clear—not a cloud to be seen, not even the slightest indication that there had been any. It was the oddest thing! The gardener's boy was walking nearby, and, acting on one of those impulses that we don't reason out but which respond to a state of mind, I said to him: 'The storm was brief today. It thundered only once.'

"'No, sir. It didn't thunder even once.'

"'How can you say no? I heard it.'

"'Not at all,' the boy replied with a stupid grin on his face. 'What happened was that the mistress, on some kind of whim, had given me orders to start the thunder run in the theater this afternoon at six o'clock on the dot, without fail.'"

Una venganza

An Act of Revenge

The whole town knew that Marcela and Dorotea hated each other. They were, give or take a year, the same age, and they had gone to the same school and played together as children. Both women were beautiful although in different ways, and they enjoyed a similar financial standing that allowed them to live comfortably. Everything pointed to their getting along well, and nevertheless, they detested each other.

Marcela was a widow and had a sixteen-year-old daughter on whom she doted; Dorotea was married and loved Jorge, her husband, to distraction. When Marcela was widowed, Jorge, a very close friend of her husband, began to advise her on everything from disagreements with relatives to monetary matters. During the long meetings that he held with her, Marcela became convinced that it behooved her to be on good terms with him because he was so smart and influential in the town. In time she also realized that he was handsomer than her deceased husband, and she gradually grew fond of the idea of making him her lover just as she had made him her adviser, so that she would have, in one man, all that she needed for her prosperity and her pleasure. Through maliciousness—in part by leading him to believe that she loved him, in part by pretending that she was restraining herself on moral grounds—she managed to drive him mad, until one day she cunningly "fainted" in his arms and made him believe that he was possessing her, when in fact, by her seduction of him, she had taken over his will and held him spellbound.

Jorge, deranged by that passion, began to treat his wife indifferently and coldly, which aroused her mistrust and jealousy and

An Act of Revenge

made her suffer a great deal. A neighbor woman informed her of the cause of his callousness, and from then on the miserable Dorotea's only concern was to win back the husband she had lost, and if she didn't manage to rescue him, to take revenge. To effect the first course, that is, get Jorge to come back to her, every act of tenderness and instance of meekness seemed inadequate to her; to accomplish the second, that is, avenge the affront and the stolen love, every act of cruelty and ferocity struck her as too little. But before embarking on a terrible struggle, she tried to recover amicably what she had lost, and one day when Jorge left town to collect on land leased by Marcela, she went with astonishing ingenuousness to the latter's house, certain that she would find her alone.

With deep feeling, forcing herself to the point of groveling, Dorotea said: "I haven't harmed you in any way. You have a sixteen-year-old daughter who ought to be the joy of your life. If you had loved my Jorge before, that love would have shown sometime. Let me have my Jorge, whom I've always adored. Don't allow him to set foot in this house again. I've come to beg you, to plead with you. If you want a husband or a lover, the town is full of men who would be proud to accommodate you, but let me have mine, don't encourage him; send him back to me, because he's mine and I've never done you any harm. I ask you by all that's sacred, in the name of Encarnación, your daughter."

And she stopped talking, awaiting a response in a posture of agonizing humility.

Marcela wavered for a moment between what her conscience was telling her and what her vanity was shouting at her, until, slowly overcome by the worse instinct, she replied with foolish cruelty, a smile on her face: "It's true. Jorge's in love with me. The devil has a hand in these things."

Dorotea, containing her anger with great difficulty, insisted with unbelievable meekness: "You'll not want for someone to love you. You're the most beautiful woman in the town. Why would you wish to make me miserable? You're not a bad person. Don't become one out of vanity."

Instead of feeling flattered, Marcela's conceit knew no bounds.

"When you beg so much," she replied, "it's because you understand that you're incapable of making Jorge happy. It's quite clear that he's tired of you, and fed up and bored. Don't blame me."

"For your daughter's sake, for Encarnación, I'm asking you. If you rebuff him, he'll be mine again."

Marcela retorted scoffingly: "My daughter has nothing to do with this, and as for him, men go where they have the best time."

Dorotea was outraged by her insults. "Good-bye. You're bringing it on yourself. I'll try to tear Jorge from your arms, even if he comes back to mine dirty and debased—and I'll get even with you."

* * *

All that Dorotea did to prompt Jorge to break up with his paramour—suffer in silence, complain meekly, attempt to entice him with caresses, excite him with disdain, make herself desirable by dressing alluringly—was futile and came to naught, because, although in love and vehement, she was one of those wives who retain a sense of shame in their innermost selves and a sense of decency in their most ardent moments of passion. Marcela, on the other hand, was born with the instincts of a courtesan and was in fact a small-town one, though only for one man, and she displayed the same sensual cunning that she would have showed off in a big city for many men. For two years the lover lived in a daze, the wife in humiliation, and the paramour in triumph.

Meanwhile, Dorotea was sought out and courted by several suitors. Some men imagined that it would be easy to possess unprotected beauty like hers; others were sincerely captivated by a lovely woman whom misfortune surrounded like a halo. And one, Lope, the caretaker of the town cemetery, fell hopelessly in love with her. He was a vigorous, coarse man with herculean strength and a face reddened by heavy drinking, and he was so smitten by Dorotea that he would not have let anything stand in his way if he could have made her his. Whenever he saw her he would say: "I'll get revenge for you!"

Dorotea never responded, but Lope neither despaired nor tired, and he kept repeating, insisting with greater determination every time: "Listen. When you can't take it any more and want to get revenge, tell me—even if you don't so much as let me give you a kiss. Come, come one night to talk to me. I'll tell you how she stole him from you. Come one night to the cemetery at ten o'clock and knock on the low window, the one by the adobe-wall door.

We'll put our heads together and hatch a good scheme, and . . . heaven help them!"

Dorotea would flee from him—horrified, persuaded that he was capable of anything—and then try to forget his terrible offers. But there were days when, her gloom exacerbated by humiliation and scorn, she had a black outlook and then, involuntarily, she would remember Lope's words.

One morning they ran into each other, and Lope said what he always said: "I'll get revenge for you however you want and whenever you want—just for the pleasure of getting revenge for you. Do you see those vaults? I have three ready for them!"

* * *

That summer a typhus epidemic broke out in the town, striking mainly the young people. One of its victims was Marcela's daughter, and Jorge, when the girl's condition became critical, spent several successive nights at his paramour's house. His behavior made Dorotea realize that, even if the time were not chosen with malicious intent, Marcela and Jorge would take advantage of it in the future if the girl survived, and that seemed to her like the beginning of a complete abandonment. She was certain that, with such a precedent set, Jorge would look for a pretext to absent himself from their home whenever he wished. When this realization sank in, she ran to Marcela's house in a fit of anger and inquired about her husband. But he hid, and Marcela answered. She was so angry, disheveled, and haughty that, rather than being anguished by her daughter's illness, she seemed irate at Dorotea's presence. Keeping the door half-closed to prevent her from entering, she asked: "What do you want? Your husband is my business manager. He's here because he should be and above all, because he wants to be. If you knew how to hold on to him, you wouldn't have to run around looking for him."

And Marcela slammed the door. Dorotea, throwing prudence to the winds, shouted at her: "Wicked woman!"

And she left dry-eyed, furious, crazed by an indefinable sensation, as if a poison ran through her entire body and muddled her thoughts by making her blood boil. Health, life, honor, and eternal salvation—at that moment she would have traded them all to get revenge.

A few days later Marcela's daughter died. Dorotea hoped in vain that Jorge would return. He sent for clothes, and that was that.

Then, eager to enjoy the spectacle of somebody else's pain, she went out to the corner of her street to watch the girl's funeral procession go by. Because people had gathered in front of the funeral home, her part of town was deserted. Dorotea walked to the end of the street, which led to open country, and sat on a stone to wait.

Without warning she heard someone walking very cautiously behind her, and then Lope's voice, midway between solicitous and terrible: "I know what they did to you, but I'm yours. Let me—let me avenge you. Why don't you want to talk to me?"

"This very day! When? Where?" Dorotea replied, unable now and unwilling to control the rancor that was making her seethe.

"Do you dare to come to the cemetery tonight? At ten. I'll be alone. Nobody can see you. I'll have a light at the low window."

"Well, have some wine too to give me courage," she added, laughing, "because I'll come."

They separated at once without anybody seeing them, and several minutes later the funeral procession passed by.

* * *

At the agreed-upon hour Dorotea set out for the graveyard, taking precautions not to be seen.

She was going along the road when suddenly, upon hearing the tinkling of a cart's mules close by, she lay down in the roadside ditch behind a pile of split cobblestones, let the carters pass and then continued across country.

Next to the cemetery's adobe wall, in the low window of the caretaker's house a light shone, but the big door was closed. Dorotea scooped up a handful of sand and threw it at the glass. A moment later the door opened halfway; Lope came out and welcomed her with a look of joyful lust, although he didn't dare touch her. They crossed a corner of the patio and entered the house.

On a table there was a piece of dried meat, two bread rolls wrapped in paper, two glasses, a bottle, and in reserve, an enormous jug of wine. The legs of a bed showed behind a coarse white cotton curtain, and at one end of the room lay various tools, hoes, shovels, and lengths of rope.

Lope, observing something frightening in Dorotea's expression—something like rage in the midst of tears that were barely held in check—made a point of being solicitous.

"Don't be silly, beautiful. You give the orders and I carry them out . . . but right now don't you see that she's probably beside herself with grief? And us . . . why don't you want us to be happy?"

Dorotea replied: "You can have whatever you want if you get revenge for me. But I need air! I'm suffocating in here! Open that window."

"No. Somebody could see you. Let's go outside. Don't be afraid—the dead are harmless."

And they went out to the cemetery grounds which consisted of the adobe wall that faced the road and three rows of burial chambers, each one with four tiers of vaults. Some were occupied and, for want of headstones, had inscriptions, letters and numbers scratched in the lime; others, still empty, displayed their fearful openings like hungry mouths. In the middle of the grounds there was a stone cross surrounded by tall cypresses that swayed slowly in the wind, and several stone slabs lay here and there. As the waning moon faintly illuminated the whole area, the wind swept in the aroma of wild flowers, and at times, when it stopped blowing, a stench could be detected, a sharp fetid odor that penetrated everywhere and brought sensations of dread and corruption. Meanwhile, in the distance, as if protesting decay and death, summer insects chirped in and out of the furrows of the plain.

Lope timidly took hold of Dorotea's waist. She asked: "Where is Marcela's daughter interred?"

"That lower tier over there. The one at ground level."

He approached it and pointed to a vault which, instead of being walled up with brick and lime, was only covered by a semicircular board.

"Here it is," he added, "number 122."

"Why isn't it walled up?"

"Because sometimes, like today, I run out of bricks, and then I put up this board temporarily, until tomorrow or whenever the mayor gives me the order slip to draw lime and bricks."

Dorotea, staring at the vault, shook from head to toe. What had crossed her mind was horrible.

"Let's go," she said, "I'm afraid."

Upon entering the house, Lope offered her a bread roll and some wine. Forcing herself, Dorotea accepted both and permitted him to sit very close, right up against her, and she even repaid with smiles the greedy glances in which he seemed to enfold her. She then began to serve him wine, making him drain one glass after another, pretending that she too was drinking and allowing him to clutch her waist. But it didn't take Lope long to let go of it; he was in a stupor and virtually tongue-tied, with his arms hanging limply and his face reddened and bathed in sweat. Then, seeing a flask of brandy on a chest, she poured part of it into a glass of wine, raised the drunk's head, and practically forced him to swallow. A moment later, Lope, rendered unconscious, toppled headfirst against the chest where he remained asleep.

Dorotea glanced around and, seeing the pile of tools, picked up a big chisel and a length of rope. Although she was shaking because of what had occurred to her earlier, she found the daring to go outside without hesitation and, her anger overcoming her dread, she headed for vault 122.

She removed the semicircular board that was being used as a temporary seal and she bared the top portion of the coffin; then, reaching inside the vault, she tied the rope to one of the handles and pulled it outside. The moon had disappeared, but in the dim starlight she saw with relief that the coffin had no lock and was simply nailed shut. Dorotea inserted the chisel at different points between the top and bottom and, using the tool as a lever, pried all around until she managed to raise the lid without splintering it and expose the body. Marcela's daughter's hands were crossed over her chest, and her only adornment was a wreath of artificial flowers.

Overcome simultaneously by fear and awe, compassion and dread, Dorotea hesitated for a moment and felt an urge to desist from carrying out her plan, but all of a sudden, as she looked away in horror, she saw the town's lights in the distance and remembered Marcela and Jorge, and once again her heart overflowed with hatred.

Then, tenderly, with gentle, careful, sensitive hands, as if she feared hurting her, she moved the dead girl, tilted her head, flexed her arms, and bent her knees a little.

Afterward, with incomprehensible compassion, Dorotea kissed her on the forehead, as if asking her forgiveness, and, leaving her in a very different position, replaced the lid, fitting the nails in the holes that they had made originally. Working noiselessly and skillfully, she shut and secured the coffin, examining it with care until she was convinced that no one would be able to discover or explain the hideous desecration that she had perpetrated. Finally, she pushed the coffin back inside and repositioned the semicircular board. She looked again. The bricks of the vault floor were scratched a little, but everybody would think that that had happened the first time the coffin was inserted.

Not long afterward Dorotea reentered Lope's cottage where the caretaker was still passed out on the floor. She put the chisel and rope back, wrapped herself in her shawl, and, going across country, returned to the town and her house without being seen by anybody.

During the walk from the graveyard to the village she was horrified at what she had done, thinking with even greater terror about what she still had to do to execute her plan fully. Remorse seemed to follow cruelty so closely that before Dorotea finished taking revenge she was already beginning to loathe herself; but when she reached the town and set foot inside the house from which Jorge had been absent for two weeks, her hatred revived and with terrifying delight she again turned her thoughts to revenge, determined to take it as she had conceived of it in the beginning.

Four days later she wrote two anonymous accusations, composed with letters cut out from newspapers so that her handwriting would not be recognized. One was for Marcela and the other for the judge, and in both she charged that the former's daughter had been buried alive; she then sent them to Madrid so that a trusted friend could mail the letters from there. Marcela and the judge received them the same day and neither suspected who the accuser was. The judge deemed the denunciation false, but Marcela persisted in demanding exhumation and witnessing it, threatening to go to the court of appeal if her wish was not granted, and the judge yielded.

The ghastly business took place without anyone discovering a trace of Dorotea's desecration, and the girl was found with her head tilted and body turned to the side, as if she had struggled with her hands and knees to get out. In vain did the doctor who issued the death certificate, as well as all the others who had seen her, swear that Encarnación had been dead.

Marcela herself had seen her dead, but she became convinced nonetheless that her daughter had been buried alive.

Las coronas

The Wreaths

There are no words with which to express the gamut of impressions that Emilia experienced as she watched her husband die almost without warning after barely a year and a half of perfect wedded bliss. Surprise, fear, and grief invaded her spirit; in the beginning she thought that she would go mad, but afterward, making a supreme effort, she displayed extraordinary composure. She laid him out, accompanied the coffin to the stairway door, and, before her relatives and friends could restrain her, ran immediately to the sitting room and pressed her face against the balcony window; she watched the funeral cortege start, and then she collapsed on the rug, yielding to the anguish of her grief when the hearse turned the corner.

As she came to, how awful solitude seemed to her! Because what greater misfortune was there than being widowed at twenty-four when she was beautiful and loved? What a frightful mark of terror the night of October 31/November 1 left on her mind! How she recalled everything down to the last detail! At twelve he asked her to arrange his pillows, which she did, and he thanked her with a kiss, the last one! At one-fifteen he lost consciousness, and at three he passed away. Poor Gabriel . . . and poor Emilia! Afterward, when she saw that one day followed another and that sorrow didn't carry her off, that she slept and experienced hunger and thirst, that she thought and reasoned as before, always subject to her body's disgusting needs, she acknowledged, with self-loathing, that the physical, purely instinctive response in human nature is both anterior and superior to every other feeling. She lapsed into a gloomy, silent pessimism.

She would spend hour after hour sitting in an armchair; not even crying, and seemingly calm, she was actually in the throes of a desperation that shook her body with nervous shudders and subjected her to mental torment.

People would tell her in vain that she was beautiful, wealthy, and, even more important, young, and that of necessity she would resign herself—if not find consolation and forget. She listened to no one. What difference did it make to be pretty if the man to whom she had given herself in body and soul was dead? What did youth mean to her except a future that entailed suffering brought on by remembrance? And the wealth that she inherited from him, his final gift to her, what was it except one more reason to pay homage to his memory? As she had earlier savored the fullness of sated passion on their honeymoon, in similar fashion she now took pleasure in analyzing and mentally scrutinizing the nature of her sorrow, delighting in the bitter voluptuousness of grief, and the more she wallowed in her distress the better she believed she was showing her love for her deceased husband. And shouldn't she mourn him if she had freely chosen him, studying his traits and qualities because he had fit her concept of what a husband ought to be? Young, handsome, very well-mannered, and rich, Gabriel was forceful with others, but gentle with his wife; he was hardworking, although not so much that he would leave her days on end, and active enough that his leisure time didn't lead him astray. Then, too, he was quick of mind in order not to make a bad impression, but affable, kindhearted, and soft so that she could control him. And after she had chosen so well, when enough time had passed to persuade her that she could not have been more right, that swift, brutal illness came, followed by the death that turned her life upside down. "You think that you won't be able to forget him," her girlfriends would say to her, "but time heals everything." Emilia would smile sadly and not answer so as not to waste her breath.

What she couldn't listen to calmly were the questions about Julián, because she always believed that his name was brought up with excessive frequency, and even with a certain malicious, sarcastic tone. What was so odd about Julián visiting her if he was her poor deceased husband's closest friend, the one who carried on his business, and the executor of his will?

There is never a lack of evil-minded people and poisonous

tongues. Besides, didn't all of Madrid know Julián? And knowing him, what sensible woman would be capable of taking him seriously?

His cheerful disposition, his joking nature, his free speech, and above all the open disdain that he exhibited toward women, drew such a clear picture of his personality that no real lady could consider him dangerous. He was so unswervingly cynical about matters of the heart that only a mad or dissolute woman would be shameless enough to allow herself to be courted seriously by him. Emilia's safeguard was in this excess of notoriety, in this aura of scandal, for she had a faultless reputation as a prudent and discreet woman. Besides, given his friendship with the deceased, in whose business he was partner and attorney, there was nothing unusual about the widow continuing to have dealings with him. Lastly, Emilia's friends could see that Julián spoke to her as he did to everybody, always cracking jokes, always poking fun, speaking in jest, in a string of constant hyperbole, without ever using those insincerely timid expressions that have a double meaning and are the mark of a crafty coward. Nor did he affect the more or less clever displays of discretion on which a man bases his amorous strategy when he proceeds with sinister designs.

For several months, during the early stages of Emilia's widowhood, Julián restrained himself out of politeness and taste, but then he reverted to his habitual language, brazenly saying whatever he wished, provoking her laughter, as if by dint of jokes he expected to distract her and cheer her up. The very boldness of his speech minimized the importance of everything that he said. Why get upset with him if everybody knew what he was like? He flirted with daughters in front of their parents, with married women in the presence of their husbands and nobody paid attention to him. In short, he was the kind who is known for his quips and sallies, the kind whose remarks are tolerated because their very levity makes it impossible to take offense. "Emilia, I want to take Gabriel's place." "Emilia, be patient . . . we should wait a year." "Emilia, it has to be someone, and if he's watching us from the next world he'll prefer that it be me." "Emilia, one day you're going to have to throw me out." And he said all these things in front of her girlfriends, openly, with harmless impudence, certain that were she to react harshly or show the slightest sign of anger she would be laying herself open to terrible ridicule. What discreet woman was going to answer him seriously? Emilia would content herself with smiling, she would call him silly or say: "What a pest you can be!"

However, when Julián continued going to see her after the will had been executed, it didn't dawn on the widow that all those visits were no longer justified. Almost every afternoon upon leaving the stock exchange he would go to inform her of the rise or drop in her securities; other days he would arrive unexpectedly for lunch. Since he was in the habit of answering letters wherever the mood hit him, he would sit down to write at poor Gabriel's desk, and lastly, knowing that Emilia didn't go out in the evening and that she played ombre with several girlfriends, he would turn up two or three times a week "bored with his club and tired of opera," humbly asking her for a little conversation and a cup of tea, and there he would remain until half-jokingly she had to show him the door. His parting words were always the same: "One of these nights I'm staying!"

Emilia conducted herself courteously and graciously, welcoming him with a smile on her face. Fully convinced that he was a harmless soul, she showed no signs of distrust. And how could she be suspicious of him if one of the things that he did was substantially increase her income in three or four stock market transactions? On the other hand, given that he was incapable of falling in love, clearly Julián would only hatch a scheme against a woman richer than he, and Emilia's fortune was considerably less than his. From which she rashly deduced that, since she was unable to inspire passion or greed in him, his jokes, flirtatious remarks, and bold behavior were just a lot of talk.

Months went by like this and the anniversary of poor Gabriel's death was approaching when Emilia's close friends began to pester her with warnings and advice that upset her.

They said flat out that Julián didn't go anywhere, that he had become serious to the point of not flirting with a single woman, and lastly, that when he spoke of her, he betrayed profound emotion even while trying to appear reserved. Emilia began to study him and it seemed to her that it was all gossip and rumor because Julián continued to make very bold remarks to her with complete self-possession, smiling and joking so openly that at any even slightly serious expression he would be able to respond, offended: "Madam! Who do you think you are?" She didn't dare take him to task as her friends advised, but they nagged so much and said so much that she decided to draw it to his attention. She had already made up her mind when she received a card from Julián in which he announced that due to a pressing business matter he was leaving for Barcelona, where he would spend two months. "Those silly friends of mine," Emilia thought, "are barking up the wrong tree. If this man had taken an interest in me, either he wouldn't be leaving or he would have come to say good-bye."

In those two months he didn't write her a single letter. He returned to Madrid and waited more than a week before going to visit her. Emilia's saint's day came, and—nothing, not even a miserable bunch of flowers.

Then, without realizing it, she began to feel mortified by a notion that was half surprise, half annoyance. Could his jokes have been deliberate? Did he then stop them because they were futile? Did he play with fire until he got burned? And above all, why would he abandon his undertaking? Little by little, involuntarily, she thought about him with such insistence that she couldn't get him out of her mind. The result of all her reflection was that, although Julián had never once spoken to her in earnest, she became convinced that he had come to love her and that he probably continued to love her. But then what was behind his behavior? Why hadn't he written to her from Barcelona nor gone to see her immediately upon his return? Did the big fool imagine perhaps that he was averting danger by avoiding the occasion for it? Blinded by vanity, she unconsciously became accustomed to the belief that she had been loved by two men: Gabriel and Julián, one deceased and one alive. Her heart, her recollections, and her tears by rights belonged to the first one; the second one ought not to have mattered to her at all, and any thoughts about him were a blot on her beloved husband's memory.

Finally, one rainy afternoon Julián turned up. It was the kind of day when only the person who wishes to find someone home alone goes out.

Emilia welcomed him with her usual affability, but didn't say a word about his silence during his trip; she didn't complain either that he hadn't come to see her right away, nor did she accuse him of ingratitude or indifference. She behaved as if they had spoken to each other the evening before. Julián's attitude was his usual one.

The manner in which he left his gloves, walking stick, and hat, each item where it belonged; the manner in which he sat down; his confidential and familiar language—in all respects he looked, not like a friend, but like the man of the house. To top it off, he invited himself to eat, saying with considerable cheek: "I'm staying here. Just the two of us. The only thing I regret is having to leave afterwards."

During the meal they talked about all kinds of unimportant things, and neither he nor she mentioned the deceased at all. All of a sudden, when they were left alone by the servant, Julián, lowering his voice as much as he could, asked: "Is anybody coming tonight?"

"I don't expect anyone. And with this rain that's coming down . . . ."

"Well, I'm glad, because as soon as we move to the sitting room, I have some very weighty concerns to take up with you. The last thing you can imagine."

"Are you joking?"

"You'll soon see what kind of jokes I play."

Emilia's heart was pounding with a rhythmic thump-thump. They went into the sitting room where they were to have coffee, and Julián was left alone for a few moments while the widow, called by her maid, entered the room that had been Gabriel's study.

"What do you want?" she asked.

Pointing to six or seven cardboard boxes that were on the table and floor, the girl replied: "Here are the wreaths that madam ordered for the first anniversary of—"

"Lower your voice!"

"They weren't delivered earlier because they hadn't arrived, but the clerk has asked if madam would be kind enough to select the one that she wants right now because many customers have put in orders."

Julián, who was anxiously pacing back and forth in the sitting room and also cutting across the living room, approached the entrance to the study at that moment and understood perfectly what the girl was saying as she crossed herself: "How pretty!

Would madam like me to take them to the sitting room where the lighting is better?"

Emilia, hearing the impatient man's footsteps so close, became flustered and confused, but she quickly regained her composure, with one puff blew the light out, and put on her most bewitching smile. Closing the door behind her so that he wouldn't learn the cause of her embarrassment, she went out to meet Julián, muttering very rapidly to her maid: "Hurry and put this away . . . and say that I'm taking all seven!"

Divorcio moral

Moral Divorce

The ten or twelve people gathered together that evening in the marquise's luxurious little drawing room were there to congratulate her on her saint's day. They had stayed on for a long time in small groups until someone said in a loud voice: "It's the truth—they're separated. He's keeping the apartment that they've lived in up to now, and she's setting up house in another one and taking their little boy with her."

"And what kind of husband puts up with such a thing?" asked an elderly lady of venerable appearance.

"Who knows which of the two is at fault, because one of them has to be," added another lady, a young one who seemed bright and curious.

"I believe," said the marquise, "that if someone is at fault it is not the husband. He was here just a few days ago and talked about his wife like a man still very much in love."

"That doesn't mean much," the young lady interrupted, "because when a husband really sets out to deceive his wife the first thing he tries to do is throw off her friends by making them believe that he adores her, hoping the interested party will hear about it."

"I certainly don't want to be critical," a foppish young man volunteered, "but he's too wrapped up in his legal work, and she's very attractive. Besides, without meaning to speak ill of her, I think she'll be pleased to have opportunities to judge just how far the power of her beauty will take her."

"She's that conceited?" a third woman asked.

"Actually," the marquise answered, "their marital discord contains an element of mystery, especially since nobody knows if he's seeing another woman or if she's capable of going astray."

A pleasant, intelligent-looking old man who still retained some of the handsomeness of his youth had been listening in silence. At this point he spoke up: "So, there's no deceit, there's no unfaithfulness, there is a child, and there is a separation. I must admit that I don't understand it. But who's the woman in question?"

"Heriols' wife—Rosita Castilla."

"Rosa? Rosa is separated?" the old man exclaimed, astonished. "Come, come now, you all don't know what you're saying or somebody has been speaking to you with a forked tongue. Rosa is incapable of doing anything that would give her husband the slightest reason for leaving her, and if he were to deceive her, she has wits, virtue, and resources to spare to put him on the right path and, if all else fails, the magnanimity to forgive him. Let me point out," and he said this in a grave tone of voice, "that there are very few women like Rosa, and when one talks about them it's important not to do so lightly."

His serious demeanor and comments caused the whole group to fall silent, except the young lady who seemed so bright, and she, without beating around the bush, gave her view: "That's all well and good, Don Luis, but it doesn't take away from what's been said. If he hasn't had affairs and she's not susceptible to . . . indiscretions, and they've separated in spite of having a child, I'm at a loss to explain it. On the other hand, she isn't wealthy, but he makes quite a bit, which means they're not going their separate ways because money is an issue. Therefore. . . ."

"Rosa would persevere in the face of adversity," the old gentleman said with great fervor.

"Come now," the lady responded, somewhat piqued, "I'm not slandering anybody. I didn't want to let it out, but I know for a fact that something's going on, something really big. Take my word for it: five days ago Rosa left her husband's house, taking with her several pieces of furniture, several trunks full of clothes, and the boy. She's living alone with her maid at 92 Guadarrama Street, I don't know which floor. Now tell me that I'm talking for the sake of talking."

"What I'll tell you," he replied, getting cross, "is that I just returned from Paris yesterday morning and haven't gone anywhere, except here, to congratulate the marquise, and therefore have no idea what may or may not have happened. But whatever it was, I'm certain that Rosa's actions were more than justifiable. She's one of the most elegant and pretty women in Madrid, is she not?" This question was not intended to please his listener. "And if her beauty is beyond dispute, which is the case, so too are her judgment and virtue."

Don Luis struggled to appear calm, but he had spoken so forcefully that no one, man or woman, ventured to contradict him, and the marquise discreetly changed the subject.

Shortly afterward Don Luis took his leave, and as he stepped on the footboard of his carriage, which was waiting for him at the door, he said to the coachman: "92 Guadarrama Street, on the double."

* * *

"Did a woman named Doña Rosa move in here a few days ago?" he asked the concierge.

"Third floor, entresol."

Don Luis had been tormented by serious doubts after he left the marquise's drawing room, and as he climbed the humble stairs of the tacky building he thought to himself: "What could have happened to her? What could he have done to Rosa for her to tolerate a change like this? Why, she's in the midst of utter poverty! What a neighborhood, what a hallway, what stairs!"

With greater speed than would have seemed possible at his age, he arrived at the third floor. He knocked, and the door was opened by a maid whose neat and clean appearance presented a conspicuous contrast with the run-down house. The entryway, overflowing with furniture, trunks, and boxes, all in disarray, indicated how recent the move was.

"Where is she? Where is she?" Don Luis asked.

Before the maid could answer, a door opened, revealing a small boudoir which was also filled with household goods strewn here and there. A woman between the ages of twenty-five and thirty appeared, a woman who looked like gracefulness personified; she threw herself into the old man's open arms, bursting into tears and weeping bitterly, inconsolably.

She was tall and slender with very light blond hair, and had large, cobalt blue eyes that were bright and lively but also calm and soft as though incapable of expressing a feeling that did not stem from love or tenderness.

"My dear Don Luis!" she exclaimed between sobs.

"Rosita, what's going on? What has he done to you? Because in your case I'm certain. . . ."

Confronted with doubt, even in the shape of such an oblique reference, she stiffened and smiled with serene haughtiness.

"But did you really suppose that I could have done something unseemly? Come, come with me and I'll tell you everything."

Rosita led Don Luis into the boudoir and they sat on a small sofa. For several moments she remained still, looking at him affectionately as if deciding on how or where to begin, and at length she said: "First, answer the question I'm going to put to you. If someone were to ask you who my father was, how he raised me, the attitudes he inculcated and developed in my spirit, how I turned out as a result . . . in short, to what extent I'm capable of goodness, honor, and virtue, what would you reply?"

"I would say," Don Louis answered in a perfectly natural tone, "that your father was the kind of man who, when in a position to safeguard a sizable fortune simply by instituting a lawsuit, preferred to lose everything in order to discharge his obligations faithfully, even those for which there existed no documents whatsoever, just his word; and I would say that later, to everyone's surprise and winning everyone's respect, he regained part of his wealth because the conduct that he displayed earned him vast credit. I would also say that your upbringing, under his exclusive tutelage, was a marvel of good sense and sound judgment, and that he made you a good person—the right words aren't coming to me—without your ever having to struggle for self-control because you had developed an aversion to evil. Above all, I would say that nature made you good, just as nature gave you blue eyes and blond hair. But what's the point of all this?"

"So your feeling is that neither fickleness nor convenience nor perversity, nor any other reason, would cause me to suffer dishonor?"

"Exactly. If you were my daughter—and I've loved you like one ever since your father entrusted your future to me—you wouldn't inspire more confidence in me. I've always maintained that if happiness meant knowing what goodness is and having a desire to be good, then you would be happy."

"I'm not saying that I'm good. How often people are unjust and bad without realizing it! What I *am* saying is that virtue, the virtue of women, does not consist solely of—how shall I explain it?—of refraining from what dishonors men and makes fools of them."

"I don't understand you."

"Bear with me."

Rosita tried to compose herself, smoothing over her ear locks of hair that had fallen loose. Then, in a voice whose alternately weak and forceful delivery revealed the nature of her recollections and impressions, she said: "You're right! My poor father! What a man! Do you remember his financial ruin? And the meal we made the day he paid up? All of us depressed and discouraged except him! 'Going bankrupt,' he said, 'has its advantages. Now we'll know who our friends are, and now I'll know if Fortune came my way on a whim or because I deserved it.' We ended up being relatively rich again. Six months before his death he sat me on his knees and said: 'If I'm taken from you now, you'll receive an income of between five and six thousand *duros*. It's not much compared with what you had before, but you can enjoy it free of worry: none of the happiness that the money brings you will have come from someone else's suffering. What you give to the poor will never be a matter of restitution.' That's what my father was like and that's how he brought me up. Imagine the impression it made on me, as time went by, to come to the realization that my husband was ... just the opposite. Some people will say I should have known his character before I married him. But what young woman can get to know a man in a year or two of courtship when the only opportunity for conversation is at the theater or at a dance? An engagement period when her sole concern is looking pretty and his is hiding his faults? During the first few weeks of our marriage I was happy. I soon realized, nonetheless, that Pepe was brusque and impetuous, although he tried to hold himself in check or was quick to regret certain outbursts to avoid making me angry.

"After we returned from our honeymoon he went back to work. During our absence a friend of his had looked after his practice. He worked very hard, but I learned early on that he felt little enthusiasm for his profession. When he left his office he was invariably in a bad humor, and what preoccupied and interested him was not the nature of the litigation nor the opportunity to display his abilities, nor even the prospect of remedying an injustice—it was the expectation and amount of his earnings. He routinely charged very high fees, and on more than one occasion this caused him serious difficulties or prompted nasty letters. I finally learned that he had a reputation for being self-seeking and greedy. He treated his poor clients rudely, showing them little or no compassion, while with the wealthy he showed no dignity. All he cared about was his fee, his fee. Sometimes he would put up with things that he shouldn't have. A certain banker, who sent payment for a bill which he considered excessive, wrote him a note in more or less the following words: 'I remit to you the amount billed. I regret that I can no longer consider myself the friend of a person who has so little regard for me.' I told Pepe that I thought the note humiliating and he said: 'What matters is being paid.' 'It would be better,' I responded, 'to charge less and retain the friendship of a man who might create trouble for you over an excessive fee.' He looked me up and down and replied: 'The best friend . . . is a *duro*.'

"I'm telling you these details so you'll see how I became convinced of what he is—a man whose only god is money. Which brings us finally, to the cause of our separation or, rather, to my irrevocable decision to leave him.

"One day a shabbily dressed woman who carried herself like a lady down on her luck turned up at the house. She had come several times before to see Pepe and he had always refused to receive her. She was let in that day because my maid answered the door instead of his servant. Shortly afterwards, from my boudoir, I heard her and Pepe arguing in loud voices. I approached his study door. She was crying and using words that scared me to death, words like 'dispossession,' 'compassion,' 'evil.' Finally, she came out, distraught and white with rage, and from the door to the stairway she said, swallowing her tears: 'If you have children I hope to God they pay for what you're doing to mine!'

"She terrified me. I returned to my boudoir and called my maid Faustina, in whom I have every confidence, as you well know. From the balcony, I pointed the woman out as she was exiting the street door. 'Get your shawl,' I said to Faustina, 'and follow her. Find out who she is and where she lives.' Pepe was in an unbearable humor the rest of the day and ordered that under no circumstances were we to let that miserable woman in again. I asked him who she was and he said a troublemaker. Anyhow, Faustina found out her name and where she lived.

"The following morning I went to see her. It was a step I took with great reluctance, but I could neither restrain myself nor suppress the desire to settle my doubts, because everything led me to suspect that Pepe must have done something really evil. Fortunately the woman didn't know that I was his wife; she knew only that he was married. The concierge of her apartment house told me that the poor devil had lived quite comfortably at one time, but had become destitute, unable to earn enough as a seamstress to support her five-year-old son.

"I climbed up to her attic room—like in a scene from a novel—and invented a white lie to talk to her. The expectation of money kept her from stopping to wonder whether I was telling the truth. It wasn't difficult to get her to open up. She was talkative, indiscreet, a veritable chatterbox, and actually *too* loose-tongued, faults that were excused by her eagerness to relate her fall from prosperity to misery. But in back of the chatter and loquaciousness was a vile deed that emerged and reared its ugly head: my husband had stolen twenty-two thousand *duros* from her!

"It's a very simple story. Her husband, also an attorney, was brought up on charges for irregularities in a lawsuit in which he had taken part, and a judgment was delivered against him. He turned to Pepe, who was a close friend of his, and, without asking for a receipt or anything else in writing, which, under the circumstances, would have been worthless, gave him for safekeeping twenty-two thousand *duros* in government securities. Can you see what's coming? He was arrested, spent a year and a half in jail, and was acquitted. When he asked for his securities, Pepe denied any knowledge of them. That is, he didn't refuse to return them, he did something more monstrous—he denied having received them. No proof existed, there couldn't be any proof. The miserable man died several months later and Pepe continued to make the same disclaimers to his widow. Afterwards I learned that Pepe had used a portion of those twenty-two thousand *duros* to pay our wedding expenses. What a foundation for a happy life together! My talk with that woman persuaded me that she wasn't lying because Pepe's very character and temperament served to proclaim his guilt. Finally, I determined to wring a confession from him, and I succeeded.

"I did something terrible, but not as terrible as his perfidy. One night I let him go to bed before I did and waited a few hours, until he was in a deep sleep. Then I arranged the light in such a way that it illuminated his whole face and called out to him in a loud voice: 'Pepe, Pepe. Gosálvez's money ... Gosálvez, Gosálvez ... what became of his money?' He awoke with a violent start, and, like the criminal who has been outwitted by the judge, replied in a rage before collecting himself: 'Where is Gosálvez? How do you know? Who told you?' I didn't need to hear him speak. The look of terror on his face was enough to convince me that the widow had indeed told me the truth. How it pained me! I swear I would have preferred to surprise him in a woman's arms. A wave of disgust and contempt washed over me. To think that he was the man who had possessed me, the one who enjoyed my first kisses of love!

"Everything that I tried to make him promise to return the securities was futile. He refused, refused obstinately, and each refusal drove us further apart. We can't get divorced, I know that—the statutes have been read to me. But I'm leaving him because I feel that contact with such a man would sully me. It's my belief, Don Luis, that honor and conscience are found in both sexes. Pepe dishonored me with his crime as I could have dishonored him with my infidelity. I'll be his legally, I'll bear his name and, what's more painful, my son will bear it, but he'll never hold me in his arms again and I'll never accept anything from him. All I ask is that I be judged by someone who's capable of understanding me."

Desencanto

Disillusion

I

Midnight was drawing near. The train station in Bourg-sur-Mer, a charming little French village next to the Spanish border, was nearly enveloped in shadows, poorly lit by four oil lamps that hung from the platform roof. Positioned higher than usual and too far apart, they gave off so little light that one could barely make out the garish wall posters in which figures of elegant women shaded by enormous parasols, guides in red boleros, and landscapes with caverns, volcanoes, and gardens advertised fashionable spas and excursions at reduced rates.

Waiting for the train that was to arrive were two men: the freight clerk, who had set down his lantern, the brightness of which projected over the pavement's blackish asphalt in the shape of a fan, and a gentleman who was briskly pacing the platform from end to end to ward off the chill.

The latter was already growing impatient at the express's delay when a whistle blew far away, and the clatter of the cars, muted by the distance, sounded like an indistinct noise; and finally, rounding the bend formed by the track at the entrance to the station, a locomotive appeared belching blasts of steam through its sides, its headlamp illuminating the double line of the rails which, polished by friction, shone like steel ribbons in the middle of the blackened ballast. The train stopped quite suddenly and a lone passenger got off, a smartly dressed man in his early thirties, who, upon seeing the gentleman on the platform, hurried over to him, dropped the luggage that he carried in both hands, and embraced him repeatedly.

Disillusion

"My dear Don Martín!"

"Luisito! You finally decided to come!"

"It wasn't possible before. And believe me—I'm sorry."

"So how long will you be with us here?"

"Three weeks, a month . . . whatever you wish."

"For my part, the longer the better. Until you get bored."

"Who's with you and Aunt Salomé?"

"Who else would there be?"

"You could have brought a friend or two."

"No. Just the three of us—your aunt, Soledad, and I."

"Oh! Soledad? And how are the two of them?"

"Well, your Aunt Salomé is getting fatter by the day—a sight to behold, a real sickness. And Soledad's as pretty as usual; that is, pretty or beautiful, no, but as pleasant and as nice as always, in spite of her strange ideas and peculiar notions."

"What strange ideas? I've heard rumors but haven't attached any importance to them. Besides, you know full well that we've had so little contact that I barely know her. And you don't know a woman after talking to her a half dozen times. But what kinds of strange ideas?"

"Nothing offensive or unseemly, which of course we wouldn't tolerate. It's that she thinks like no other woman and says what she thinks so openly that it leaves you flabbergasted, and frequently, although she's a very bright and very good woman, she does what no other dares to do. Do you understand? At times even imprudent things."

"I understand. You're saying she's not cut out to be Caesar's wife."

"That's right. What she needs is a man of superior intelligence who can curb, who can channel her excessive love of freedom."

"So she excites fear."

"At the least she gives cause for concern, which explains why, being so likable and well-off, she hasn't married. And it's getting late because, mind you, even though she doesn't look it, she's almost thirty."

"How does she get along with Aunt Salomé?"

"Very well. First, because she was so admirably brought up, and second, because she's so kind and so unusually helpful. Poor Salomé, like all sick people, is demanding, unpredictable, even selfish and inconsiderate, but in spite of it all Soledad is more and more affectionate with her."

"She obviously loves her."

"Very much. Listen, even though she may be dressed to kill, to go where she really wants to go, if she realizes that she's needed or that Salomé is bored or sad or upset, she doesn't go but gladly stays with her. The other night she was invited to the dance at the casino; you should have seen her, because the women here dress up as much as they do in Madrid. Well, Salomé had one of the breathing fits that make it seem like she's suffocating, and Soledad, without saying a thing to us so we wouldn't stop her, sent word that she wasn't going. Her friends came for her anyway, but nevertheless she stayed behind, just as she was, dressed to the teeth, keeping us company. This is a very unusual woman."

"Most unusual. Especially if she's at an age when she has no time to lose."

"I don't think she's in a hurry to get married. She's very particular."

"What I see," said Luis speaking slowly, "is that between the care needed by Salomé and Soledad's presence, I run the risk of being in the way. Tell me frankly: do you think it's better for me to go to an inn? Even if I still have lunch and supper with all of you almost every day . . . frankly."

"By no means! In the first place, that would prompt Soledad, believing that she was imposing on us, to want to leave. Besides, everybody knows that you're the son of my best friend and that I was your guardian. Can there be anything odd about your coming to my home? Aside from which, I do as I please in it. And as for scruples or prudery on Soledad's part, don't worry. She's not one to pay attention to appearances, gossip or rumors."

"Then it's settled."

"Now, if you're ill at ease—"

"The most that can happen is that I'll like her too much and have to flee from danger."

"Or that you'll be lured by the abyss, as they say in plays."

"That danger exists only in adolescence and after the age of fifty, and I'm thirty-four."

"How mistaken you are! Love doesn't ask anyone how old he or she is."

They were talking in this manner, waiting outside the station, while a porter loaded Luis's luggage in the front of the coach that awaited them; when he finished they got in immediately and the horses set off at a good trot.

Although there was no moon, the brightness of the stars was so intense and the atmosphere so clear that the countryside could be seen plainly. The highway, lined on either side by tall sycamores, stretched along a plain dotted with those houses so typical of the south of France—white, low, with doors and windows painted ocher or red, at whose entrances stand a few trees, and on whose façades there are almost always signs and posters. Then, alternating with cornfields and meadows, came adobe walls and fences behind which, among clumps of leafy trees, rose huge buildings—villas constructed a half century ago without exaggerated claims to luxury, but comfortable, spacious, and surrounded by vast gardens. Finally, as one approached the town, there loomed among expensively worked iron grilles and stone walls the much more luxurious modern structures, some planned with a genuine artistic sense, others with abominable blunders in layout and ornamentation, all of them attesting—with towers and cupolas, terraced roofs and overhangs, bay windows and balconies—to the affluence and at times extravagance of owners and architects who, through elaborate shapes and a combination of stone, marble, cement, and brick, sought to flaunt wealth rather than show good taste. A few of the properties that Don Martín was pointing out on both sides belonged to Spaniards who boasted of their riches in this way, which was their undeniable right, but which moved one to think with sorrow of the old, forgotten ancestral homes in Spain, of the dilapidated seignorial mansions which, far away from France, are coming apart, taking with them as they collapse the glory and memory of Spanish art and history. A strange kind of patriotism: showing off in your neighbor's house instead of improving your own.

As they climbed a hill, which slowed the horses and lowered the jingle of their collar bells, the formidable roar of the sea could be heard in the distance; and beyond the horizon, against the blackness of the sky, an intense brightness began to shine at brief intervals, a brightness that would quickly disappear in space only to reappear and flash anew as if a secret mechanism moved it.

"The lighthouse," said Don Martín. "We're getting close."

Several minutes later, passing by the hamlet of Bourg-sur-Mer, they turned onto a boulevard formed by new chalets, each with its own small yard, separated only by fences not yet covered with ivy and other barely developed climbers.

As the rolling swell of the sea was heard closer and closer, Don Martín said: "The beach is very near. It's where Soledad spends most of the day."

"Are all these chalets occupied? And by what kind of people?"

"Almost all, and by 'all kinds,' as the French say. You'll see the woman we have for a neighbor. I don't know if it ought to be tolerated, but this is a republic."

"Those birds, if they have colorful plumage, nest where they wish. Neither the Paris of the eighteenth century nor the Paris of the Second Empire was a republic, and they've never been better off."

The coach pulled up in front of one of the chalets and Don Martín and Luis got out. They climbed the short flight of steps and entered a small drawing room on the first floor which was poorly lit by a single electric lamp that sat on a central pedestal table covered with books and illustrated periodicals. Next to it, spending the evening together, were Salomé in one armchair, with her hands folded, and Soledad in another, reading.

The room was bizarrely furnished. No doubt due to the peculiar mixture of poor taste and excessive economy, as well as to a desire to take advantage of the old and little knack for selecting the new, its owner-lesser had tried unsuccessfully to match pieces of furniture and appointments so diverse that they offended the eye: two enormous armchairs upholstered in green rep that were ugly a half century ago, both with a round crocheted tidy on the back; a trumeau in a gold frame above the fireplace, the painting depicting the decapitation of Mary Stuart; and on the wall several illuminated lithographs which were views of the castle in Blois. Forming a contrast with all this was a set of modern English-style chairs in imitation mahogany; the very latest device for the electric light that hung from the ceiling; a brightly colored rug that stood out jarringly against the dark inlaid floor; and two vases so modernistic as to be ridiculous, with figures of such long-legged and thin women that, according to Soledad, you could not put flowers in them because they dried up, ashamed of such company.

"Don't look at any of this, which is hideous," Don Martín said upon entering. "If, as we expect, I take the house next year, it'll be on the condition that it be refurnished or I'll take the one next door occupied by the *traviata*, which, I'm told, is very nice."

Luis, paying no attention to the furnishings, had approached Salomé, warmly taking and shaking her hands and saying, to be gallant: "Why, you're no heavier than before!"

In fact, as her brother had said at the train station, the poor woman was a sight to behold. Her obesity had begun to show when she was fifteen and it increased so rapidly, despite drugs and treatments, trips and consultations, that at the age of twenty she was already resigned, for the rest of her life, to being a nuisance to others and herself—as she used to say, a person smothered by fat.

"You're very kind," she replied. "You say that to comfort me, but I'm not taken in. I'm worse than ever; I can barely move. There isn't a stairway that doesn't creak as soon as I grasp the handrail, and they had to set my bed practically on the floor so that I can get in without having to raise myself."

The pity that she inspired increased when one considered, on looking at her, that were she not disfigured by her corpulence she would have been attractive.

She had delicate features and a ruddy complexion in spite of her age, and blue eyes, a soft, intelligent expression, and silky blond hair. But these were attractions noticed only by people who knew her well, because everybody else, on the other hand, made fun of her enormous face, her broad back, and her unsteady and almost wobbly step, which gave the impression that her feet could not manage with the weight that they supported.

"Listen," she said to Luis, "I know I'm a sight, but you can get over the effect that I produce by looking at my niece, so feast your eyes on her!"

"Good heavens, Aunt Salomé," Soledad said, "don't embarrass me. You're not that heavy and I'm not that much to look at."

The praise was somewhat fulsome. Soledad was not the kind of woman who at first sight generates excitement but rather the kind who captivates you once you get to know her. Although she was thirty she barely looked twenty-five, but her physical charms were not enough to drive anyone crazy. She was on the small side, had a somewhat pale complexion, dark auburn hair, and blue eyes—like many a woman you encounter in the street who does not stand out as either pretty or homely. Her best features were her hands and feet, of which she took good care, going without gloves whenever she could and always wearing becoming shoes. She had refined taste in clothes, knowing how to choose styles and colors that best suited her, but her real strengths were her character, her disposition, and her upbringing—the combination of qualities that shaped her highly pleasant nature. There were times when, from the inflection of her voice and the hard stare in her eyes, one suspected that she would be more likely to err on the side of excess energy than surplus tenderness, but for that to be the case she would have had to be unfairly provoked because the constants of her makeup were gentleness and kindness. Besides, there was absolutely no coquetry in her; that is, she never tried to be wooed or admired, never sought the tribute of flattery or the gratification of the flirtatious remark, which might explain what did please her. When she understood that a man was favorably impressed by her affability, intelligence, grace, and elegance; when she was complimented on her hair, her shapely foot, or her hands—her most attractive features, which she knew—then she was visibly and sincerely gratified, and contentment played on her face, enlivening her eyes and lips with a singularly bewitching smile that almost made her beautiful, causing whomever was looking at her to think that this petite, plain-looking woman, just like those modest little flowers that leave the hand saturated with a strong perfume, could, given the chance, return a hundredfold the love that she might awaken.

Luis refused supper and consented only to a cup of tea with cookies, which Soledad helped to serve him, and then, out of sheer amiability, he said: "This is icing on the cake. I get to see you and Don Martín as well as this young lady. It's been a while since I've had the pleasure of seeing her."

"I spend only the spring and fall in Madrid," Soledad said, "which is when I believe you travel to Paris. We couldn't run into each other."

"Believe me, I'd rather spend the whole year there. Spain is impossible."

"We don't agree," Soledad replied evenly, but clearly expressing a contrary opinion, and adding: "Paris . . . one month a year, every year. But to live . . . where one was born."

"Still, for a man with money Paris is a delight."

"Well, I believe that men, as wealthy as they—you—may be, have an obligation to do more than just enjoy life. I mean, I, if I were a man, even if I were living it up, even if I had a lot of money, and precisely because I did, I'd consider myself obligated to do something beneficial to my country. Really, to complain about backwardness and then go abroad just to spend and have a good time."

"Why would you have us go abroad?"

"To have a good time, of course, but also to study what's done well so as to take advantage of it in our native country."

"Oh! You're a patriot?" Luis asked with a touch of irony.

"Yes, sir," she replied in mock seriousness. "Not a patriot to get all excited about people rushing into the street and shouting 'Long live So-and-so' under any pretext, but a patriot in another sense."

"Do explain. I'd like to know how patriotism is understood by you ladies who spend here or buy everything that you wear here."

"I'll tell you, yes, sir. I've thought about it time and time again. We buy everything here because the men who govern in Spain aren't doing anything to make it possible for us to buy there."

"You asked for it," Salomé said, laughing.

"Go on, go on."

"Don't make fun of me, because I'm not good at arguing, but aren't there good silks in Valencia, for example? Aren't fabrics produced in Catalonia? Aren't there cows in Santander and the Basque Provinces? Well, what are all of you doing so that in Valencia they can learn to weave and dye the way they do in Lyon, or so that Catalan fabrics, which you say crumple in a suit as soon as they get wet, are like the ones in England? Who has tried to make Pas Valley butter taste like the butter in Normandy? As for what we women wear, what sense of style are the poor dressmakers of our country going to have when they haven't seen anything or learned anything? As a general rule, they make perfectly grotesque pieces, but believe me, if they came here to learn it would be a different story. Don't doctors go to Germany and artists to Paris and Rome?"

"A regular speech! Spanish dressmakers would learn a lot of mischief if they went to Paris to study. We'd rue the day!"

"That's making light of things. Besides, for women to engage in mischief they don't need to leave their own country: it's enough that you men keep them ignorant and defenseless instead of training them so they can learn how to live and support themselves. They live miserably. That's what all of you like, and when a woman is desperate a man appears to protect her if she's pretty, and if she isn't she becomes a servant or dies of hunger."

"You're a sociologist!"

"Nothing of the sort; I won't talk about what I don't understand. What I can assure you is that when I pay thirty *duros* or a hundred francs to one of these Frenchwomen for a hat, it annoys me because I would gladly pay as much to a woman in my own country."

"Well, I don't concern myself about that. We're not going to change the situation. Live and spend where one feels like it, that's what I say."

They continued to chat for a time without saying anything worthy of being recorded, but among the commonplaces spoken by both there was one difference: hers was typical of a woman who was trying to talk with good intentions about something she did not fully grasp, while his, in addition to ignorance, revealed the indifference and selfishness of the man who believes he has a right to enjoy life without troubling himself to go after it.

Don Martín had picked up a newspaper, and the colossal Salomé, settled in an armchair and almost asleep, woke up as she dozed off, saying: "I'm going to bed."

Soledad, as she was saying good night to Luis, affectionately helped Salomé to her feet and retired, accompanying her aunt. Don Martín also said good night and they all withdrew to their rooms.

Soledad did not stir the slightest interest in Luis that night. She struck him as a woman with a very ordinary figure—dressed tastefully, to be sure—and, in particular, as somewhat of a know-it-all; nothing more.

As she was going to bed Soledad thought that Luis was probably one of your average males, with no personality. Neither intellectually nor perhaps morally did he show signs of amounting to much, which was a shame, because on the physical side he had the features that can appeal most to a woman. He was what's called a fine figure of a man: tall, vigorous, and healthy-looking; handsome without a trade of effeminacy; very dark-skinned but not sallow; black hair and neatly trimmed beard; eyes that, if not so expressive that they spoke by themselves, were sufficiently lively so that he did not appear listless; and dashing in appearance and stylish without affectation, the kind who at least knows how to choose a tailor.

Without being captivated by him or losing sleep over him, Soledad thought of Luis as one of those men to whom any woman of good taste can give her arm, delighting in doing so and being envied by other women.

II

Don Martín and Luis took long walks; Soledad, although she was criticized for it, liked to go off alone to explore the surrounding area or would frequently accompany Salomé in a carriage without being bothered in the least by all the attention they attracted because of the poor woman's corpulence. In the evenings the men would go to the casino for a while or to the station to watch the arrival of the express train; the women stayed at home, one reading, the other dozing. During meals, Salomé, as if instinctively making up for the long periods that she spent alone in unavoidable silence, chatted a great deal with Luis, which meant that since his arrival he had not had many opportunities to talk to Soledad, nor was there anything that prompted him to seek them out. Based on what little she contributed to the conversation, she continued to strike him as a passable woman who dressed well and said strange things.

Although Soledad was becoming persuaded that Luis had not set the world on fire and that he was not a saint, she nevertheless took pleasure in looking at him when nobody could notice; and as he, except for politeness, was not showing the least indication of trying to charm her, she also began to feel slightly mortified in her self-esteem as a woman, wondering with a certain amount of bitterness if maybe her thirty years would now deprive her of all appeal.

One morning, well before lunchtime, Luis came back from buying newspapers, and when he opened the iron fence of the yard that surrounded the chalet he ran into Soledad. She was dressed in white piqué, wore very pretty shoes, carried a book in one hand, an enormous red silk parasol in the other, and was on her way to the beach.

"What's this?" he asked. "You two go out so early?"

"*I'm* going out. To the beach, until we have lunch, which I do almost every day."

"Alone?"

"Why not? Aunt Salomé doesn't like to go out early. I sit there, and if I don't find agreeable company, I read; and if I do find it, I have someone to talk to me."

"And you go alone?"

"Of course. I'm not a child."

Luis hesitated a moment and then asked: "May I accompany you?"

"Why not?"

At the beach, in the shade of the bathing establishment, beneath which projected numerous large red and white striped canvas sunshades, staked and secured to the ground with taut rope like tents, there was a multitude of people: groups of women, almost all of them dressed in white; men who were staring at them more or less furtively or openly; wet nurses and maids whose clothes and headgear proclaimed their French or Spanish origin; and scores of children, most of them barefoot, some wading into the water up to their knees to fill their toy buckets, ignoring their mothers' shouts and warnings, while others, with their hands and play shovels, dug trenches and built mounds of sand, which were undone first by waves that washed up in a rush, then completely destroyed in the undertow by millions of tiny pebbles. Women in bathing suits, scarcely covered by oilskins and towels, walked up and down planks that descended from the establishment almost to water's edge; some wore espadrilles or sandals, others went barefoot, revealing feet deformed by tightfitting shoes, and all were deprived of the charm of their hair by the bonnets and head scarfs which they used to keep it from getting wet. A confusion of sounds arose:

children's screams, adults' voices, vendors hawking pastries and newspapers, and the laughter of young women hearing flirtatious remarks; and in the midst of it all, a gray-haired beggar with artistic pretensions coaxed from his violin a popular Italian tune that, while sounding tasteless to the young people, perhaps evoked the sweetest of memories in the old. The shrill whistle of a steam launch became an invitation to take a cruise around the bay, and rising above this din with relentless regularity was the continuous sound of the surf breaking upon shoals. In the distance, standing out on a small promontory, among chalets ringed by pines and tamarinds, rose the lighthouse; the August sun shone with all its magnificent power; and beyond the horizon, disappearing in the crystal atmosphere, a long, undulating trail of smoke marked the passage of a ship and streaked the immaculate cobalt blue of the sky.

Soledad and Luis descended the steps that went from the establishment to the sandy area, and, choosing a spot, sat down a little apart from the mass of people.

The person closest to them was a woman by herself—blond, very young, and very beautiful, although too big. Scorning fashion, which at the time had dictated white, she was exquisitely dressed in pink, and was sitting, if not exactly in a showy, daring position, then in a somewhat studied one. She had her chair firmly anchored in the sand, tilting backward a little, and her right arm rested against the back of it, turned in such a way that the slats did not conceal her figure; her feet, propped against the crossbar of another chair, showed under her skirt, not so much that they seemed to be on display nor so little that one had to look for them. In her lap were a white leather bag and a book, which she read now and then, although it did not seem to interest her very much.

Soledad and Luis observed her on the sly, the latter for her figure, the former for her figure and for her dress. The woman in question did not move and modestly kept her eyes down, like someone who knows she is being scrutinized from head to toe.

"Very good-looking, don't you think? That's our neighbor," Soledad said in a low voice.

"Our neighbor? Oh, yes," Luis replied, recalling that as they left the station the day of his arrival Don Martín had spoken to him about her. "Now I remember: the one in the chalet next door."

"She's delightful, although a little big. On the other hand, she dresses splendidly."

"But you can tell a mile away that she's not as innocent as she looks."

"Some scoundrel's fault," Soledad quickly retorted.

"You assume—"

"Always! Men are either the cause or responsible for all the good and bad that we women do."

"And vice versa."

"True, but we don't usually do harm except when we're passionate, while you men do it for pleasure, even out of vanity or self-esteem."

"So you imagine that every one of these—"

"It's the result of something evil done by one of you. But stop discussing that now and look at her. What hair! What lips! And what pretty feet!"

"You're right. And a good judge. I've never heard a woman sing the praises of another one like that."

"She really is beautiful, and being as refined and stylish as she is there's no one here to compare with her. And she looks like a good person."

The interested party, who, judging by the expression on her face, undoubtedly understood Spanish, failed to contain a smile of satisfaction on hearing the last words of the dialogue spoken by Soledad, but she did not raise her eyes from the book.

"Believe me," Luis continued, "as a rule, these women are bad."

"Well, in a certain sense of course they're not good, but nevertheless it's one thing to live in that wretched manner and very much another to be capable of good feelings."

"Women, honorable unmarried women in particular, can't talk about such things."

"Of course we probably don't have all the facts and have to ignore a great deal. Nevertheless, don't kid yourself—with our hearts or with our heads we women judge everything."

"There can't be many as indulgent as you."

"You're right, and I suppose it's because I imagine that left on our own almost all of us, men and women, would be good. It's our fellow human beings who cause our ruin."

"Believe me: women of her type are the most dangerous of 'our fellow human beings.' Don't feel sorry for them."

"Well, I do—very much so."

"You ought to sit on one of those boards that work to prevent the white slave trade."

"We single women, even at my age, aren't involved in such things. A single woman, officially, doesn't know of its existence, and it isn't good for her to know; she finds out when it's unavoidable."

"Well, well," said Luis, smiling, "we're on a ticklish subject."

"Whatever you say. Let's talk about society gossip or you pay me compliments. With women there is no other conversation, because I assume you don't wish to discuss fashions."

"With the people I see here there's plenty to talk about."

"Do you like gossip?"

"It depends. Digging deeply in the lives of others, no, I don't like it—nobody interests me enough for that. Now: to comment on what's being said, and even amuse myself a little by it, yes, that's very useful. Besides, one finds out about everything and can stay away from the people to be avoided."

"I believe," Soledad interrupted him, "that to accept or reject people because of what's said about them causes a person to commit great injustices and in order not to be unjust one needs to be tolerant."

"If it's about us—men—yes, but you, that's different. When, for example, certain things are said or known about a woman, it's best not to have anything to do with her, not countenance what one suspects is wrong."

"I think that when one is absolutely certain of those things, you're right. The trouble is that they're rarely known for sure. In incompatible marriages, for example, very often we don't know who's at fault. Appearances condemn both parties, but to make a flat assertion, to contend that he or she was right or wrong . . . you almost never can."

"For that reason one should accept the prevailing opinion."

"How horrible!" exclaimed Soledad. "That *would* be exposing oneself to the greatest injustices and also be a surrender of one's own view. Under that system I suppose you'd even have to accept slander."

"That's not what I'm saying."

"The prevailing opinion can be perverse, odious, mistaken."

"Then again, we're not going to spend our lives investigating the reasons for other people's conduct, and slandering is not common. What happens is that certain pieces of gossip are accepted fairly easily."

"So it's all the same. As long as it's not known to be the truth, I think it's slander when someone repeats something bad that's said about a person."

"By that standard you'll always have to compromise and socialize with everybody."

"No, sir. What may be sufficient in many cases to keep me from striking up a friendship with a woman or even a break with her, for example, is what I'm told of her behavior by serious, reliable people whom I know to be genuinely honest. But the other way, based on gossip, idle chatter, and tales, or mere appearances, no, sir—not a chance! And in the serious, basic concerns of life you'll see that I'm right."

"What I see now," said Luis, glancing around and observing that almost nobody was on the beach, "is that it must be lunchtime and we're practically alone."

"You're right about lunch. Poor Salomé! She'll be starved! As for our being alone—don't worry about it because I'm not the least concerned."

"A sign of the fact that there's no particular person whom you can displease by accepting company," Luis said jokingly.

"No, there isn't, but if there were I would have chosen that person and made myself so clear that it wouldn't matter."

"That's asking for a lot of trust."

"As I see it, the necessary amount, since a certain feeling to which you seem to allude, without trust ... well, it's not *that*."

They headed back to the chalet, keeping silent for a time, like people who instinctively try to take stock of the impressions they have received in a conversation and the ones they have made. Luis reflected that few young women thought as freely, or at least they did not let it show, and this freedom annoyed him, although he found nothing reprehensible in her manner of expressing it. What he felt mainly was a certain vexation, almost a touch of humiliation on seeing that a woman was capable of more bravery of conscience and spirit of justice than he for dealing with life's ups and downs.

Soledad held to her initial impression that Luis was an ordinary man, but, nevertheless, his type, his figure, his voice, even his manner of dress, afforded her immense pleasure; and putting into words the opinion that she was forming of him, she thought to herself, "What is there about him? He's nothing special, yet I enjoy his company. I wonder if he likes me." As she saw him walking smartly at her side, with a firm step and full of vitality and charm, moving and wearing his clothes with natural grace, she was beginning to perceive the contradictory, annoying sensation of being attracted to a man who did not come close to having the qualities that she had always dreamed would be had by the one she called hers; and afraid of such a lapse of judgment, she realized how very intelligent women can fall in love with men unworthy of them.

They were nearing the chalet when, breaking the silence that was irritating for both of them, because each one feared that the other would read his thoughts, Luis said: "This is a delightful little town, a nice place to be, and the food's marvelous, but, really, a woman like you must get very bored here."

"I don't know what that is," Soledad replied, almost laughing. "I'm accustomed to being sad; bored, never—the two are very different things. Boredom is a sort of stupidity into which the spirit falls when it's incapable of feeling or thinking. And who doesn't find something in life about which to be saddened or gladdened? I'm almost willing to say that boredom is a kind of selfishness; nothing at all can matter to the person who gets bored, because such a person lacks ideas and feelings."

"You're practically a philosopher and amuse yourself easily."

"Not much is needed to philosophize, according to you. And above all, I didn't come here to amuse myself but to keep Aunt Salomé company."

"That's a work of charity, because the poor thing is impossible. She must get bored for sure, even though you don't believe it."

"She doesn't get bored, she suffers. This is a woman who's not all that old—many at her age are vain and flirtatious—and very intelligent, and kind, and pretty, because blown up and all, you can still see the daintiness of her features, and so wealthy—"

"Yes," Luis interrupted, "as wealthy as her brother."

"Oh, a lot more! You don't know that the other brother, the older one, left almost everything to her?"

"I didn't know."

"Everything that he had or could. Her income's greater than Don Martín's."

Luis, listening to her very attentively, was struck by an idea, a mixture of dirty suspicion and incipient greed: first, his mind racing, he wondered if perhaps Soledad was being solicitous and caring with Salomé out of self-interest, hoping to be her heir; then he thought that if that happened one could certainly tolerate her outspoken approach to life, her nerve, and her brazenness.

"Yes," repeated Soledad, incapable of guessing what he was thinking, "very wealthy and unable to enjoy a thing. Since extreme obesity like hers looks ludicrous, nobody wants to be with her, nobody accompanies her, not a single friend dares to sit with her in a theater box and, although she sometimes makes a joke of it and even says that she could be taken to a fair and be exhibited in a booth for money, she has bitter days. With me she relaxes and lets her hair down. You can see that I don't do much of anything."

Luis listened to her with a desire to smile mischievously because it seemed natural to him that she would be driven by selfish motives; he came close to letting her know his reaction with a joking remark, but, fortunately for him, did not say a word. Besides, perhaps a certain kind of prudence contributed to his silence: the base but instinctive prudence of a man who, in the recesses of his mind, is beginning to hatch something that flatters or suits him.

Upon arriving at the chalet they noticed that Salomé was leaning out of one of the windows, and when she saw them she spoke to Soledad, shouting more than talking: "Listen, sweetie, lunch won't be for a while yet, and Martín hasn't returned. You could do me a big favor and go over to Rue Thiers to get me some of the pastry that I like. Come on, honey."

Soledad nodded with her pretty head, and, turning to Luis, said: "Let's go to the bakery. It's very close."

They started walking again, and after a few steps Luis asked jokingly, in a tone that attributed no importance to his words: "So it doesn't matter to you that we're seen keeping company?"

"Keeping company," she repeated sharply, "no. You mean together, because it's not exactly the same thing. With you or another man, what difference does it make? I don't care if I'm seen with someone or if I'm criticized because occasionally I go out alone. What I won't allow is being seen in unacceptable company."

"You're an independent spirit."

"Precisely. And as for going out alone, isn't it ridiculous that a woman my age, because I assume you know I'm thirty, be with a hired *demoiselle* or with one of those poor old ladies who on certain occasions get in the way and on others show no respect?"

"Seeing that it's not the custom—"

"Well, when customs are foolish you make a break with them. Let's see: why do women who are in my situation—with practically no family or with very elderly parents who don't leave the house—why do they have a chaperon or something similar? So it can be assumed that they're not doing anything unseemly, that they're being watched, isn't that right?"

"Certainly."

"In order to inspire confidence, so that men, and especially girlfriends, won't believe that we can make ill use of freedom."

"That's it."

"Well, I think the whole thing's utterly absurd. Just because some poor woman's paid this or that amount monthly—not much more than a maid—what authority is she going to have to avoid anything? She'll go where she's taken or wait where she's told and cover up what she's ordered to cover up, and I don't say keep quiet, because that's so much more difficult. And what I assure you is that I'd never pay any mind to a man who didn't have complete confidence in me."

"You're marvelous. The trouble is that men don't think like that."

"What I am is frank. The stylish girls and single women that you see in the streets with a shabbily dressed miss who makes ten or twenty *duros* a month, or with a matron getting on in years who looks like one half of a pair of Civil Guards, do you know what those women think even if they don't say it? If they're good and discreet, they put up with the so-called 'watch' unwillingly because they know that their virtue doesn't need a lookout; and if they're frivolous, then they don't stop at anything—what they do is convert that same lookout into an accomplice, or at least into an accessory."

"I repeat: you're marvelous . . . and I'm not convinced."

"Be honest; you think I'm daring. But tell me: now, for example, I'm going to the bakery and you're accompanying me. What harm is there in it? What can people gossip about?"

"You're right. In most cases it's the most innocent thing in the world; in others. . . . Suppose that I . . . that is to say, not me, but some man in my situation, he could take advantage of this opportunity now to talk to you however he liked, however he wished."

"And I would listen to you, or to whomever, say the things I should listen to, but just as soon as you overstepped yourself even a little," and with the thumb of her right hand, making a very amusing gesture, she touched the nail of her little finger, "I'd answer you in such a way that you'd never again want to come near me."

"You wouldn't avoid an unpleasant scene?"

"Why would I do that? I'd create one for whomever was disrespectful to me. You know all too well, you men, that rude remarks or nasty things are said only to women who tolerate them. Nobody's ever said them to me."

"The point is there can be things that, without being rude, just expressions of longings, of desires . . . in short, certain natural, excusable instances of boldness that a lady shouldn't . . . well, you get my drift."

"That depends on the nature of those longings and instances of boldness. A woman knows full well the kind of feeling she awakens, what she can accept and what she should reject. Don't trust the easily frightened ones."

"Whom do you call easily frightened?"

"The ones who out of natural simplemindedness or self-interest or coquetry, which is worse, are easily shocked. What's in a woman's interest is for a man to talk, to talk a great deal—"

"And compromise himself."

"—to reveal his inner self. That way a woman can get to know him and take a liking to him if he deserves it, or disabuse him in time, as the case may be."

"Which means that you would pay no attention to anyone without—"

"Without first learning as much as I could about the worth of whomever spoke to me in a certain sense."

"And have you been spoken to often in that way?"

"You're curious," she said, entering the bakery whose door they had reached.

They bought the pastries and began to walk back, both of them silent. When they were nearing the chalet, Luis said: "You didn't want to admit to me if you've had to do that kind of character study."

"What kind?"

"The one you referred to in order to learn the worth of whomever . . . whomever has courted you. Because you won't try to convince me that you haven't had anyone to love you, and perhaps someone whom you have loved."

"In all honesty, like—yes, a few have liked me. Love me?—I'm certain that not a one has loved me, nor have I myself ever been very interested. Am I being clear?"

"Or perhaps you were loved and didn't realize it."

"It is very difficult, my friend, to be mistaken about such a thing. We women usually take it all in: truth, lies, what we're told out of flattery, out of self-interest, you name it."

"Well, seeing you and listening to you, it makes no sense to me that you've not been truly loved. You must be very difficult to please."

"Perhaps you're right. I mean, what's happened to me has been . . . but what nonsense we're talking. Anyway, the idea is to pass the time . . . amuse ourselves."

"Fine, if all this is just a joke . . . all right. But what I want is for you to tell me what you were going to say."

"What?" she asked, making one of those feminine faces full of charm.

"You were on the verge of opening up and being candid and you held back."

"And you're asking me to do so? All right, then, I will. A fiancé, an honest-to-goodness fiancé, a man who intended to become mine, to whom I promised myself . . . that one is yet to appear."

"Incredible! That's hard to believe!"

"Gospel truth."

"Explain it to me because I don't understand."

"Very simple: in the first place, since I'm not beautiful, and not poor either, I'm very distrustful."

"Oh! You don't consider yourself beautiful?"

"You're not going to show bad taste and flatter me, are you? Let me finish: in the second, I haven't had a fiancé because, although a few have courted me and I didn't discourage them, I've never let things reach a certain point. I'll explain myself."

"There can't be anything more interesting."

"You make fun of it? Never mind, but understand right now: whenever I realized that I was beginning to love, whenever I believed that I was loved, I did everything in my power to get to know through and through the man who was courting me, undaunted by the possibility of disappointment, and to have him get to know me, and I discovered that he or I had not done well on the test, that one of us was mistaken. A very bitter pill, right? But a very healthy one. And I never agreed to go any further. Neither deceive nor be deceived. As long as I don't meet a man whom I consider worthy of my affection and can convince myself that I really love, I'll stay single. With what I have I'll endow a half dozen beds in a hospital, and they can bury me a virgin. Do you want more candor?"

"For the latter to be the case it'd be necessary for you to meet only men who have no judgment whatsoever."

"Why?"

"Because men with a mind will quickly appreciate your merits."

"Thank you for the flattery."

"It's not flattery, it's that I'm surprised that you say things so openly."

"Yes, I am sincere. I assure you that never, regardless of the circumstances, would I try to mislead someone by faking traits I don't have nor would I take a liking to a man I didn't know thoroughly; I would open up my heart and soul to him and demand that he do the same; we'd both have to know what each was capable of doing for the other. I can't imagine approaching true love and marriage any other way."

"The manner in which you reason is delightful, but when you take life so seriously and lend so much importance to everything, the disappointments are fierce."

"On the other hand, they have the advantage of being timely

and preventing worse things. Well now: I've just about given you a lecture, but we weren't going to discuss fashions and politics."

They had arrived at the iron fence. During lunch they spoke very little; Martín and Salomé carried the conversation. Luis continued to be mortified by the certainty that Soledad, so independent and resolute and frank, would consider him subject to ordinary concerns and incapable of understanding her; and with a certain smug, petty rancor he said to himself: "I'd clip your wings for you." For her part, Soledad was annoyed with herself, fearing that she had talked excessively, but at the same time she was hoping fervently, beyond reason, that she had made a favorable impression on him—a hope she had not experienced with anyone before.

III

The days went by. From that morning on Soledad prudently sidestepped any conversation with Luis that might lead to familiarity or intimacy. She did continue, as was her wont, going out alone, never bothering to mask her thoughts out of a futile respect for others, but whenever Luis attempted to accompany her she avoided it if she could do so graciously, and in the afternoon, she had the girlfriends with whom she took walks come to the very door of the chalet. She behaved as if she feared getting close to that man, although, without realizing it, she began to take meticulous care in her toilet and in the way she dressed, choosing outfits, color combinations, and accessories that flattered her the most; she even tried different hairdos, which in some cases is the greatest sign of preoccupation that a woman can display.

Salomé, who chatted frequently with Luis and was nobody's fool, soon picked up on what was happening, and after watching Soledad and becoming convinced that she had been right, gave it considerable thought and prepared to intervene in a situation which she deemed serious for her niece.

Three weeks after the foregoing events, Soledad was shut up in her room late one night; very solemn, very sad, and showing signs of having cried, she was nearly finished rereading, as if to make sure she had expressed her thoughts clearly, a long letter she had just written to a girlfriend. The letter, a faithful reflection of her state of mind, read as follows:

Bourg-sur-Mer, 28 August

Dear Pepita,

Because you really care, and because you're more like a sister than a friend, I'll keep you posted on everything that's happening to me and everything that I'm feeling.

It can't be said that we're courting; he hasn't proposed to me; he hasn't been silly enough to make what we call a formal proposal, something I've always believed should be replaced by mutual and unspoken understanding, by the reciprocal consent sought and obtained by the man and woman who like and are beginning to love each other. But I still don't know whether he's dispensed with the proposal because he understands that it would strike me as ridiculous or whether, cautiously, he wants to enjoy his freedom in order not to become involved so that he can back away whenever it suits him. Nevertheless, he *is* becoming involved and he's involving *me*, because I've gotten myself in a situation from which I'll emerge either to be his or to do something, in order to remain free, that will justify his calling me coquettish. I'm sure that he likes me and even more sure that I like him. And the fact is that—now I'm really opening my heart to you—upon admitting it, I'm not happy with myself.

You've heard me say a thousand times that I can only conceive of a woman falling in love with a man who's her superior. I believe that, if not exactly admiration, something very similar to it should weigh considerably in our love; I think that, when we fall in love, to some degree we're looking for support, and it can only be given to us by someone who is superior to us; we repay it in tenderness, in obedience, in self-denial; but it seems to me that none of this is possible when a woman sees herself as more intelligent, more moral, and stronger, and with more heart and more willpower than the one who's to be our director in life. I'm not saying that every woman ought to love in this way, but I would like to. And I can't, because leaving vanity and self-esteem aside and speaking honestly, I'm afraid I'm his better. I'm not a genius, and I understand what he doesn't; I'm not a saint, and I forgive what he doesn't; he should have more experience than I, and he judges things in life with an impetuosity of which I'm incapable; in a word, I'm convinced that, if we got married, our guide, the head of our house would have to be me, or I'd be miserable.

In spite of which, I like this man a great deal. You see what a contradiction? I wake up thinking about him, I go down to the dining room hoping he's there, and when I say or come up with something that pleases him, that brings us together, I experience a delightful impression. Afterwards, alone, if I make, so to speak, an examination of conscience, I get angry with myself. It may be shameful, but it's true: the fact of the matter is that I like him.

He's of average height; well-built; has eyes that deceive you because they express more intelligence than he possesses; his beard, which must be very soft to the touch, is neatly trimmed; his teeth are like pure snow; he dresses stylishly, but without a hint of affectation; and his whole person exudes cleanliness and neatness. I assure you he could serve as a model for any painter who needed a dashing figure of a man to set alongside that of one of those famous love goddesses who have filled the world of poetry with their names. If he were the male lead in a theater, he'd be one of those who make us forgive all the blunders of passion. Do you understand what I'm saying?

Well, all this delight from looking at him, I won't say that it vanishes, but in my eyes it lessens considerably as soon as he talks; it's not that he says a lot of foolish things nor that he commits serious gaffes, it's just that his thinking and mine are almost never along the same lines.

You can see that I have cause to despair and be distressed. This'll be resolved according to God's will, but, for now, I see no cure for my state of mind. Feel sorry for me—I'm very deserving of it. I'll write to you again soon.

Much love from your best friend,
Soledad

It could not have been long before the best friend felt a need to pour her heart out and seek solace by sharing more confidences, because a week later she wrote to the very same friend the following letter:

Bourg-sur-Mer, 4 September

Dear Pepita,

This is going from bad to worse. I don't know what's happening to me. I summon reason to my aid, I try to reflect coolly, and it's for naught. If I had any courage I would leave this place . . . but I don't have any! So that you'll have some idea of my situation, I want to tell you what happened to me a couple of days ago. You know who came to the casino in town to give a few performances? Nerval, that beautiful actress who interprets modern drama like no other. Naturally, her repertoire is not the sort to be seen by Cistercian nuns; she does pieces that, rooted in truth, more or less successfully portray the world we live in.

Need I mention that many mothers said they would not take their daughters? The very same daughters who know about everything that goes on in the homes of their friends, and at times, what's worse, what goes on in their own?

Poor Aunt Salomé is passionately fond of the theater. There's no better treat for her than for someone to get a box seat and take her there first thing in the morning so she won't be seen, because, as you know, she's so fat that she attracts attention. She sits halfway back and leaves when nobody's left in the galleries, after having spent an entertaining evening. The day of Nerval's debut I went out bright and early and came back with the best box seat I could find. You should have seen the look on Luis's face when I told him at lunchtime. "You mean you're going to go? A lady like you?" The truth of the matter is that to avoid upsetting him—and you'll understand from this that I'm more involved than I ought to be—I would have backed off, but how was I going to tell Salomé that I would not be accompanying her, knowing as she does that I'm not shocked by plays and that I had taken the box for her? So we went to see Nerval, who, by the way, is adorable. Martín and Luis went with us, the former out of sheer indulgence as he does not like the theater and prefers to go to bed early, and the latter I suppose to be with me as well as to see Nerval, who is lovely. But as he disapproved of what I had done, he wished, undoubtedly, to make it known to me in a way that removed any uncertainty.

Five or six times he brought up the fact that mothers had left their daughters at home. Poor things, how they would have enjoyed themselves! I wisely kept quiet and he continued to find fault, although in moderation. Finally, he let the cat out of the bag. During a scene in which two lovers kiss, he said: "Good grief! Look at that! I don't understand why any self-respecting woman would come." Listen, my dear Pepita, I realized full well that he didn't dream this up to insult me and that it was a mere venting of his hypocrisy and bad taste, a result of the sanctimoniousness so prevalent today, but just the same, I was hurt so much by his lack of tact that I nearly burst into tears. The curtain fell and I sat at the back of the box. Noticing it, he asked me: "What's the matter? The play doesn't lend itself to tears." I refused to answer him. The rudeness of his language and his lack of sensitivity, which prevented him from seeing the hurt that he caused me, became confused in my bitter frame of mind.

And as things in life get entangled and complicated, especially the trivialities, if there are trivialities in love, a much more unpleasant incident occurred. When the play ended, we remained in the box seat waiting for the people to leave, because of Salomé's desire not to be seen. We were the last ones; it was very late and there wasn't a soul in the galleries or the foyer. As we passed by the restaurant, which consists of two rooms, one large and one small, we saw that the first was empty. And thinking that, given the hour, the second one would be too, Salomé said: "Martín, treat me to chocolate." So we went in and each one had what he wanted. All of a sudden we heard talking in the small room, and a few minutes later two people came out: a stunning, stylish woman, not at all flashy, and a man with a very good figure giving her his arm. As they were approaching us, I looked, albeit discreetly, with that curiosity that we don't know how to suppress on seeing a pretty dress. The woman looked at me too, hesitated a moment, like someone who's reluctant or doesn't dare to greet you, and slowly turning her head, spoke in a low voice to her escort; but I had recognized her and understood her embarrassment, so I got up, ran over to her, and, cutting her off, took her hands and kissed her affectionately. It was Beatriz Morales, our classmate. You know the story. She was rich, and her husband ruined her and then ran off with a governess they had engaged for their little girl. After five years of abandonment, and it's said almost of destitution, Beatriz found a man who loved her, and the three of them live together, because the man is becoming, out of love for her, the girl's true father. It caused a big scandal in Madrid. Since then some people greet her, others don't; I hadn't run into her until now. "You were going by without saying anything to me?" I asked her. Smiling with a kind of sweet sadness, she made a gesture that meant: "And how was I going to know if you wanted to say hello to me?" She then introduced me to her gentleman, and right away, kissing me joyously, said, "Thank you so much. You're always you. I shouldn't have had any doubts. We'll get together in Madrid." "I'll visit you," I replied, "and I hope you're happy." And so we said good-bye: she, undoubtedly contented, I pleased with myself. It all happened in an instant, much faster than it takes to describe.

As I was returning to the table that we occupied, I saw that my Aunt Salomé was nodding toward them as they were leaving; Martín had tipped his hat; and Luis, pretending to be lost in thought or distracted, was staring at his patent-leather shoes. I understood all too well that Salomé and Martín were being polite out of consideration for me; and I also realized that Luis's moral sensibilities had been disturbed and that he regarded what I had done as reprehensible; he was unable to hide it.

The following morning he told me so quite frankly, in a scene between us that I'll never forget. We were alone in the drawing room of the chalet waiting for lunch—he, very serious; I, very sad. Unwisely and unnecessarily he brought it up; we spoke almost bitterly; he defended his intolerant way of thinking; I defended mine. Abruptly he said: "You were wrong: society is what it is, and you have to bow your head." "I bow my head," I replied, "when it's necessary; what I'll never do is ignore my heart or my conscience. That woman deserves pity, respect, and above all she's my friend . . . and nobody tells me what to do."

All of a sudden—imagine my surprise!—he rushed toward me, took both my hands, squeezing them furiously, and with his face twisted, midway between passion and rage, said in a tone that could just as well have sprung from love as from arrogance: "But don't you see that I love you and can't live without you? You have to love me!" And letting go of my hands to grasp me by the waist, he drew me toward him, trying to kiss me. Flushed from embarrassment, I pulled away from him without screaming, without uttering a word, and ran to shut myself up in my room. The impression that I received was tremendous. What could have happened inside that man? Did he behave like one in love? Was he an animal? What he seemed like to me was an animal in love. It took me a while to compose myself, and when I went down, Martín and Salomé were already in the dining room. The worst part, my dear Pepita, is that after all this, I'm sad, and depressed, but not indignant. So there you have it: he and I don't think alike in any respect—not about what is of little consequence—like an actress or a play—nor about what is of great consequence—like a matter of conscience; he's been indiscreet, intolerant, rude, brash . . . and I continue to like him. You don't understand it? I don't either. It's absurd, but it's the truth. Look, when he squeezed my hands so brutally, just like one of the male servants with a maid, I pushed him away out of dignity and modesty, but his pressure felt like a caress. There is something pulling me toward him with a powerful force, and nevertheless I realize I would be unhappy being his.

Now you know everything that's happening to me. I expect nothing good to come of it, and this love of mine—because it is love!—is something of which I'm almost ashamed and I fear it will be the beginning of my unhappiness. Only two things can save me: for him to do something detestable, thereby disillusioning me—imagine the distress!—or a burst of independence and firmness on my part, for which I'm slowly losing strength. You'll be able to grasp what's happening to me by this last admission. If I were to deal with him from a distance, through correspondence or wireless telegraphy, I'm certain I would act to my advantage, but seeing him, having him at my side, I don't know what will become of me.

Good-bye, Pepita. Keep to yourself the anguish of your best friend,

Soledad

IV

Thanks to those people who hear everything and tell everything, it is known that after what Soledad related in her letters, Luis—perhaps ashamed of what he had done, or perhaps to execute a plan that he had devised—suddenly left for Paris, saying that he would be gone for a few days to take care of business matters but that he expected to return soon. From there he wrote to Soledad and to her aunt and uncle: to the former, asking her forgiveness, offering to explain upon his return what had prompted boldness of such magnitude on his part, adding that he hoped she would forgive him once she knew the cause of his excessive behavior; and to Martín and Salomé announcing his decision to marry Soledad if she was willing.

Salomé then—and this was a powerful factor in all that happened afterward—shut herself up with Soledad and had a lengthy conversation with her, at the end of which the niece left her aunt's room with a grave expression on her face, like a person who has just listened to something that she needed to know and having heard it unexpectedly, is very upset by it. And it is rumored that the last words spoken by the kindly and forthright obese lady were these or ones very similar: "If it had been someone else, I might have held my tongue, but you being the woman you are, thinking as you think, and me knowing you as I do, I believe I've done what had to be done." To which Soledad responded more or less: "You did the right thing and I thank you from the bottom of my heart. I'm certain that the decision I make will meet with your approval." From that point on Soledad seemed constantly preoccupied, and although she tried to hide it, she spent entire days overcome by a profound and persistent sadness.

One morning, after an absence of eight days, Luis returned from his trip. When he arrived at the chalet and entered the yard, followed by a porter from the station with his trunk and hand luggage on a cart, Don Martín was sitting there reading a newspaper and greeted him warmly but without going to extremes, as if they had seen each other the night before; and in order to avoid talking about Luis's wedding plans or other things, Don Martin left him alone and went to his room, saying he had to dress. Luis inquired about Salomé and was told that she had not gotten up. He made no attempt to see Soledad because first he intended to talk to her aunt and uncle to ask them to intercede on his behalf.

Lunchtime came and Salomé and Martín were waiting for him in the dining room.

"Tell us, tell us. Paris must be beautiful," Salomé said.

Luis either did not hear her or paid no attention. He had just noticed that there were only three place settings, and pretending genuine interest while actually foreseeing the imminence of something that could be humiliating for him, he asked: "What's this? Soledad's not eating? Is she ill?"

"No, she's not ill," Don Martín replied.

"Then why aren't we waiting for her?"

"God only knows when she'll show up."

"You can't bring her to reason," added Salomé in such a sweet voice that there was practically no anger in her reproach.

"But what's going on?"

"Typical of Soledad."

"He'll find out in the end; it's better we tell him straight off," added Don Martín.

"And after all, even if it is bizarre and highly irregular behavior, it shows her heart's in the right place," Salomé said.

"Please tell me!" Luis exclaimed.

"It is bizarre behavior, as she says, which everyone will criticize in his own way . . . so God help us. You already know," Don Martín continued, facing Luis, "that a very beautiful woman lives in the chalet next door."

"Lovely," interrupted Salomé.

"The prostitute. Soledad pointed her out to me at the beach, but what connection can there be between the two of them?"

"You'll see," said Martín, "and brace yourself, because this niece of ours does the oddest things. For sure there isn't a soul in this town who hasn't talked about her. Maybe some people are defending her, but I don't know . . . I don't know."

"She's been imprudent, that's true," said Salomé, "but, of course, only a person of generous spirit would do it."

"Will you please tell me!"

"Well," Don Martín slowly continued, "you should know that the prostitute, whose name is, or so she says, Yolanda de Saint-Bris, had taken the chalet adjacent to this one from August to the end of October; she arrived a week before we did. She was living with the gardener and his wife who have two children and are responsible to the owner; with a cook whom she hired here; and with the maid that she brought from Paris and who, from what people say, hadn't been with her very long, which explains what she did. You left here on Wednesday, didn't you? Yes, well, the next Friday, according to my information, mademoiselle Yolanda fell ill. She spent a difficult night, was worse, much worse, the following day, with a terrible fever, so they sent for a doctor. He came—one of the two or three who live here supported by the Spanish colony; he examined her, made a face and returned that night. In short: smallpox. A fierce attack! As soon as the servants learned of it, the first one to clear out, and I do mean clear out, was the little maid brought from Paris: hearing the doctor say it was smallpox, exclaiming in terror 'Mon Dieu! Mon Dieu! Oh, la petite vérole,' calling the gardener to tell him that she was very frightened, and leaving—that all happened in an instant. And when the cook, who didn't sleep over, arrived and found out, she left her food basket at the gardener's cottage and hasn't been seen since."

"Good grief!" Luis interrupted.

"The gardener's wife, after a row with her husband, who refused to leave with her, took their two children and went to the house of relatives. And there was mademoiselle Yolanda with all her cruelly threatened beauty, her jewelry, which is exquisite, and her smallpox, with no help except the gardener.

"When the doctor returned, she was alone with that one charitable man. The doctor—what was he going to do? He said that of course she would have to go to the hospital, running the risk that on the way she might take a turn for the worse. And now here comes the incredible part.

"The neighborhood heard all about this—our servants before anyone else. Soledad's maid, that pretty Aragonese girl that she's had for five years and thinks the world of, tells her the story; Soledad gets indignant and says that those people are terrible, that it's inhuman, and, all of a sudden, stopping at nothing, asks her maid: 'Carmen, would you have the nerve to go with me and take care of that poor woman?' 'I'll go wherever my mistress goes.' 'Then what are we waiting for?'"

Luis, placing his hands on his head, exclaimed: "For God's sake! And you allowed such an absurd thing? Of all the.... Couldn't you send for and even pay for a nurse?"

"Yes, of course," continued Don Martín. "But who was going to stop her? She went next door and spoke to the gardener, who gaped at her in wonder; she then waited for the doctor, who can't get over his astonishment since finding out that Soledad is a lady no less, because at first he thought she was of the same ilk as the patient. Picture the poor woman's surprise! In any case, the lady and her maid have been at it for five days, exposed to what you can imagine."

"Good grief! I've never heard anything like this in my life."

"When they told the prostitute that she had to be taken to the hospital, it was a heartbreaking scene. The doctor asked her if she had any family; she didn't say a word and burst into tears."

"Who knows if someone like her has family!"

"Poor thing!" said Salomé with compassion. "The fact is that Soledad has even exposed us to this contagious disease . . . but she and the girl are remarkable."

"Madness," Luis mumbled.

"And now you know it all," Don Martín continued. "Soledad comes to eat at whatever time she comes, or she doesn't come and sends Carmen over for the food. She's spent three nights without going to bed—for a woman she doesn't know!—and is doing for a harlot the same thing she'd do for a member of her family."

"She's touched in the head."

"Of course, the one you have to hear is the doctor. You have to see with what respect and admiration he treats Soledad; he says that if rewards for virtue aren't for these cases, he doesn't know what good they are."

"Oh, sure," replied Luis, "and catching a disease is also for these cases. Both of you amaze me. With the way people are, it must have caused a real scandal!"

"What do you mean, scandal?" Salomé asked. "Nothing of the sort. It may have been unwise, something out of the ordinary, but deep down . . . ."

"Yes, very deep down. For whatever reason, do you think it's prudent for a lady like her to go into the house of such a woman? Won't whoever finds out believe that to do a thing like that it was necessary to know her before . . . to be friends? Just try and put a stop to the malicious talk!"

"A lot of attention she pays to that!" exclaimed Salomé who, because of her innate kindness, was delighted with what her niece had done although she did not dare to say it openly.

People commented on the matter in different ways. Let it be said in honor of humankind that praise outweighed criticism. It is also known that when the danger had passed and Yolanda de Saint-Bris had almost recovered, a not unattractive woman came to get her and accompany her to Paris. The moment when the Madrilenian lady and her Aragonese peasant said good-bye to the French sinner was a scene to be described by a pen of gold; perhaps it was one of those moments of sublime, intangible poetry that a writer should not spoil with commentary, because when reality is so supreme, art cannot add beauty to its beauty.

V

The following week, Luis, spying on Soledad during one of her long late afternoon walks, came upon her unawares and pretended to run into her by chance at some distance from the town; he caught up with her in a magnificent forest of pines whose trunks, struck by the nearly horizontal rays of the setting sun, looked golden. The afternoon was gorgeous; nearby you could hear the formidable roar of the sea as it pounded between the cracks of the rocks; from time to time you could also hear—though muted, as if muffled by that mighty voice of nature—the small, weak, strident sounds of the whistles of locomotives and the horns and sirens of automobiles; daylight was fading rapidly, and the turbulent surface of the sea darkened continuously, intensifying the whiteness of the foam that formed on the crests of the waves. On the broad and nearly bare hillock that Soledad had reached to watch the sunset, a little girl was tending three goats that kept stopping to nibble at the little bit of damp grass that grew in the saline climate; there was no one else.

Soledad, attired in exquisite simplicity, the lines of her graceful bust shaped by a white flannel dress that the wind pressed against her body, was walking slowly; after a time she sat upon a big rock.

All of a sudden she heard her name being called behind her.

"Have you been following me?" she asked on seeing Luis.

"Why lie? Yes. Don't you think we should talk?"

"As much as you wish . . . maybe for the last time."

"First of all, have you forgiven my outburst of the other day?"

"Why go back over that? Yes, you're forgiven. Actually, I didn't think you needed forgiveness. I imagined . . . who can say? That you didn't know what you were doing . . . that maybe you had had four glasses of cognac with your coffee instead of one. In short, let's say no more about it."

"About that, no; about my hopes, yes."

"Your hopes? Not about them either, even less so. We can be

very good friends, although perhaps, given how differently we think about a lot of things, we would need to rely more on tolerance than trust."

"Good manners erase all the differences."

"Except those that spring from the heart, from feeling. Why persist in being somewhat in love today and miserably married tomorrow? When happiness comes within our grasp, it is folly not to seize it, but to seek misfortune is madness; no, leave it be, let it go away, and one day we'll be glad."

"You sincerely believe that you would be unhappy with me?"

"I'm certain, and you with me. Let's not indulge in wishful thinking. We're alone, no one can hear us, no one will know what we say, so let's speak honestly, especially me, even if you believe that I'm breaking what you and others call social conventions."

"Say as much as you wish."

"To show you that I'm being frank: I have no doubt that you like me a great deal."

"A very great deal."

"And you don't displease me."

"Then—"

"But we don't go beyond that, and marriage, as I see it, is something more than the union of a man and a woman who like each other. It should be—call me romantic, I don't mind—the blending of two spirits, of two natures capable of viewing in the same way; and to suffer and enjoy, they should have the same weapons and make use of them in like manner. It shocks you that a woman should reason in this fashion, doesn't it? When one isn't beautiful, she has time to think about everything. In short, I believe that your ideas, your weapons for the battle of life, aren't mine; instead of using them together to fight for our happiness, believe me, we would end up brandishing them against each other. Let's be sensible. Neither one suffers any damage to self-esteem. Nobody knows that we felt a mutual, passing attraction. Are we still friends?" she asked, extending her hand to him.

Luis did not feel regret or anything like it, but he did experience the profound setback occasioned by a frustrated enterprise, and nervous now, he responded: "Fine. This means that after having forgiven my outburst of the other day, which was born of the love that I feel for you—and your forgiveness which shows that you had some feeling for me—one rumor, one piece of gossip was enough for you to deny me happiness."

"I'm not happiness for you nor has there been what you suspect."

"Allow me to insist; no doubt you've been told that, maybe with some degree of passion, I condemned what you did a number of days back during the prostitute's illness."

"There's no point in discussing it. I know, beyond question, that you criticized roundly what I did for that woman. Poor thing! A few conversations at her bedside taught me more than the experience of living many years. She may remember me with gratitude; I'll remember her with the satisfaction of having done something good. You can see that I come out ahead—I have something more certain than she. But let's talk about us."

"My criticisms were based on propriety, on your decorum."

"Stop right there, my friend. The only keeper that my decorum needs is me."

"But people are people, and those things can't be done."

"Don't you see that we'll never agree? People, when they're right, are very respectable, but when a person acts out of conviction, what others think shouldn't matter much."

"And the disgrace?"

"So if I were disgraced, as you say, and even if you were firmly convinced that it was unjust, you wouldn't marry me? Honestly."

"Honestly—maybe not; but we're not in such a situation."

"The more we talk, the more we draw apart."

At this point Soledad hesitated a moment, stared at Luis, and, like a person who has wavered somewhat before speaking, continued with a certain gravity: "Well, I'm of the opinion that when happiness and the future are at risk there's a right to speak plainly."

"By all means do."

"But it has to do with a very delicate matter. I wouldn't want you to take offense. It's almost like putting you to the test."

"You can't offend me and I'll do well on the test."

"Then here goes. If I offer to alter my way of life, if I'm sensible, don't go out alone; if I learn to respect people, and, as you sometimes say, to talk without saying what I think and feel . . . well, you know what I mean, will you, in exchange, agree to do what

I ask of you? It's a test, almost a condition, and I beg you not to be the least bit offended by it."

"Go ahead and ask."

"First I'd like you to understand fully what marriage is to be for me: an intimate union, based on mutual esteem . . . the same thoughts, the same feelings . . . each side having the best possible opinion of the other, and thinking that nothing can be done by one that won't be approved and defended by the other."

"That's what you said before. Now I don't know where this is going to end."

"All right. I know that you have an interest in a business that produces a great deal but, to tell the truth, one on which I wouldn't like our life to be built."

At this point, Luis, beginning to feel uneasy, understood that he was going to hear something highly mortifying, while Soledad, calm and serene, found the courage to go on by remembering everything that Salomé told her after learning of the wedding plans that Luis had in mind.

She then continued: "Yes, a big business, I know, but not a very attractive basis for a life, a position. Forgive me. I find it repugnant—not very worthy of us. Do you understand?"

"I'd rather not."

"I've already said that I'm not trying to offend you. It's a judgment of mine, perhaps a scruple, but before becoming tied down for the rest of my life. . . ."

Luis did not utter a word, and his silence was the silence of one who, hostile and quick to be aggressive, does not succeed in responding on the spot and is plotting an answer that will injure and wound.

"I'm referring to the moneylending business," Soledad added gingerly. "Would you give that up out of love for me?"

"Madam," he replied with his face distorted. "And you believe that you're not offending me? Do you know what you're saying? All that my partners and I do—because I'm not alone—is perfectly honest, proper and legal; we work under the protection—"

"Yes, I know, under the protection of the law. But it's money that smacks of tears; I don't want it for my home."

"It's unbelievable that a person as bright as you can think that it should be the woman who inquires like this into the source of what the man provides to shoulder the responsibilities of marriage."

"And it's also unbelievable to me that there are women who don't want to know the source of their husband's earnings. I'd like the water that I'm to drink to be clean and the money I'm to spend to be even cleaner."

"Allow me to say," he interrupted her, "that I was mistaken. I thought we would talk to each other like lovers and I find myself with a public prosecutor."

"Enough. The one who was mistaken was me."

Luis still contained his anger for a few moments, but was beside himself. Incapable of understanding Soledad, he only saw an affront in what was no more than an expression of moral greatness and anxiety in a woman who was trying to determine the extent of the love that she believed she had awakened and which she doubted.

"You're quiet?" she asked.

"I ought not to answer. I think we can consider this conversation ended."

"Do you see how we can't get along? I shouldn't, perhaps, have spoken up, but I've dispelled my doubts. You neither love me nor understand my idea of a life together. I repeat: I had no intention of offending you—and no hard feelings, I hope."

"No hard feelings," he repeated ironically. And though pale with anger, he added with the utmost coolness and calm, as if he had finally found in the dirty recesses of his mind the sentence that could hurt the most: "All of that was suggested to you by Salomé and it's as base and malicious as would be the suspicion—which, of course, I don't harbor—that you look after her, and accompany her, and pamper her out of self-interest, hoping to be her heir. The people who call me moneylender and usurer perhaps call you adulatory and greedy."

He sat there contemplating her with a sardonic grin of satisfaction at having found a way to mortify her unerringly and cruelly.

Soledad, standing up and moving away from the rock where both had been sitting, looked him up and down with a stare that was worse than a slap in the face and said at once: "Believe whatever you like; I know now what I ought to think. We were free before, we're free now."

"In that case," he replied, "I'll leave here tomorrow."

"I don't even think," she said calmly, "that it's necessary for us to return to the chalet together. We can take our leave here."

"At your service, Soledad."

"Good-bye."

Luis walked at a brisk pace and arrived first; Soledad took her time, gazing at the grand spectacle of the sun, which, like an orb on fire, was sinking below the choppy, dark green surface of the water.

During the meal they spoke about inconsequential matters, as if nothing had happened between them; the next day Luis, using business as an excuse, left.

Soledad wrote to Pepita, telling her everything and concluding with this paragraph:

> So there you are: the story of my dreams has come to an end. Why did I entertain them? I don't know. The afternoon scene was painful. But how many tears this disillusion must have spared me! Fortunately, I was able to control myself. I feel for the women who don't. I'm resigned, almost glad. What I regret is that my youth is coming to a close and I've not found the companion of my dreams for old age. I'd like him to be worthy of my spirit, and if not, let him stay away. He may never come. Maybe that's why your unfortunate friend, who loves you so much, is named after solitude.
>
> *Soledad*

La Vistosa

The Overdressed Woman

I met Enriqueta, known as the "Overdressed Woman," when she was having an affair with my friend Perico. His insane jealousy, together with the fact that she loved to talk, caused me to keep my distance from her; I wanted to avoid anything that could have led to my being accused of an offense that I was incapable of committing.

Our joint business ventures made it necessary for Perico and me to see each other often, so I would frequently go to eat with him—that is, with them, because he lived conjugally with Enriqueta. I've known very few women as pleasant and, above all, as perceptive. She quickly took notice of the extreme circumspection with which I spoke to her, my determination to steer clear of any undue familiarity, and the exquisite care that I exercised to ensure that we were never alone. Undoubtedly mortified and assuming from my excessive cautiousness that I harbored a thinly disguised contempt, Enriqueta tried to dispel the notion that I might be ill-disposed toward her.

One evening, when I expected to find both of them at home, only she came to greet me. Not until after I was settled in her sitting room did she inform me that Perico had gone out, and when I attempted to leave she added, in a half-serious, half-mocking voice: "Oh, no you don't, my friend! We have to talk. Even though Perico is consumed with jealousy, which explains why you always speak to me indifferently or brusquely, you're a complete gentleman, and I know for a fact that you are neither hypocritical nor intolerant. On the contrary, you're broad-minded and indulgent of certain sins, and I haven't the slightest doubt that when you treat me—treat me coolly, with an open display of dislike, it's because you have a very low opinion of me."

I tried to interrupt her, but she wouldn't let me and continued as follows: "You've probably heard a lot about me. I can just imagine. Virtuous women have detractors who slander them out of spite and frustration, and even pride, so aren't we going to have our backbiters, those of us who are . . . not so virtuous? But I don't want you to have a low opinion of me. The things that people must have told you! That I'm self-seeking, greedy, selfish, cold, and insensitive to such an extent that through my fault a man committed suicide. I mean, I almost put the revolver in his hand, saying to him: 'Come on, why don't you kill yourself?' Well, my conscience is clear. I'm cheerful, as part of my stock-in-trade, when I'm not alone; and I do have my *ways*, as people say, because for want of consideration you have to have something in life in order not to die of sadness. So listen and judge me as you see fit."

She turned serious and, in a pitiful mixture of actual honesty and shamelessness, told me her story.

"I never knew my mother. My father was a merchant, and retired with an annual income of four thousand *duros*. He had a somewhat older but much more wealthy friend, the banker Don Ulpiano García Pignorado. You must have heard of Don Ulpiano. At his death Papa named him my guardian; I was fifteen at the time. My father believed that Don Ulpiano was honest and that he possessed a superior mind. He could believe in his honesty because during Papa's lifetime the banker suffered no financial reverses, which are what serve to put real probity to the test. As for considering him a person of superior intelligence, there's only one way I can explain it. My father was weak out of sheer kindness, one of those men who don't mistrust anyone, who don't say no, and Don Ulpiano had a rough, harsh nature. Papa, confusing harshness with energy, genuinely admired, and maybe even envied, a trait that was just the opposite of the one that formed the basis of his own nature.

"One episode will be sufficient to give you an idea of what our friend Don Ulpiano was like. He had an only son, very young, and not too bright, who, on account of the wrong crowd and the stinginess, negligence, and indifference of his father, began to go bad. He got into debt and signed an IOU for four thousand *reales*. Don Ulpiano, instead of keeping him on a tight rein in some other way, and in spite of the fact that he had no other children, packed him off to London to work in a bank for a pittance and ordered that he be watched closely.

"When I became an orphan, Don Ulpiano, instead of taking me into his home, entrusted me to the care of an aunt, my father's sister, who until then had lived alone on a small widow's pension and on what Papa used to give her from time to time. He arranged, in addition, to have two thousand *reales* given to her monthly to cover my expenses; the rest of my income went toward building up the capital. Four years went by and during that time the two thousand was paid punctually. Then, all of a sudden, one month he gave us only half, and the following month, nothing. I had just turned twenty and had had a fiancé for a year. We were going to get married, and with the consent of my guardian I was preparing my trousseau, for which four thousand *reales* had been set aside. I prefer not to discuss my fiancé. When I think of how much he duped me, of how blind I was, I understand why so many marriages go sour. Believe me, in many instances the engagement period is a time of lies, hypocrisy, and pretense. Sometimes it's the man who's dishonest; other times, the woman; and quite often both are complete fools. In our case I was the fool.

"One day, when I still didn't suspect the reason for the delay in the monthly payment, I came across an item in the newspaper: one of the most solid banking houses in Madrid had failed. The banker's first name and surnames were indicated by initials, U.G.P., that is, Ulpiano García Pignorado. My aunt and I ran to his house. He had flown the coop. A few days later, a lawyer whom I consulted, a friend of my father's, dashed all my hopes. In the first place, my father, on making his will, had absolved Pignorado from surety, and secondly, my small fortune was in government bonds and bearer bonds. I was utterly ruined.

"But let's get back to my fiancé. He took stock of the situation. I suited him fine so long as I had my three-thousand-odd *duros* of income, but I lost them, so . . . good-bye, my love! He looked for a pretext—unfounded jealousy—and dropped me. Consider the position I was in: accustomed to living well, no concerns about the future, and all of a sudden . . . nothing, I mean nothing. By pawning and selling everything in the house at a loss, and supporting ourselves only on my aunt's widow's pension, we scraped by for a few months. Then came the cruel, unrelenting misery, and with a vengeance. I'd rather not talk about it. People say I'm pretty. Back then I was! I'll show you a picture of me that dates from that time and you'll understand that certain things cannot help occurring. Look: either a woman is brave enough to jump from a balcony or she isn't. I didn't have the courage. I don't want to reveal to you how . . . what happened to me . . . in short, how I met my first lover. If I had fallen in with a decent man I assure you he would have been the only one.

"Two years later I found out that Don Ulpiano had returned to Madrid and was spending freely and living on a grand scale, without going into business or having any known source of income. Everybody knew that the bankruptcy of the past was a fraud, but I had no recourse—the laws were completely useless. And I didn't bother with them. Don Ulpiano's second period of prosperity didn't last very long because the great big swindler died, and besides, why did I need to appeal to him? He would not have been able to undo the damage that he had done to me. At the time I was in love—don't laugh, in love—and even smitten, with a man as good as gold. Unfortunately, his family separated us and with him I lost my chance to be sensible and relatively honest. After him I began an affair with the Viscount of Manjirón, Pepe García, the one who killed himself because of me.

"He had just returned from abroad and was making a real show of spending a great deal, literally squandering his money. I don't know if it was because of the way I dressed—bright colors, outlandish dresses—or because of my type, but I was called 'the overdressed woman' or 'the overdressed blond.' In any event, he saw me, took a liking to me, and began to shower me with gifts. At first he tried to get me to go and live with him; then he gave up on the idea, realizing that such an arrangement is impossible here in Madrid, because although this society tolerates the affairs of married women, there's no tolerance of an unmarried man and an unmarried woman living together, no tolerance of two people who don't dishonor or degrade anyone. In the end he set me up in a sumptuous apartment and spent lavishly on my personal needs. From shoes to hairpins, it all came from Paris.

Did he love me? I'm convinced that he didn't. Had there been another one, even more demanding and more expensive, he would have wanted her because, you see, I didn't mean much of anything to him; in fact, I don't believe he was all that taken with me as a woman and a woman only. It inflated his ego for people to know that I was his, that he paid for my life of luxury, and that I cost him a great deal. He 'kept' me out of vanity. If I had told him that I wished to live on a fourth floor somewhere, modestly, he would have left me high and dry.

"Pepe was a hard, gruff man, difficult to get along with because of his suspicious nature, like someone who's been brought up in a loveless environment, far removed from trust and affection. What pleased him was spending, showing off, and attracting attention. He acted like an upstart, a parvenu, and was incapable of tenderness and sensitivity, even in moments of the greatest intimacy. Can you conceive of love, even if it's a travesty of love, without openness and trust? That was Pepe, in a nutshell.

"I've never indulged in wishful thinking, and know full well that my standing, my life, what we might call my past, strip me completely of the right to certain demands. But by nature, by instinct, and by temperament, I'm affectionate, unassuming, and would rather give in than give orders; and most important of all, I would like to guard against the crudeness of material love, and envelop it and surround it with something exquisite and pure— I would even say poetic if I weren't afraid that you would laugh. The love of women like me is sheer pretense, right? Everyone knows that it's a sham, so the more I dream the better off I am. There was no way to reach the viscount. The only thing he enjoyed was being talked about, even if it were unfavorably; he didn't like pleasure for the sake of delighting in it, but for the sake of having others envy him for it.

"After two years together I had a whim: I wanted Pepe to take me to Paris. This was when he was setting up his stables, and he flatly refused, but so harshly, so bluntly, that I was humiliated.

"'The horses come before you,' he said.

"At the time Pepe had a crony who accompanied him everywhere, and very often he would come to eat with us. Half-jokingly, but with serious overtones, this friend of his used to say to me: "'Oh, Enriqueta! If I had money, you'd be living a very different life!'

"I never knew what to say. He was one of those men that a woman regrets not having met sooner—a picture of happiness that arrives too late. Well, this friend, speaking one afternoon about Pepe's refusal to take me to Paris, said: 'I advised him to take you. Besides, he could find a better horse handler there than here, but he's stubborn. Tell him one thing and it's enough for him to do the opposite. Just like his father.'

"Then he went on to tell me that they had known each other since childhood, and that afterwards, as young men, they had worked together in London at the same bank. Finally, that his father, Pepe's, had sent him to England on account of something stupid that he did here, and that his father, evil personified, had faked bankruptcy, ruining a lot of people. I listened in astonishment; I asked him a thousand questions; I talked to him about my father and my family; I voiced my doubts; I asked more questions; and what emerged was that Pepe García, Viscount Manjirón, my lover, was the son of my guardian, of Don Ulpiano, the man who had brought about my downfall and my degradation. It's easy to explain why I didn't realize it sooner. My guardian's name was Ulpiano García Pignorado, but everybody in Madrid referred to him by his second surname; Pepe, naturally, put his mother's surname after the paternal García. Besides, when my guardian died, Pepe came from London, collected his inheritance and went back abroad. He traveled widely, and in Rome, for a donation that he made to the Pope during a pilgrimage, he obtained his title under the name of an estate that he owned near El Escorial. When I met him everybody in Madrid called him Pepe García, or Viscount Manjirón. What would have led me to suspect that he was Don Ulpiano's son?

"From the moment that I found out, I couldn't stand the sight of him. The life of luxury that he was giving me, his wealth, his loveless gifts, his meaningless caresses—it all seemed like an unbroken chain of sarcasm, a brutal, savage mockery of fate. His father had robbed me and caused my ruin, and he, partly with my own money, was putting the finishing touches to my undoing and depravity. Perhaps these sentiments were not entirely justified but they took hold of me and wouldn't let go. I decided to break it off with him immediately, and without explanations, which he would have been incapable of understanding anyway.

"At the time there was a rich playboy in Madrid who, although not as wealthy as Pepe, competed with him in that stupid life of ostentation and vain display. He had made amorous overtures to me a number of times, and I was certain that whenever I wanted to—for the sake of humiliating my lover—I could twist him around my little finger. I got in touch with him and stipulated that we go off to travel, that he take me to Paris, and we reached an agreement; for his part, he insisted that we remain in Madrid for eight days and that during that time Pepe not set foot in my apartment.

"I gave him my word and that very afternoon began to keep my end of the bargain. I wrote to the viscount who, in my eyes, as you can imagine, was now only the son of Don Ulpiano, and made a complete break. Nothing held us together; he knew what I was, and he had no claims on me. I was doing plenty by informing him. He came to see me and I didn't let him in; he tried three or four more times and I stood my ground. Under no circumstances was I going to give in.

"It became known by all the people in Madrid who concern themselves with these things, and Pepe's anger knew no bounds. The indifference, unfaithfulness, and desertion of a woman whose favors were a matter of money constituted an unbearable humiliation for him. Now I feel sorry about it—he must have suffered a great deal. Unquestionably, the blow to his self-esteem poisoned his thoughts; pride and anger—and who knows what else? perhaps everything negative—must have fermented in his imagination, as weakness, despair, and a misplaced sense of humor ferment in the minds of others. I believe he killed himself in a fit of madness.

"After four days had gone by without our seeing each other, the night watchman on my street, who of course knew him, unlocked the door to the apartment house for Pepe. It was twelve-thirty at night, he came up and knocked, because I had had the lock changed on the door and his key was for the old one.

"Knowing that he would ignore my maid, I myself spoke to him through the peephole.

"'Is it true that you're going off with him?' he asked. 'Don't you realize that you're making an absolute fool of me?'

"I said that it was true and told him to forget about me. I also said that there could be no humiliation for him because the betrayal and unfaithfulness of a woman like me didn't dishonor anybody. He went wild. I closed the peephole and walked away, tapping my heels, then retraced my steps on tiptoe. His mind must have already been clouded, because, beside himself and pressing his lips against the peephole slot, he said 'Open up! I'm going to kill you!'

"I didn't say a word and a few moments went by in silence. All of a sudden a shot rang out and it reverberated in the stairwell as if it were a thunderclap; then I heard the sound of a body hitting the wood floor, and right after that, what must have been the revolver as it fell from his hand. Fortunately for me, at that exact moment, two gentlemen, along with a servant who was lighting their way, were coming out of number three. Their statements saved me; I don't mean from a formal charge, but from a lot of trouble and bother at the very least. After I pleaded with them they agreed to wait inside my apartment for the magistrate, who arrived at two o'clock in the morning.

"Pepe lay flat on his back on the staircase landing. He had left his walking stick propped against the wall, and his hat, which he had evidently thrown, was found on the lower flight. He shot himself in the right temple where you could see a very small hole from which flowed a trickle of blood that dribbled between his neck and shirt. It was a horrible sight!

"The magistrate didn't question me very much because of the statements given by the men, and besides . . . I think he liked me.

"You can see that it wasn't my fault that Pepe killed himself, just as I couldn't overcome the aversion that sprang up in me when I discovered who he was. He never loved me and I never loved him. There was no betrayal."

Afterward Enriqueta became momentarily lost in thought, then she suddenly ran both hands over her face and finished her story in a voice fraught with bitterness and cynicism: "He spent a lot on me. So what? It's a known fact that women who live as I do are born to put ill-gotten gains back into circulation."

La prudente

The Prudent Woman

I

I first saw her at the Royal Theater. She caught my attention because she was dressed entirely in white and her figure stood out conspicuously against the red background of the box seat. She wasn't wearing a single piece of jewelry—no necklace, no bracelets, not even earrings. Her only concession to vanity was to show off her lovely hands, on which there were neither gloves nor rings so that the admirable form of her fingers could be appreciated. The one adornment on her dress consisted of a small bunch of very pale violets fastened to the left side of her décolletage. With marvelous flair she worked an enormous fan made of black feathers—but not a black as deep as the ebony of her eyes—whose movement would momentarily conceal her bosom and the lower portion of her face. Her complexion, slightly dark, reminded me of the ivory hue of magnolia petals, and when she set the edge of the fan's black feathers against her lips, her wet mouth, glistening and crimson, looked like a ruby blossom. Her clear forehead and nearly straight nose lent her profile the appearance of a head in relief on an ancient coin. Strictly speaking, she couldn't be considered beautiful because her features were irregular, but on the other hand she was a perfectly delightful creature. She appeared to be twenty or a few years older. Her principal charm lay in her manner of looking at something: she was one of those women who are adept at and capable of expressing as much as they want with their eyes. The pretty, slightly furrowed brow, a certain languor in her posture, and a barely noticeable grimace that she would make from time to time betrayed her intention to appear indifferent to everything around her. Was it genuine disdain? Was it studied aloofness? Maybe by looking at the surface of water one can determine what its depths contain, but who would be capable of divining a woman's spiritual state from her face?

There were two other people in the box with her: a gentleman who spent the evening reading newspapers and a lady dressed in luxurious extravagance. They were her parents, but the truth is that they didn't look it. Neither one showed signs of enjoying the music, in spite of the fact that the opera being performed was sublime.

I spent a good part of the evening watching them. How different they all were! The parents, common and ordinary; the daughter, elegant and aristocratic. Looking alternately at father and daughter I entertained thoughts that were not very favorable for the mother's conjugal fidelity; it was difficult for me to believe that such a refined young woman was the work of such an unpolished man. However, perhaps my suppositions were unjust, because plants with the roughest textures usually produce the most exquisite flowers.

When the performance ended, I went out to the foyer and waited for them at the bottom of the staircase. She came down ahead of her parents, revealing her feet, which were as pretty as her hands; wrapped in a magnificent white plush coat trimmed in black fur but with her head bare, she glanced from side to side with an indifferent, almost scornful, air as she descended. But her arrogance seemed to be infused with sadness and her disdainful carriage was very much like a mask of melancholy. A romantic would have been able to fantasize to his heart's content by contemplating that splendidly dressed figure of a woman who evoked thoughts of misfortune and by gazing at the expression on that face filled with attraction but devoid of joy.

I asked a friend who she was.

"She's the daughter of the couple in back of her," he replied. "Very wealthy. She'll inherit several million *pesetas*. Nonetheless, she hasn't been married, nor is she to be married, nor does it seem likely that she ever will marry." And since I made a gesture of surprise, he added: "Don't go thinking that she's lost or squandered what Dumas called a girl's capital. It's said she's very cold. Look. I don't want to tell you the cause of that obligatory virginity. What's delightful is to hear it from her own lips, as I have. Try to get yourself introduced, do what you can to win her confidence, and if some day she agrees to relate to you the reasons behind her decision to die a single woman, you'll be much amused. Manolita is what today's novelists call a human interest case."

II

That night the image of Manolita paraded constantly before my eyes. There were moments when I wondered if my pleasure in remembering her was the beginning of falling in love, but I soon became convinced that it was not, because the following day I hardly thought about her.

A few weeks went by, and then one evening I ran into her at a party given by a family who were friends of mine. She seemed more beautiful to me, and just as sad as the first time that I saw her. With a severity unbecoming to her age she was dressed completely in black and, of course, was elegance personified.

I asked our host and hostess to introduce me to her, and Manolita and I proceeded to talk for quite a while, or rather, I sought reasons and pretexts for her to talk. She was very discreet and, without making a show of it, expressed herself with a certain freedom of language which, given our customs, wasn't too ladylike. On the other hand, she spoke ill of nobody, and whenever I tried to turn our conversation into gossip to observe her, she would immediately fall silent, foiling my every attempt, or would very cleverly manage to change the subject.

Naturally, that evening I didn't dare ask her anything about herself, but realizing that I hadn't gotten off on the wrong foot, I told her that it would give me great pleasure to be received in her home. She responded by introducing me to her parents, who then invited me to visit them.

When we took our leave, Manolita said to me: "I suspect that we're going to be good friends."

And it seemed to me that she pronounced the word *friends* as if adding mentally: *but just friends.*

III

Sure enough, we were—as soon as she became convinced that I wasn't wooing her.

Manolita's tastes were the same as mine, but her sentiments were superior because she was a woman. The really remarkable aspect of her character, however, was the lofty, noble idea that she had of her own dignity, the self-respect on which she based all of her actions and words. Her good qualities were founded on the belief that ignoble and base behavior was unworthy of her. Integrity for Manolita meant not saying or doing anything she couldn't confess, and she was such a marvelously tactful and gifted conversationalist that she was bold without being cynical and modest without being hypocritical.

In a very short time we became good friends, just friends and nothing more, which allowed us to be extremely candid with one another. And thanks to this candor I came to know her in a way that men can never get to know the woman they love, because a woman who's loved does everything she can to seem better than she actually is.

Once we were close I realized that she would never marry. There is nothing that alienates us men from women as much as the fear of being morally beneath them, and suitors who approached Manolita had, in advance, the certain knowledge of their own inferiority. This created a big drawback for her because no sooner is a man persuaded that the reasoning of his fiancée, wife or lover is superior to his than he develops an antipathy toward her without anybody being able to prevent it.

So when Manolita believed that I wasn't in love with her, and above all, that I didn't aspire to her fortune under the pretext of marriage, she regarded me with favor, which I tried to encourage. I gained her trust and, little by little, learned even her innermost thoughts. Finally, one evening at a social gathering in someone's house, by chance we found ourselves alone at the far end of a drawing room, sitting on the same sofa. The other people present began to play ombre, paying us no attention whatsoever. If they had believed that we were in love, somebody would have come over to disturb us, but thinking that we were bored, they left us alone.

I don't recall how the conversation started. As it happened, within a short time the subject turned to how risky the choice of a husband is for a woman.

One thing led to another and I reached a point at which, not having intended to question her, I blurted out: "The truth is that the majority of women are as unsuccessful in choosing a husband as they are in selecting dresses: they marry and deck themselves out as if advised by the devil. On the other hand, there are some who possess an abundance of sound judgment with which to attract and hold sway over men of real merit, but they don't do it." And swept along by momentum, I added: "Take you, for instance. Why are you single?"

I was afraid, as soon as I had asked, that she would stand up and rebuke me for my daring by stalking away, but she didn't. Undoubtedly she understood that my indiscretion was the result of the interest that she aroused in me.

She made herself comfortable on the sofa, rested her pretty feet on a cushion, and, certain of not being overheard, looked straight at me and said: "Now then. I'm going to tell you why I am, and most likely will die, single. If I don't do it, others will, and it'll be worse because they'll distort the truth."

"Let me say," I interrupted her, "that if I've committed an indiscretion I'm sorry and I ask your forgiveness."

"Don't you write novels? Well, listen to this one. The difference is that all of it, all of it is true. It's happened to me. I'm the protagonist.

"Although I don't look it, I'm twenty-four. I spent my childhood and the first few years of adolescence in a private school run by nuns—may God forgive them!—where my parents tried to have me educated. And I say *tried* because I walked out of there without knowing how to greet people or turn up a hem, but able to write with awful spelling, speak broken French, and pray a great deal—why, of course! What little I know I've learned as a result of my liking for books. I would spend winters at the wretched old convent and summers with my parents, but as summertime is the season for travel, I can assure you that I never became acquainted with my home nor with the life that was lived in it. For example: they would take me out of school on

June 15, two or three days later we would depart on the express train north to Biarritz, then spend the month of September in Paris and at the start of October return to Madrid, in other words, to school. During Christmas vacations my home would look like a warehouse full of everything on God's earth—all we did was give and receive gifts, decorate rooms, and prepare dinners; at Mardi Gras it was pretty much the same thing—dresses in one place, dummies in another, and fabric everywhere. On my mother's saint's day there would be a formal meal; on my father's saint's day, another little celebration. Oh, and I'll have you know that on the days I was taken out of the convent at nine o'clock in the morning, I was taken back again at nightfall. So I never once spent a full week at home during the school year.

"The very day that I turned fifteen I received a most welcome piece of news—that I wasn't returning to school. Shortly afterward I put on a long dress and went to my first dance. A society columnist wrote in his newspaper that I had made my debut. That night, because of the novelty, I had a very good time. But now, the last dance I've attended is the one that strikes me as the dullest. What's behind this indifference with which I look upon what the French call *le monde* and what we call high society? I don't know. The fact is that a book, a play, the opera, or conversation with my intellectual betters are infinitely more appealing to me than getting dressed to kill, going out with a low neckline on cold nights, and having to suffer the asinine remarks of anyone disposed to make them to me.

"And there's one other thing that I enjoy in a way that I can't explain, but don't make fun of me or call me romantic. My greatest delight, when I'm in the right frame of mind for it, consists of seeking seclusion for a few hours to talk to myself about hopes and memories and fantasies; and I ask myself questions about the oddest things, and I answer myself, and I get lost in reverie, carried away like a peaceful and somewhat dejected madwoman.

"On the other hand, and I'm not exaggerating, all my mother has to do is mention a dance or a reception to me and I start shaking like a leaf. I've often wondered why I differ so much from other women in this regard. I'm beginning to think that I'm not on a par with them. It's one of two things: either I'm a woman of greater worth, much greater worth, because I'm so difficult to entertain, or of considerably lesser worth, because I don't know how to savor the pleasures which are a source of delight to so many who have a reputation for cleverness. Thinking about this, I sometimes say to myself that perhaps society isn't to my liking because generally it's made up only of idle, unimaginative souls and petty people who do nothing except speak highly of themselves and ill of their neighbors. Artists and writers, who study and work with the mind, the ones I'd like to meet and get to know, don't frequent these houses, so when they paint and describe what goes on in them at times they're considerably wide of the mark. And the things they could learn!

"But forgive me for rambling like this. You want to know why I haven't married? Nobody's told you about the scandal I caused? Well, it was horrible, a ferocious affair.

"At one of these dances that I've referred to, I met a thirty-two-year-old man, clever and as handsome as a man can be without looking effeminate. I thought him kind, well-bred, and even educated and serious compared with the hordes of young gentlemen for whom a poorly tailored dress coat constitutes a tragedy. To make a long story short, he courted me for several months, really pulling the wool over my eyes. You know of course that the engagement period is the time to cover up faults. I was foolish; without knowing him all that well I consented to his asking for my hand. Papa and Mama looked favorably upon the marriage and inquired into his financial state; it turned out that he was rich. It didn't occur to them to investigate further. Making inquiries about his moral makeup, putting to the test the nature of his feelings—nothing along these lines was considered. I wish I could have done all this on my own, but will you tell me how I would have managed? How can a young lady engage in a similar line of inquiry—a young lady who doesn't go out unaccompanied, who mixes, superficially, only with her own kind, and who has nobody she can trust?

"Was I in love? I believed I was. At the very least that man aroused in me a feeling of sweet anxiety, an urge to dwell on him and share his life, a fervid desire to be everything to him, to such an extent that frankly, I thought it was love. And actually what I was doing was confusing the need for love with love itself.

"My trousseau was magnificent. Two rooms were taken up with a mélange of dresses, fabrics, laces, lingerie, and jewelry that my girlfriends looked at again and again and commented on and criticized, half-astonished, half-jealous. I admit that instead of going from shop to shop and from store to store, I would have preferred to handle things differently, less ostentatiously. For example, I would have done part of the preparations at home and asked my fiancé for his advice in order to familiarize myself with his tastes and preferences to blend them with mine. But it wasn't possible.

"So let's get to the scandal. One morning—my parents hadn't risen yet—the maid came into my room saying that some young woman was very insistent about wanting to see me. 'Who is she?' I asked. 'She refuses to say.' 'Was she sent by someone I know?' 'No. She's just very eager to see you.' 'All right, tell her I'll see her.' I thought that maybe it was some skilled dressmaker, seamstress or embroiderer who, informed of my trousseau, was asking for work. So I instructed the maid to bring her in. She was a very refined and frail sort with a slim little figure and big, beautiful eyes set in a childlike face of small features, but in early decline from a life of hardship and privation. You know the type—one of those young women who, if there were any justice in Divine Providence, ought to be born in the midst of silks and exquisite dresses instead of spending their lives sewing them for others like me. Just by looking at her I realized that no one had sent her and that she had come on a mission of her own, strictly her own. She said firmly, but not haughtily or insolently, that she wished to speak to me alone. I signaled my maid to leave us, and . . . now get ready, because here comes the juicy part.

"She threw herself at my feet, broke out crying, and, between sobs, her words literally wetted by tears, said to me: 'Miss, you're going to marry Mr. So-and-so, aren't you? Well, for two years he's had a love affair with me and we have a ten-month-old daughter. Don't think I've come to ask you to call off the wedding. I know I have no right to do such a thing. All I ask is that you and he give the baby and me something to live on before you marry. We have nothing, nothing other than my work and you can't imagine what it's like for a woman to live off her work. Right now, thank goodness, I'm healthy and I earn a little, but what about the day I get sick? And what if I die? For the love of God, miss, check and you'll find that it's all true, and by what you hold most dear in the world, see that the baby's provided for. . . .'

"Why continue?" Manolita asked. "It goes without saying that

The Prudent Woman

I took pity on her! Do you know what I did? For three or four mornings I went out accompanied only by our steward. I acted like a police agent and gave out money, talking to whomever I thought could help me. Result: everything that she had told me was the unvarnished truth. And I found out more, a great deal more, which she had had neither the time nor the courage to tell me. My husband-to-be was a scoundrel in the fullest sense of the word. I don't know what other women would have done in my place, but I refused to receive him, to listen to him, even to talk to him. I mean at all—I didn't so much as write to him. His entreaties, supplications, and threats were to no avail. My father had to come to an agreement with him. The only times I've seen my former fiancé since then have been at the theater or on the street, from a distance.

"I gave that poor mother two government savings bonds, one in her name and the other in the baby's, for an amount equal to all that I had spent on wedding preparations. Oh, and I counseled her that on no account and under no circumstances should she ever marry that man, or allow him to recognize the baby, going on the assumption that it's better to be left fatherless than have one who's forced into it out of a sense of obligation.

"It caused an unheard-of scandal. My girlfriends called me stupid, Papa got furious, and nobody approved of my conduct, not even my own mother! This happened a while ago, quite a while ago, and since then no man has given me the time of day. So it's one of two things: either they think the wedding was called off because of something—speaking plainly, dishonorable for me, or men avoid us women when they see that we're capable of thinking for ourselves and being strong-willed."

When she finished her story, Manolita dabbed her eyes with her handkerchief and, smiling bitterly, said to me: "Come on, be frank and tell the truth. Isn't a woman better off single than married to such a man?"

The cardplayers rose from their table, and in the midst of the general conversation that followed we were unable to continue our private talk.

* * *

Since then, whenever I see an indifferent, haughty Manolita at dances, parties, and soirées, with her pretty brow wrinkled as she strives to appear disdainful and cold, I think about the contempt that she must feel for people, and about how much she must suffer; and I'm reminded of an Arab tale that relates the adversities of an angel who was condemned by Muhammed to live among lepers.

Sacrificio

Sacrifice

I
PARAGRAPHS FROM A LETTER

May 1870

You're right, it's true. As girls we grew up together and you've been my best friend, my only friend; nobody is more entitled than you are to know the reasons and motives behind my decision. I needn't remind you of the years of my life that you've shared; first, we had the same playthings, and later, the same dreams, which you, fortunately, have been able to realize. You'll recall that everything at home was pretense and appearance, and the situation in my family began to deteriorate at the same time that you got married and went traveling in style from place to place. Papa had good jobs with the government that never seemed to last very long, then periods of unemployment that never seemed to end. His political life came down to this: while our party was in power we sinned on the side of undue luxury; when the party wasn't . . . we lived a life of deception and hardship. Sometimes we owned a carriage, other times we found ourselves owing for the very shoes that we wore. When Papa died my mother wasn't left a widow's pension and, consequently, when she passed away, I had no right to an orphan's pension either. In other words, if it hadn't been for my Aunt Florentina, who very willingly took me in, I would have ended up in the street. With everything in the house—furniture, clothes, inexpensive jewelry—sold for practically nothing, I wouldn't have had enough to live on for a year.

You know what Florentina is like: a very generous and good person, proof of which is what she did for me in the beginning, but she is also a person given to falling in love with a vengeance. As long as a man wasn't involved she had a heart of gold, but on seeing another woman courted, envy made her capable of anything. Surely you remember what Papa used to say about her: that when she was a child she liked toy soldiers more than dolls, that as a young woman she had a different beau every month, and that after her husband died in a fit of temper, she made more conquests as a widow than Napoleon. I've heard it said that there was one house where she let herself be wooed by every one of the male guests, from the schoolboy who went out only on Sundays to the grandfather who was Espartero's* adjutant. This is not meant to slander her, it's to give you the background so you'll understand what follows.

Florentina was very kind to me for eight months. More than once I had to refuse when she offered to spend money to buy me useless things. But the situation soon changed. A handsome young oculist came to live in the apartment next to ours; undoubtedly he was just beginning in the profession because he had few patients. We got to know him by chance. Florentina started to have problems with her eyes and called him in, even though we weren't acquainted, because the ailment was slight and he was the specialist who was nearest at hand. The visits became frequent, and in a few weeks the doctor had become a friend. You can't imagine a cleverer and more congenial man. Soon I was convinced that he liked me, and that the real purpose of his visits, longer each day, was me. On the other hand, I didn't realize that this was not to my aunt's liking. I had heard a great deal about the excessive ease with which she could fall in love, but I never imagined that it could be so extreme, nor much less that she would allow herself to be dragged down by it to the point of becoming cruel and base.

Beginning with our first conversations Mariano spoke to me like someone who is determined to be fully committed—that is, to get married. He was hardworking, intelligent, seemed to be in love and sincere; I believed him and, what was worse, I fell in love too. I'm not ashamed to confess it: I loved him because he appealed to me and because I considered him worthy of my affection. Besides, I was persuaded that, being poor, I couldn't aspire to a better marriage; in a word, my heart and my head drove me toward him. Mariano had told me that in order to marry we would have to wait at least a year, which was how long it would take him to obtain a position in some hospital or other; and fearful that my aunt would not receive him at home because she would be unwilling to tolerate the inconveniences of the courtship, we agreed to keep our relationship a secret. But one night she surprised us talking across from our windows, and from that moment on my unhappiness was sealed. What shameful emotion took hold of her? Was it jealousy without love? Stupid envy? I have no idea. If that woman took me in with the intention of caring for me until I got married, why did she behave the way she did? None of this makes sense. What is certain is that she considered herself humiliated by the mere fact that Mariano paid attention to me and not to her.

Mariano had a serious fault which I, blinded by love, neither noticed nor criticized. My aunt, more experienced, caught it right away, and she set out to channel it to her own advantage. That fault was vanity, a peculiar vanity mixed with professional ambition, which, as I later observed, is very common among men of science. To this vanity, which you and I will never understand, Mariano sacrificed me, and I believe that he would have sacrificed his own mother. His golden dream, his most cherished ambition, was to own or lease in Madrid a villa where he could set up and direct a French-style *maison de santé* for the treatment of eye troubles. He based his eventual glory and success on this plan. Hidden behind the curtains in the study, I heard the shameful pact with my own ears. There was no doubt they had already discussed it extensively, because he pretended to be as loving with her as with me, and she looked at him with all of the expression that her eyes, not yet recovered from a relapse, would allow. I don't know what made me angrier, the flattery that they were lavishing on each other or what they were saying about me. That I was silly, that my beauty was the ordinary good looks of a twenty-year-old, that I was incapable of running a home, and that I had pretended to be in love with him as a last resort; finally, that what he needed was a reasonable, judicious woman capable of helping him to become a man. In a word, that very week they intended starting marriage proceedings at the rectory and negotiations to purchase a villa in the Argüelles district, where Mariano could set up his *maison de santé*, his small luxury hospital, or whatever it was. As far as I was concerned. . . . I still break into tears of sorrow: my aunt would send me to live in Getafe, where she had a house, assigning me a small daily allowance on condition that I never return to Madrid.

My greatest bitterness consisted of knowing that I was, or that I had been able to be, in love with that wicked man. My disillusionment was profound. A few minutes were sufficient to convince me of his infamy, of my error, and of how irreparable was my misfortune. I would need many days and many sheets of paper to explain to you how much I've suffered. What kinds of thoughts have I had? What direction have they taken? Even I don't know. But what I do feel today is not spite for the evil of one man, it's an aversion toward all men. They look for nothing more than the satisfaction of their vanity in beautiful women, and I'm not one, since I could not bring him to love me; money in the rich ones, and I have nothing; patronage in the fortunate ones, and I'm in no position to support anybody. What do I have left? I don't have the courage for certain things, nor do I feel resigned to wait many years for death, which strikes unexpectedly those who fear it, yet does not respond to those who summon it. I'm going, therefore, to meet it. My resolution is irrevocable. Within eight days I'll enter the order of the Daughters of Health, who are like Sisters of Charity, and on completing the novitiate year, if I can endure it, I'll be assigned to a hospital.

I feel capable of tolerating the greatest suffering, of seeing and alleviating the greatest misfortune. The only thing that frightens and intimidates me is the idea of feeling love again. You'll probably say that my decision is not prompted by pious motives, but what importance do the mysteries of my soul have when I'm preparing myself to console others in their misfortune? Cholera, typhus, smallpox, plagues and wars—I fear nothing, and trust that one of these will end my life. Good-bye. Remember me as your best friend remembers you.

María del Amparo

II
EXCERPTS FROM THE DIARY OF DOCTOR FLORALS, MILITARY PHYSICIAN IN THE ARMY OF THE NORTH DURING THE CIVIL WAR
1871–1873

17 August

We had set up a field hospital in the paper mill at Ortolaeta, which was almost destroyed, and in adjoining buildings. In spite of the distance we could hear the cannon shots perfectly, and the air was filled with the smell of gun-powder. Soon after the firing had begun, they started to bring in the wounded. The first ones were a chasseur with both legs fractured, who died during the night, and an artillery captain with a gunshot wound in his back, the bullet having lodged in the lumbar vertebrae. Never have I seen a more dashing figure of a man nor one of more quiet courage. Unfortunately the wound was of such a nature that I attempted in vain to extract the bullet, and he fell into a state of deep prostration.

The medical supplies that I had requested arrived the following morning, along with two nuns. One, forty years old, anemic, almost tubercular, seemed to have come more to be cared for herself than to help her fellowman. The other one, between twenty-five and thirty, was supremely beautiful and very slender; she had big, sorrowful eyes, white skin, perfect features, and a highly intelligent appearance. The only thing about her that displeased me was her disdainful expression, the air of scorn with which she looked at men—that is, at strong and healthy men, because for the wounded she was all solicitude and tenderness. Since she struck me as brave, I entrusted the poor captain to her care.

He became delirious in the early morning. I have never heard anything like it. The hapless man saw or believed that he saw a woman, and he called out to her sobbing, crying, roaring, and cursing—sometimes in highly tender terms, at other times with coarse expressions. She could have been his fiancée, his wife or his lover—in short, someone he loved very much—because he kept repeating: "Julia, kiss me; Julia, kiss me."

The nun looked at him, her appearance seemingly impassive and serene, but observing her well, you could see her suffering. There was a moment in which she drew back, turning her face away, as if she were trying to hide her emotion. Suddenly, with an almost convulsive movement, the captain extended his arm and succeeded in seizing her, first a sleeve of her habit, and then her hand, while continuing to say: "Julia, kiss me; Julia, kiss me."

Seeing that the nun's eyes were clouded with ill-contained tears, I asked her, pointing at the wounded man: "Do you know him?"

"No, sir," she answered.

"Well, he," I replied, "undoubtedly believes that you're someone else."

And all the while the captain kept repeating deliriously in a very weak voice: "Julia, kiss me; Julia, kiss me." Everything that I did to calm him down proved useless. He was prey to an emotional disturbance impossible to combat.

"Nothing can be done, right, doctor?" she asked me. "You don't know who he is either?"

"I don't recollect his name, but I've run into him occasionally in Madrid and I believe that the one he's calling was a woman of ill repute, who deceived him miserably. Forgive him, Sister, but this unfortunate man without doubt remembers her and thinks she's in his presence. For him now, you are that Julia."

And his voice, fainter each time, repeated: "Julia, kiss me; Julia, kiss me."

We were alone. The dim light of dawn competed with the reddish glow of the lantern on the table, and through a large window we saw the branches of walnut trees gently moving in the wind. Suddenly a contraction of supreme anguish appeared on the wounded man's face, and sighing weakly he repeated for the hundredth time: "Julia, kiss me; Julia, kiss me."

What happened then was of a sublimity that my pen is incapable of describing. The nun removed her headdress, which resembled a large dove with wings extended, revealed her forehead crowned with short, black hair like a boy's, and immediately, bending her head toward the wounded man, kissed him calmly and lovingly. Afterwards she turned away from him, and again putting on her headdress, which had fallen to the floor and was stained with blood, she knelt near the cot and began to pray.

I took my hat off in front of her out of respect.

Shortly afterwards the captain calmed down and even slept. All my science is unable to explain how that happened, but I have never obtained with any medicinal substance such a restorative and untroubled sleep like the one induced by that woman's lips.

In my latter years I was sent to Seville as chief medical officer, and I had to visit the supreme commander of the army, a man of around fifty but still quite handsome. He received me very cordially, conducted himself much more graciously with me than required by official courtesy, and invited me to dinner without my guessing the reason for such kindness. Shortly before the meal was announced, he introduced me to his wife. She was a graceful, extremely elegant woman of singular beauty, in spite of her prematurely white curls. I called forth recollections, I stirred up memories, and moved by an overwhelming curiosity I asked: "General, were you wounded in Ortolaeta around '73?"

She then, looking at me affectionately, held out her hand, and clasping mine in hers as if we were lifelong friends, asked me: "And me, doctor, don't you recognize me?"

Cura de amores

Love Cure

Pedro Proaza never knew his father. His mother, who claimed to be a widow, lived a happy and disorderly life until the age of forty or so and then had to go to work. She was a seamstress off and on; she was employed in a linens warehouse to take measurements and orders; and she spent a year as a single gentleman's housekeeper. But she never succeeded in ingratiating herself or settling down anywhere because she did everything grudgingly. Her erratic, vagabond nature was above and contrary to the self-discipline that work implies. As a young woman, because she was pretty, and even as a buxom, middle-aged woman, because she was sly, she had known how to avoid that self-discipline, but with the onset of old age, just when it was bound to be most distressful to her, she had to earn a living. She refused to suffer such a great misfortune and protested by dying, because she undoubtedly died from the terrible agony, from the profound, repressed bitterness that the unavoidable submission to somebody else's will caused her. Gossips in her neighborhood said that bowing to the wishes of others could not have been what anguished her the most, since she had always lived that way; rather it was seeing herself denied the pleasures and comforts that such acquiescence brings with it. In short, she was very flighty and when she could not continue in her ways she breathed her last.

Fortunately for him, her son had been taken in tow ten or twelve years previously by the deceased's sister, who was the exact opposite: an honest, responsible woman. This aunt served in the household of the old dowager, the Duchess of San Clemente de la Moras, and sometimes ironed this lady's finery, sometimes read to her, and always enjoyed her complete trust. The duchess, out of affection for her servant, took the boy under her wing, first by paying for his education and later by having her son the duke employ him in the office that managed his holdings.

The duke was a grandee—of the old school when it came to the pride and inborn haughtiness of the nobility—but he also had a keen mind, was kind in the extreme, and so wealthy that, without leaving his own land, he could traverse eleven provinces in Spain. On the first floor of his venerable mansion, covering an immense paneled door painted in light blue tempera, stood a folding screen; nailed to it was a wood sign that read: "Administrative Office of the Property and Lands of His Excellency the Duke of San Clemente de las Moras, Count of Calderuela de Nieva." It was in this office, where five employees already worked under the direction of a general manager, that Perico got a job.

At first, nobody paid attention to him; he was considered one more unnecessary clerk who had been taken on to please the duchess. But not long afterward, the manager began to notice that the young man was punctual, reserved, respectful without being obsequious, and unusually serious for his age. He entrusted him with several assignments and tasks, and Perico carried them out admirably; he confided in him, and Perico knew how to keep the information to himself; and at the end of a year there was no one in the family who did not love him for his natural ability and even more for his character traits.

The duke and duchess had Perico exempted from military service, provided him with free time for his studies, and increased his salary and authority in the family's affairs, with the result that at the age of twenty-four he was in a position to manage them.

"He's a gem—if he doesn't go bad," the manager told his master and mistress. "When I die you won't need to look for someone to take my place."

To which the duke said in reply: "It's true, he does possess exceptional qualities. Only one thing about him displeases me."

"What's that, your Lordship?"

"Well, for his age he's reticent, gloomy, and given to melancholy. Sadness in young people does not augur well."

The old duchess, endowed with a kind heart, and much more

perceptive and observant than her son, said: "What's weighing that young man down is his parents. He realizes that nobody knows who his father was and that he would be better off not knowing who his mother was. But he's loving, gentle, and affectionate. You should see the fuss he makes over his aunt, who took him in as a child—and us, the ones who made him a man, well, he adores us. The melancholy that makes him taciturn and so somber will be driven away by time . . . and some woman."

The duchess was right. If Perico had grown up on the streets or had been taught a trade, the battle with hunger would not have allowed him time to think. The duke's family's protection, which satisfied his needs, left his imagination free, and as he acquired an education and polish, he felt more acutely the unseemliness of his origins and the lack of a maternal bond. The melancholy that inspired distrust was shame at someone else's shortcomings, a longing for the propriety ignored by others.

Perico's physical portrait can be drawn by saying that he was uncommonly tall and had an attractive appearance that featured big blue eyes and a pointed blond beard; except for his hair, which he wore short, his person had something reminiscent of the image of Christ as it was conceived by painters of the German Renaissance. His sad air of calm and the nobility of his bearing gave him the appearance of an illustrious gentleman fallen on hard times by a twist of fate. Such was the Pedro whom the duke and duchess loved and held in esteem, as much as the rich can love and hold in esteem a person in their service. They even considered him a rare example of good sense and good judgment. "He's always in his place, he never oversteps his bounds," they frequently said in praise of him.

But Perico, nevertheless, was not in his right mind—he lived under the sway of a mania firmly rooted in his spirit. Love had gained a foothold in his heart, but love not for any specific woman but rather for many, all who caught his fancy: one day he would love one woman, another day another one, without ever talking to them, without ever possessing them, keeping his imagination continuously focused on their charms, of which he considered himself the master, and changing lovers at the drop of a hat.

Perico worked at the office all morning and, during the winter, until four in the afternoon; during the summer, until five. The general manager who gave him his orders left at these times, so he was free until the following day. Unless inclement weather made it impossible, he would go and take a stroll—always to the place in vogue, to sites frequented by the aristocracy. He would observe a woman who excited him, gaze at her, and for the next few days seek her out again with his eyes, looking for opportunities to see her up close, until he committed her to memory and stamped her figure on his mind so that he could evoke and contemplate it whenever he wished. Endowed with prodigious energy to latch onto and retain mentally the facial features and singular characteristics of the ones who attracted his attention, he managed to make them spring to life in his fantasy; he would keep them captive in his mind's eye as though they inhabited a mysterious harem where, without having to speak, he could satisfy his slightest whim and have them brought to him in a state of submission, and, if he wished, in love. He was like the miser who had the faculty for daydreaming about piles of money.

He would pass by a beautiful woman and examine her, looking her up and down out of the corner of his eye; then he would walk by her again until her face, body, and gait, if she were on foot, or manner of reclining, if she were in a carriage, were stored away in the deepest recesses of his memory for him to call forth at will without rearranging a single hair or changing a single aspect of her expression. There were women with whom he carried on these unilateral, disembodied romances for three or four months; others tired him in a fortnight or sooner. His capacity for retaining images and his ease in evoking them verged on the magical: thinking of the particular woman's name and instantly conjuring her up as if she were alive were one and the same. In this way he courted the most elegant, aristocratic ladies in Madrid, and, making some exceptions, a few of the wealthiest and most beautiful, distinguished women of the middle class.

This madness, if such it deserves to be called, was characterized by a meek, innocuous posture, but it did not pass unnoticed. Several of the ladies singled out by him had observed Perico, and by turns they knew that he was a poor but peaceful lunatic who contented himself with watching them, not once exhibiting a sign of insolence or brazenness. He was not harming anybody— except himself, because such mental activity, outside of office time during which he held it in check, had predisposed his mind to greater disturbances.

Perico lived like this for several years, sharpening and perfecting, on a daily basis, his ability to retain the images of his chosen ladies in order to delight and delude himself with them when, all of a sudden, what was a mere speculative phenomenon passed into the realm of reality.

One day on a narrow, out-of-the-way street, and at the very moment that she was exiting the back door of a church, he saw an arrestingly beautiful woman. She was dressed in half-mourning—black with mauve bows; she was blond, slender, walked gracefully, and looked about twenty-five or thirty. A moment's glance sufficed to divine in her the woman certain of her beauty, accustomed to having her way and expert at making herself desired, but also capricious and prodigal of her charms once she decided to turn them on. All this was suggested by her big, bright, blue eyes, her languid but insistent gaze, and the contour of her body, which seemed to quiver at every step.

Perico got a close look at her, and her beauty made such an impression on him that surprise was written all over his face. The woman, fully aware of the effect she had produced, felt flattered, but her admirer's modest appearance did not meet with her approval. Perico struck her as a handsome man, but not a gentleman as regards his clothes. They then continued walking in opposite directions. Perico turned around to look at her from a corner and saw her get in a magnificent berlin that was waiting for her; afterward, the carriage passed by him just when she was lowering the glass window.

The poor devil lost his appetite, sleep, and peace of mind. He quickly understood that his impressions this time were very different from previous encounters. At first, the woman's face and body, reproduced in his mind by an act of will and with his usual facility for recall, pleased him no end. Her image came to him as obediently as the others, but when he tried to erase it from his consciousness, if only to conjure it up again, he could not. This woman's image would not go away—quite the opposite; it lingered and persisted, acquiring by the hour, by the moment, more vivid features of reality. It hovered in front of him, no longer like a desire that materializes in midair but like a tenacious apparition that, lovingly and relentlessly, pursued him.

On the other hand, the fact that she had realized the effect that her beauty had produced in him bothered Perico beyond measure, because he considered it impossible to look for her and follow her without being discovered. Already in that love there existed no secrecy, none of the mystery on which his sweet aberration was founded.

Driven, nonetheless, by a force greater than his will, he returned to the narrow street, haunted the area, and was fortunate enough to see her. What he failed to do was escape notice. Although he tried to control himself, admiration showed in his eyes. But the surprising part was that *her* expression underwent a change, revealing the vague outlines of pleasure. She did not put on a face of annoyance like the aristocratic lady who is bothered that a man of inferior social status is looking at her amorously; what she expressed was the profound delight of the woman who is gratified and flattered at having inspired a sentiment that is all the more sincere because the man who experiences it needs to realize that he should not expect to see it reciprocated.

A long time passed. Perico went on seeking her out, eyeing her, and contemplating her, without ever trying to get close to her.

* * *

And this is where Perico Proaza's adventure would remain, shrouded in mystery, if what occurred subsequently were not revealed in the following letter, written by the widowed Countess of Bocangel to her cousin, Madame Coeuratous.

Dear Hortensia,
When I tell you that upon my return to Paris I won't live the wild, frivolous life that I led before, or that, to be precise, *we* led, I've said all there is to be said. I'll shop for clothes, but the idle pursuits and indiscreet behavior are things of the past.

I'm truly in love, and—would you believe it?—me, the most sought-after and courted of women, *après toi*, chased by wealthy, elegant, genteel Don Juans—I've had to proceed to the *search and seizure*, as I believe they say in legal terminology, of the man I love, who is poor and has no sartorial taste whatsoever. When I became convinced, after he had followed me around for weeks, that he would not even dare write to me, I decided to find out who he was. I had made up my mind to look for a way to overcome the obstacles between us, unless, of course, his kind of life made him absolutely unworthy and out of the question for me.

I soon learned that he worked for my aunt, the old Duchess of San Clemente de las Moras. I went to see her, and the praise that she heaped on him suggested a course of action to me. "I know all that," I replied immediately, "and since this man is a gem and the management of my assets is in a deplorable state and I'm almost ruined, I've come to ask you to lend him to me, to let him come to my house whenever he wishes, however he wishes, and for whatever amount of time he wishes, to see if he can put my affairs in order and get me out of trouble and arrears."

She summoned him on the spot. For both of us it was a moment of trial.

When he left the sitting room, the duchess talked to me for a long time, relating certain strange quirks that he had: that he fell in love with every woman he saw, and that, apart from his gifts as an administrator and organizer, he was a crackpot. How should I know? All kinds of peculiarities and absurdities—she's the one who must really be cracked!

The most difficult thing fell to me: to convince him that I was not a fickle, impetuous woman. The following morning, when he appeared at my house, I said to him, with downcast eyes and as troubled as I could sound: "Yesterday, when I went to see the duchess, I had no idea who you were . . . but surely you understand that this cannot be."

Then, with admirable aplomb, he replied: "I do not understand you, Countess. You knew who I was?" Disconcerted, I then asked him: "But did you not know who I was?" To which he answered with astonishing calmness: "Yesterday was the first time that I had the honor of talking to you . . . and even of seeing you."

The predicament was solved: by his pretending that he didn't know me, I was spared embarrassment at having sought him out.

In the course of time I became convinced that the duchess was right: in Perico's mind there was something sickly, feeble, and dangerous, as there is in my heart—and well you know it—something anomalous, perverted, and unhealthy.

But each of us is curing the other: I do it by making his platonic daydreams come true, and he does it by infusing poetry into what for me never had it until now. Today I understand that the intimate and supreme happiness of love is not in inspiring it, but in experiencing it. What a great pity it is that when we really do love we cannot eradicate the memory of when we thought we loved. Goodbye, darling cousin. Envy me now as other times I envied you.

Love,
Teresa

Elvira-Nicolasa

Elvira-Nicolasa

Elvira and I had just finished eating supper in a small, private room of an inn where she liked me to take her to have shellfish and white wine. In an argument triggered by jealousy and in the heat of recrimination, I let slip an offensive expression. I must have said something very harsh to her, evidently a very obvious truth, because then, her talkativeness roused by the insult and her tongue loosened by the alcohol, she reclined on the divan with provocative indolence and turned serious.

"Oh? You think I'm that bad? Well, as certain as I'm sitting here, coquettish, fond of making you men hopping mad—because that's what all of you deserve—proud of having ruined some and made fools of others, I have done one good deed in my life, even if you don't believe it, and would have done more if I hadn't been so miserable during my childhood."

I felt threatened with the eternal tale of an ordinary seduction, but hearing it was preferable to watching her get drunk, so I sat back to listen and she continued as follows: "I'm going to tell you the story. In the first place, my real name isn't Elvira, it's Nicolasa. I hail from a town near Madrid and at the age of eighteen I ran away from home, thinking that I couldn't possibly be worse off anywhere else. I had become a nursemaid to my stepsister, and nothing would have been more unbearable than her insolence, my stepfather's crudeness, and my mother's bad temper. As long as she remained a widow I was able to endure my mother's unpredictable nature and the consequences of her greed, but after she remarried, life turned into hell for me; in addition to being an unloved daughter, to which I was accustomed, I became an unpaid servant, which struck me as the height of tyranny. Old *Pelusa*, as my stepfather was nicknamed, was as irritable and avaricious as the woman who had taken him for her second husband.

"Nevertheless, I still spent a few years resigned to being a beast of burden and the one who did all the dirty work. Then, when my stepsister Inesilla got older, her pranks showed such a deep-seated animosity toward me that I began to wonder what the future held in store.

"I was the first one in the house to get up and the last one to turn in; I would awaken from a deep sleep to water the horses and mules, then spend an entire day washing clothes, measuring seeds, and carrying bundles of one thing or another; in short, I was exhausting myself with work, and without a single complaint. What I couldn't abide were the jokes in bad taste, the haughty impulses, and even acts of perfidy that that beast of a stepsister would dream up for the sole purpose of tormenting me. She was so evil! Her dirty tricks were not the mischievous antics of a child, but real instances of cruelty. She would take the bread that I kept in case I got hungry between meals and feed it to the pigs; on the sly she would oversalt the stew to see me catch hell afterwards; the very least that she would do was swear at me like a trooper, using all the foul language she had picked up, and spit in my face, without my stepfather or her stepmother putting a stop to her vile behavior.

"Finally, I got fed up. One day they sent me to the fountain with her—she was nine years old then. The wicked thing pretended to go willingly, but halfway there she slipped away through the arcade on the square and ran off to play in a courtyard with some little friends of hers. There she stayed for three whole hours while I was going crazy looking for her. I don't have to tell you what happened afterward when, late that afternoon, we returned separately. I thought they were going to kill me. My stepfather tied me to one of the upright beams that supported the patio trellis and beat me with a stick until he got tired. When he let me go I went up to the attic that served as my room; I didn't want to eat, and I lay down without undressing. All of a sudden I hear noise, glance up and see Inesilla at the transom, looking down at me and sneering and laughing and clenching her fist to add insult to injury.

"'Why did you do that?' I asked.

"And in a very cheerful voice she replied: 'Because I really enjoy it when they knock you around.'

"From that moment on I thought only about getting out of there."

As she spoke, Elvira's eyes misted with tears of anger. I didn't dare interrupt her story, and she went on: "Yes, my friend, from that night date all the awful things that I've done in my life—and it'll be the cause of the ones I do in the future. I made a bundle with the few clothes I had; I removed almost thirty *reales*, which represented all of my savings, from the hiding place where I stashed them; and before daybreak I headed across open fields and took the road to Madrid. I entered the city by the Extremadura road and Segovia Street. Seven years have passed and I remember as if it had happened this morning."

"Where did you go?"

"To my Uncle Manuel's house. Actually, he wasn't a relative or anything close to it. He was my stepfather's nephew once removed, and I rather liked him because the few times that he visited the village he treated me like a human being. One day he prevented them from giving me a thrashing; another day, during a meal, when he saw that my stepfather didn't want to give me meat, he gave me his portion; and, furthermore, one other time when he was there just a few hours, he went to the fountain and gave me two colored handkerchiefs and a silver needle case without anybody in the house finding out about it."

"He obviously liked you."

"You'll see presently.

"He lived alone with an elderly woman servant in a big old house on Mancebos Street. I went there, explained to him what had happened, and asked him to help me find a house where I could work as a domestic. He said he'd do what he could and told me, seeing that I didn't have the money to go to an inn, to stay there a few days until I found work."

"What was this man's age? And how old were you then?"

"Manuel was forty, and I, as I said before, was eighteen."

"You don't have to say another word."

"You've guessed right. Within two days I realized that I had put my head in the lion's mouth. But will you tell me how I was to ward him off? What I was to do and where I was to go? Like a girl from a small town and like girls from everywhere, I knew all that has to be known. I recognized the danger at the outset; what I didn't see was the way to avoid it."

"So what happened?"

"Just imagine. You know that I'm an avid reader and that I devour novels. I've even read *Don Quijote of La Mancha*, and there's a woman character in it who experiences the same thing that happened to me. Do you remember when Dorotea, speaking of her love affair with Don Fernando, says more or less the following: 'As a result of my maid's leaving the room then, I ceased to be a maid and he turned into a traitorous and perfidious scoundrel.'* Do you remember the episode? Well, it was the exact same thing. Using some excuse, Manolo got the old woman out of the house and—"

"So he was traitorous and perfidious and you ceased to be what you had been."

"Of course, what he did was despicable, but afterwards he grew very fond of me. At the time I wasn't as hard as I am now. I'm certain that if he hadn't died he would have married me."

"He died?"

"Two years later."

Elvira interrupted her story for a moment, tried not to cry, as if ashamed to show feelings, and continued: "I'll omit the details, but right on the heels of Manuel's death his brothers kicked me out. This wretched life that I lead began then, and at that I'm one of the luckier ones.

"Starting to work and getting the chance to stop was a matter of six months. Needless to say, I had a devil of a time finding a job, and as soon as I wanted to walk a crooked path there were more than enough people to push me along it. But you're familiar with that, and besides, you know almost everybody who's had anything to do with me.

"What you don't know, nor does anyone else, is that three or four years after I went to the bad, when I already had my own apartment, furniture, expensive clothes, fine jewelry, a carriage some months, and two maids to serve me (to this day what surprises me the most is seeing myself waited on), just then, having all of that, things I have never dreamed about and you might find this hard to believe—"

"Get to the point."

"Well, I was overwhelmed by sadness. What do you think got into my head?"

"Marriage?"

"Of course not. I still don't have enough money for that. I got it into my head to visit the village."

"Repentant?"

"I don't know for sure. Sometimes I thought I was, sometimes I thought I wasn't. Actually, what I went through is extremely difficult to explain. It was a nameless melancholy, a desire charged with sadness."

"In all probability you were affected by the insipid sentimentality of some novel. Why, even now you're talking like a serial heroine."

"Don't make fun of what I'm saying. It may have been the best urge of my life. And let me finish.

"As if I had forgotten how much I had suffered up to the age of eighteen, as if I had been spoiled at home, and disregarding so many bitter memories and several scars that I have on different parts of my body, I wanted to go back to my village, see the places where I had grown up, the corners where I hid to cry, the cellar where they used to shut me up, the attic that they called my room, the stable, the mules, the fountain—everything, in a word, that should have been hateful to me. Finally, and I understand that it was an utterly crazy notion, I even wanted to see my mother, my stepfather, and that rascal of a little girl. What got into me? As they say in plays, I don't know, but when I thought about it I would say to myself mentally *my family*. Mother's bad temper seemed excusable on account of the work and hardship of life in a farmhouse; my stepfather's brutality became less abhorrent in my eyes when I remembered that he wasn't my real father; and as for my stepsister's acts of cruelty . . . it was as if they hadn't taken place. What I mean is that I remembered them, but I didn't hold a grudge against her. I repeat: I've never fully understood my disposition at the time. It was somewhat similar to the homesickness experienced by Galicians when they spend a long time outside of their native land, but mixed, even though I shouldn't say so, with a certain generosity of spirit that drove me to excuse and forgive all the wrongs that I had suffered. In short, I returned to my village for a visit."

"But didn't they know back there how and on what you live? It didn't occur to you that they could have shamed you and—"

"Of course they knew everything! Very seldom does anyone come from the village and not go to my apartment to ask me for something. I'm not exaggerating when I tell you that I've done more favors for my village than a congressman—I'm almost tempted to call it my district. As for a frosty reception, it wasn't a concern. If I were going to ask for a handout, maybe; but loaded down with packages, trinkets, and gifts . . . no, sir!"

"And they were shameless enough to . . . ?"

"I went in a simple, gray flannel dress and wore no accessories, but since I'm so absentminded I forgot to remove these diamonds from my ears; I was carrying a handbag trimmed in silver and my umbrella had a gold handle; to put it in a nutshell, all they had to do was look at me to realize that I wasn't going to ask them for a thing. Nobody recognized me at the train station, but as I crossed the square I heard three or four people say in amazement: 'Nicolasa! Nicolasa!' Then I noticed that, keeping well behind, two girls of my acquaintance were following me, one with a child in her arms and, you know, that one made me envious."

"Of course she would."

"I arrived at my house. Imagine their surprise. After the initial moment of shock, my mother smothered me with kisses, my stepfather cried with real feeling, and Inesilla took my handbag and began to examine it."

"What a turnabout!"

"My stepsister had blossomed into a fresh, attractive beauty with big eyes and sleek hair! What you would call a striking young woman. She had a hard face, a serious expression, and a disdainful smile, but on the whole, she was wonderfully robust. In a word, what a flower is before anyone handles it."

"And what happened?"

"Nothing. I handed out my gifts: two rolls of white linen for my mother, coral earrings for Inesilla, dress lengths for both of them, a silver cigar case and chain for my stepfather—everything that I had brought. They gave me the best room in the house and didn't ask a single question about how I lived or how I supported myself, and they treated me as best they could."

"Did people from the village go to see you? And if so, what did your parents tell them?"

"People came all right! My stepfather told them I was the governess of a nobleman's daughter. In all, I spent three marvelous days there, gay as a lark, without having to put up with you and others who never leave me alone here, in a bedroom all to myself; and when I returned, I sent my mother and stepfather six thousand *reales* to buy a pair of mules."

"All this is very interesting, but I'm still waiting to hear about the one good deed that you've done."

"It happened at the very moment I was saying good-bye. I didn't want them to accompany me to the station, and we were in the hallway—my stepfather looking for the hundredth time at the silver cigar case, my mother crying, Inesilla tying a bunch of wildflowers, and me with my eyes full of tears—when, without warning, my stepfather took me by the hand and, leading me to the rear of the dining room, closed the door behind us after letting my mother in. Inesilla stayed outside. I thought to myself that they wanted another pair of mules."

"And what was it?"

"I couldn't believe my ears! My stepfather, like all of them, knew what kind of life I lead; in my mother's presence and with her consent, he moved his head in my stepsister's direction and said to me: 'Listen, Nicolasa, now that you've had a run of luck, why don't you take Inesilla with you?'"

"How atrocious!'"

"Just imagine! And I had gone to the village to immerse myself in integrity. For a moment I was shaken. That lack of a moral sense, that corruption awakened in my memory, at one fell swoop, all the bitterness of my childhood, all my suffering. Don't think I'm exaggerating: I experienced once again the pain and shame of all the blows I had received in that house. I remembered the last day that I spent there. I could picture myself sprawled out on the straw mattress while Inesilla was enjoying my misery; her cruel, mocking voice seemed to echo in my ears, and, naturally, with the recollections the resentment came back and with the resentment the desire for revenge. Revenge—and what revenge!—was mine for the asking. To bring my stepsister to Madrid with me. Just imagine!"

"And what did you do?"

"I was no doubt inspired by God. I looked at them in a way that they couldn't have understood, and, going out into the hallway, said: 'I want to believe that you don't know what you're asking.' Cleansed of hatred, I kissed Inesilla on the spot and returned to Madrid free of resentment and illusions."

"I believe you!"

"This Elvira who's sitting across from you did that, this Elvira experienced that. Nonetheless—and maybe I'm a fool—the honest-to-God truth is that some days, when I have more money and believe that I'm more cheerful, all of a sudden I forget that I'm playing the part of Elvira and I become Nicolasa."

La amenaza

The Threat

I

The midday bell rang and shortly afterward the door began to discharge, in waves of a human flood, the tired, silent throng that made up the shops' work force. There was no talking; the men ignored the women, the girls avoided the boys' signs of attention, and the children did not stop to play. The strong looked worn-out, the young aged before their time, and the old half dead. A caste doubly oppressed by its own ignorance and other people's selfishness!

The multitude scattered like a cloud that is broken up and dispelled by the wind. It dispersed first in swarms, then in groups, and afterward in pairs that usually split up in silence, some heading toward home, others entering small inns and taverns, spreading out and disappearing, all of them confused and swallowed by the hectic movement on the outskirts of town.

One of the last workers to leave was Gaspar Santigós, alias Gasparón or the Big Guy, because he was a very tall and very well-built man of tremendous strength. He was so burly that he looked like Hercules in overalls, but his gentle face, clear brow, and honest expression earned him great popularity.

He set out in the shade of an adobe wall, crossed two or three streets and one square, and, taking a shortcut through alleys and empty lots, came out on an esplanade of giant elms. Their interlocking branches formed a shady dome under which sat a neat, attractive, young woman who was waiting for him with a basket in front of her, a little boy in her lap, and a dog at her side. The animal ran toward his master, the child extended his tiny hands, and while Gasparón was removing various items from the basket and breaking the golden-brown loaf of bread, the young woman, looking at him all the while, set the salad aside, took out the bottle of red wine, napkins, and wooden spoons, and then emptied a potful of yellowish, steamy stew into the white earthenware soup dish bordered in blue.

II

When the back-to-work bells rang in the distance, Gasparón drank the last of his wine, rolled a cigarette, kissed the child, tossed the dog a piece of bread, and, giving the young woman a quick squeeze around the waist, like a miser who fondles his treasure, returned to the factory.

He disappeared behind the door, crossed a courtyard full of piles of iron ingots, and entered a long, spacious work bay. Large windows admitted light, and outside of the steamed-up panes one could make out blackened walls, mounds of coal, spluttery fire sparks from forges, and tall chimneys that belched the heavy, sooty smoke of bituminous coal in a torrent of thick clouds. Overhead and along the length of the bay ran an interminable and complex network of gleaming steel, burnished iron, levers, rods, and pulleys linked by leather belts that went up and down, twisted and crisscrossed, and spun dizzily like mad members of a living mechanism in which nothing could stop without the whole assembly being paralyzed. The parquet floor shook from the vibration of the steam boiler whose blasts were heard nearby; and from other shops, lowered in volume by the shouting and the distance, the sound of the forging of iron and the whirring of machines mixed in with the singing of women.

At the end of that bay another one identical to it started up, and spanning the courtyard that separated them was a narrow little wooden bridge, alongside which a mammoth flywheel rotated on its shaft.

When he was midway across this bridge Gasparón saw that an apprentice was running toward him from the second bay with so much momentum and velocity that he could not stop himself. With no time to turn back, and sensing that the two of them would not fit on the tight walkway, Gasparón drew himself up and stood to one side. The boy came on the dead run, swerved the wrong way, collided with him, and fell flat on his face; with nothing to grab hold of, he nearly tumbled over the edge of the narrow planks that formed the floor of the bridge suspended above the courtyard. Gasparón, more heedful of someone else's danger than of his own, reached out a hand to him; the boy, panic-stricken, clutched it with such strength and such fear that he caused the worker to totter. As he lost his balance, Gasparón tried to regain it by shifting his weight and instinctively raised his other hand behind him, but unluckily a spoke of the flywheel caught it and snapped his forearm.

Afterward the boy said that, despite his terror, he heard a crack that sounded like a piece of wood being split with an ax. But Gasparón still had the strength and presence of mind to move back a few steps and haul the apprentice up; and after setting him down safely on the bay floor, he collapsed, overcome by the excruciating pain. His fellow workers picked him up and, because the factory did not have an infirmary, carried him seated in a chair to the nearby hospital, where that very afternoon his arm had to be amputated at the elbow.

The convalescence was long. First it consumed their savings, then the loan taken out on their Sunday clothes, his cape and her shawl; after that they were helped by friends and neighbors; and lastly by a contribution from the Workers' Strike Fund. Another job was out of the question, for he had lost his right arm.

III

Some forty days after the mishap, Gasparón's wife showed up at the factory payroll office. This was a small room divided by a partition of wood and wire netting, and through the windows you could see a well-dressed old gentleman in a clean shirt who was sitting next to a safe and reading a newspaper. Near him, and within eyeshot, two men were bent over huge ledgers spread open on pine desks.

"What brings you here?" one of the clerks asked as she approached them.

"How's Gasparón coming along?" asked the second.

"How do you think? He's maimed!"

"Why have you come?"

"To collect his pay."

One of them picked up a notebook and began to thumb the pages, mumbling "Gaspar, Gaspar . . ."

"It's under Santigós. Drills department, section two," the woman said.

"You're right. Gaspar Santigós. Here it is."

"He's the one," she added with a sigh.

The clerk began to write figures on a piece of paper and, without taking his eyes off them, asked: "Was he paid the week before the accident?"

"Yes, sir."

"Well, it's . . . it must be—"

Then the gentleman in the clean shirt dropped his newspaper and, without looking at the young woman, asked: "What day was that?"

"The twentieth of last month. A Wednesday. At two o'clock," she answered sadly.

"Well, there can't be much doubt," the old man replied. "Monday, one; Tuesday, two; and Wednesday—two and a half days, at four and a half *pesetas* a day which comes to just a little over eleven *pesetas*." And he turned his back on her.

The clerk took a small basket from the cashbox, counted the money, and gave it to her without another word. Gasparón's wife left in tears and you could still hear her footsteps when the old gentleman in the clean shirt said harshly: "Don't forget to record that Gasparón is *off the payroll*."

IV

When the workers learned that Gasparón had been paid for only *two and a half days,* a storm of protest enveloped them and whipped them up to a frenzy. The injustice of it all provoked outrage.

The delegates of the shops met one night in the back room of the Frenchman's Tavern, and to help them form a more complete picture of the situation, Gasparón was also asked to attend. The one-armed man related his misfortune in a perfectly natural tone, showed them his scarred stump covered with clumsy sutures, and then, for the duration of the meeting, pestered his

The Threat

friends to roll cigarettes for him because he still had not become adept at doing it with just one hand.

A grimy oil lamp burned uselessly, barely lighting the room. It was nearly impossible to see bodies, shapes, and faces. Voices seemed to come out from among shadows like protests and anonymous threats.

"I've been working in a shop for fifty-two years," the first man said, "and I know more than all of you because I've seen a lot of factories in my day. I started at the age of twelve. I've always maintained that owners should be forced to support those who can no longer work. If not, look at the result: callused hands and an empty belly."

"Although I haven't put in as many years," said another man, "I've got more experience in these matters. Our best bet is to agree on a course of action, keep it secret, and sabotage their raw material, their manpower, their machinery, everything that we can; and waste time, and do a bad job of smelting and a worse one of weaving. In a year every factory would lose its standing."

"And every worker his living."

"An eight-hour workday!" several voices cried out in unison.

"Some consolation—to be dogs for eight hours a day instead of nine."

"A raise in pay!"

"And they immediately raise the price of clothes, bread, and rent. If they could, they'd charge for the air we breathe."

Then another voice, silent until this point, was heard—a voice that betrayed a small body and evil intent.

"We didn't come here to debate, but to get revenge. Do you have the courage? Yes or no? I know where there are three sticks of dynamite, each one five and a half pounds: one for the models warehouse, which is worth a fortune; one for the owner's house, the back part where his family lives; and the third we keep for whenever it's needed. We'll draw lots to see who does it."

A long silence fraught with apprehension followed this ghastly proposal. Some feared the idea of destruction, others the prospect of retaliation; in spirit virtually all of them were accomplices, but not a one said, "I'm game."

Suddenly Gasparón stood, puffed twice on his cigarette, and, positioning himself under the dim light of the lamp so that they could see the unshakable resolve on his face, spoke as follows:

"All of this is futile or it's monstrous. Live on the dole? A retirement pension? Take money from them? You're dreaming. And a strike? What for? To give in when we run out of food, be in debt up to our ears, and return to work? The dynamite idea is a cowardly atrocity. I don't want anyone killed on my account! Leave the revenge to me. It'll be a good and lasting one."

A few grumbled, the rest agreed willingly; the pusillanimous among them acted out of fear, the hotheaded because they glimpsed something terrible and mysterious in Gasparón's eyes; but all of them acceded to his request. The meeting then broke up immediately, like one of those storms that carries in its bosom a thunderbolt and does not shoot it earthward.

V

The following day Gasparón started to beg in front of the magnificent house in which the manufacturer lived. There he is, day in and day out, next to the railing with gilded points on its bars, near a window covered on the inside with the broad folds of silk curtains; there he is from sunrise to sunset showing his scarred stump, the tattered bulk of his body silhouetted against the marble façade, and always wearing around his neck a little placard that reads: DISABLED AT THE FACTORY OF DON MARTÍN PEÑALVA.

Entreaties, threats, promises: everything that has been tried to get him to leave has been in vain. There he is when the rich industrialist, the new lord of modern feudalism, goes out on business and pleasure; when his wife returns from church; and when his daughters, elegantly attired, go to soirées and parties.

That mendicant at the door of that mansion is a living affront, and he is also a dire prophecy.

The hand with which he begs seems to threaten.

Un sabio

A Wise Man

Don Luis Romillo was worth a fortune. As a child he had been sent by his parents to Mexico where his guardian, a maternal uncle, placed him as a clerk in a big commercial establishment. Because of his honesty, hard work, and ability, in time he became one of its partners, but he grew tired of living far from the land of his birth. So after he inherited a sizable fortune from his uncle, he returned to Spain, taking up residence in Madrid. During the first few weeks of his stay in the capital he lodged at an inn, but he quickly became disenchanted with the bad service and decided to set up house in his own apartment. Despite his wealth he did so with great modesty—not out of parsimoniousness, but because he was a man of few needs and by nature hostile to ostentation.

At first he had no dealings with the other tenants. He was served by an elderly married couple, received no visitors, retired early, and whenever he met a neighbor on the stairs would limit himself to a polite greeting and avoid conversation.

One night, on returning from the theater at one o'clock in the morning, an unusual hour for him, he came across his two servants on the landing of the floor where he lived; they were talking to a pretty woman who, with tears in her eyes, was thanking them for a favor they had done her. On seeing their master, the elderly couple made way for him and quickly stopped talking while the weeping woman hurried up the stairs.

The servants' initial response when Don Luis asked questions about the young lady was to conceal the truth, but when he pressed them they had to admit the cause and reason for their meeting. The young lady whom he had seen—because, although humbly dressed, she had the look of a young lady—lived in the topmost and cheapest of the building's rooms with her aged, ailing mother. They were very poor and their only sources of income were the old woman's meager widow's pension and what little her daughter earned from embroidering. The shop for which the latter worked had failed and she had not gotten any jobs for two months; reduced to the scanty sum paid by the widow's pension, the two impoverished women received barely enough to eat on. As long as they had something to pawn they got by, but then the mother fell ill and the doctor prescribed costly medicines. Don Luis's maid knew all of this because she used to talk to them about the care of the flowers with which they brightened their windows and whether this or that plant could or could not flourish in pots and whether they required a lot of water or little water. This kind of conversation had led to greater familiarity, and the young woman ended up developing as close a relationship with Don Luis's maid as can exist between a well-bred albeit poor person and another further down on the social scale.

In any case, one afternoon Miss Juanita, as the young lady was called, had asked Don Luis's maid for a cup of broth for her mother; subsequently she asked for similar favors until Don Luis found out by chance, thanks to the meeting on the stairs after his return from the theater.

After he became aware of the miserable women's sad situation, Don Luis instructed his servants to help them as much as possible and not turn them down when they sought small favors. He then went some time without thinking about the misfortune that existed so near to him, until one afternoon when he saw Juanita leaning out of a window.

Gaunt and almost anemic from undernourishment, she was shabbily dressed, wore no jewelry or any other accessories, and looked saddened and melancholy from being down on her luck, but she had strikingly beautiful eyes, lovely lips, lustrous jet-black hair, very fine skin, very fine features, and a graceful, shapely figure. From looking at her there was no doubt that within three months of eating properly, walking, being free of worry and not working, Juanita would blossom into a very handsome woman. She was a plant that sprouted in poor soil with insufficient sun and water, but a plant that a knowledgeable gardener could, with minimal effort, cultivate and develop to transform her weakness into strength and her decline into luxuriance.

The day after he saw her at the window, Don Luis showed up at Juanita's house and without beating around the bush inquired if she wished to undertake embroidering a considerable quantity of linens that he needed. When she accepted with understandable enthusiasm, he asked her to do the buying for him because he lived alone and knew nothing about certain kinds of purchases: so many sets of sheets and pillowcases, so many towels, so many tablecloths and napkins—in short, a tidy sum in white goods. Don Luis added that, inasmuch as he wanted everything embroidered with exquisite care and skill, and in a very short space of time besides, it would be a good idea to take on a helper, in effect setting up a small workshop. It goes without saying that his requests were accompanied by sufficient money to pay for the materials and daily wages, and that as a result Juanita and her mother's difficulties disappeared overnight.

From that point on, Juanita went down to Don Luis's apartment regularly to give him an accounting of cash received and to explain the progress of the work, and from time to time he went up to the garret where Juanita was embroidering continually. It should be noted that, modestly dressed in black and surrounded by so much white material, she looked enchanting.

Juanita's transformation was very swift: her cheeks took on a soft, rosy hue; her lips turned deep red; she filled out; and her breasts rose. In a word, she became desirable, as the *Song of Songs* puts it. The bad side was that the changes—the greater comforts that she enjoyed, the better clothing that she wore, and Don Luis's visits—were the source of endless and mean gossip. The doorkeeper, the servants, and the neighbors all believed that the elderly gentleman collected payment for his generosity by enjoying Juanita's charms, which was a barefaced lie, because it did not occur to him to propose such villainy nor would the poor women have accepted.

Don Luis had something else in mind. He was in love with her, but his plan did not consist of seducing her, but of taking her for his proper and legitimate wife, and what he was doing was creating the means to see her frequently, observe her, become convinced that she was a good person and then tell her that he loved her and ask her consent to speak with her mother and formalize the relationship. His error consisted of imagining that gratitude could be changed into love, and above all it was a mistake to go continually to Juanita's house and never let on that he *did* love her. He was a man accustomed only to business dealings; he had never attempted to win the love of any woman, and he believed that for Juanita it would be a very simple and straightforward matter to answer him instantaneously when he asked, "Will you marry me?"

And since he did precisely that, what was bound to happen, happened.

One night Don Luis entered the attic apartment, sat next to Juanita, took her hand—much to her mother's surprise—and spoke as follows: "Juanita, you're a gem, a real find. I think you're capable of making the most demanding man happy. I'm fifty-two years old, in good health, and enjoy a rather sizable income. Will you marry me? Oh! And I don't have a bad temper."

The poor thing let the needle fall from her hand, dropped her embroidery on the floor, glanced at her mother, who was dumbfounded, and burst into tears.

That night there was no conversation, nor was it possible for Juanita to respond, given her distress and her mother's fainting spell, so Don Luis left to tell his maid to make linden tea. It was tea that he himself would end up drinking because no sooner had he left in search of his servant than Juanita began to recover, and since she felt that she was suffocating, she unbuttoned the top portion of her dress and undid her corset to breathe more freely. Don Luis came right back up again and, because the garret door had remained open, he entered without knocking, surprising the young woman with something besides her neck exposed, and that something was so wonderfully white, lovely, and well-shaped that the poor man experienced an indefinable shock; his legs gave way, he turned pale, he had to sit down, and finally, without knowing what he was doing, he took the cup of tea, which she had not yet touched, and slowly drank it all, while the young woman, confused and ashamed and turning her back to him, laced her corset and buttoned her dress.

The following day Juanita's mother called on Don Luis and told him that her daughter very gratefully accepted his proposal. Two months later the couple had found and set up a delightful apartment; it was going to cost them twelve thousand *reales* a year and they had spent five thousand *duros* furnishing it.

Everything was all ready and the necessary arrangements completed at the rectory, when one afternoon Don Luis went up to the garret. Juanita and her mother were not in, but the doorkeeper was there; the women had given her the key to take up packages that they expected to be delivered.

"I'll wait here," said Don Luis.

The doorkeeper went down to her cubbyhole and Don Luis was left alone; he sat down, looking around at the shabby furniture that Juanita would soon exchange for other pieces more in keeping with her fine beauty. But after a while he tired of merely taking things in and got up to begin a meticulous examination: the cheap sewing box alongside which his intended had worked so much, the dining table where so many inexpensive dishes had been served, the mother's bed with its very unpretentious but clean bedding— in short, everything. Finally, he had a whim: to see where his fiancée slept.

It was a tiny bedroom whose only contents were a bed covered by a calico spread, a small trunk, and a side table; on top of the table he saw, much to his surprise, a filled inkwell, a pen, a folder made from a folded newspaper, an addressed envelope, and an unfinished letter. Inside the open drawer were two thick packets of letters still in their original envelopes and bound with colored strips of cloth that had tied the boxed linens before Juanita embroidered them.

Don Luis could not help himself: he untied one of the packets and scanned several of the letters. They were all in the same handwriting—a man's handwriting!—had the same signature, began and concluded with words and promises of love and affection, the prospects of kisses, and they were addressed to Juanita. Blind with rage, he finally picked up the letter that lay on the table, the one written by her. The closing was missing, but even incomplete, what it said sufficed to give anyone pause. The most important paragraph read as follows:

> Don't tire yourself out: stop writing me and humiliating me and making me feel worse than I already do by saying over and over again that you love me with all your heart, as I love you. I'm getting married so that my mother can die peacefully, in a decent bed and with proper care, instead of dying in a hospital, because I'll go blind from

the constant crying and working and won't be able to support her if she lives or bury her if she dies. And don't ever, ever think that I'll be capable of cheating on Don Luis. I don't love him because I love you, do you understand? But even if I'm torn to pieces and burned at the stake, I'll never betray the man who gives me his name. I'm returning to you. . . .

She had not written more.

That explained why *his* letters were carefully tied in packets for return.

Don Luis sat down on Juanita's trunk, his head slouched, and he felt two big teardrops roll down his face. Then, all of a sudden, he stood up, dried his tears with a corner of the calico bedspread and, leaving everything undisturbed, exactly as he had found it, he walked out of the bedroom and went down to his apartment, pausing first to make a mental note of the address on the envelope in which that admirable letter would be mailed.

Don Luis spent a miserable night, but he was so good-hearted that a peaceful melancholy, and not fury, invaded his being and calmed his spirit like a sedative. As he dressed the next morning he took notice of his skinny, spent body, burned out from work and weighed down by the years; he remembered the delightful white shape that he had glimpsed during Juanita's distress, smiled sadly and mumbled: "It's too late!"

The following day Juanita and her mother did not receive their usual visit from Don Luis, nor the day after that either. Finally, four days later a friend of his went, at his request, to see them and inform them that he had embarked on a very long journey and that he had entrusted him with giving them a roll of papers and a letter. The papers were government bonds that would yield an income that was more than enough for them to live in comfort, without worrying about the future. The letter read as follows:

Juanita,
    You're much too good, and it was foolish of me to think that you could care for me. For your virtue and beauty there's but one reward in this world: love. The only thing that I wouldn't be able to give you! I've learned that your boyfriend is bright, hardworking, and honest; and he's young and handsome besides. All the two of you needed to be happy was a little money, and I'm giving that to you. Accept it without embarrassment, just as I've accepted, without resisting it, the lesson that was given to me in your bedroom by chance,

which in this instance deserves to be called Providence. It was meant to be! I'll write in a few months, and if you have a baby I'll come back to be his godfather.

Juanita married her boyfriend—who, despite having her for his own, loves her more with every passing day—and before their first wedding anniversary she gave birth to a baby boy who has his father's looks and is as beautiful as she is.

Don Luis did not return to Madrid for four years, but he came back cured of his passion, which was all the more dangerous for being late.

Today, when the weather is nice, you can see him strolling toward Retiro Park in daylight hours, holding the smartly dressed little boy by the hand. The child calls him grandfather and his parents, strange though it may seem, are grateful. If someone asks him who the little boy is, he replies: "My heir."

And then in his peaceful monologues as a prudent man he says to himself, thinking about the past and relating it to the present: "Juanita's an angel, but ... would she have been one, married to me?"

Narración

Pepita

In the year 1900 Pedro Fuentelcésped traveled to Paris with his wife Mercedes, making her believe that the object of the trip was simply to spend a few weeks there visiting the World Fair and seeing how the products of his factories had been displayed in the Spanish exhibits. The fact of the matter was that he wanted her to be examined by a renowned specialist because she was very sick, even though she had no idea of the extent and gravity of the illness.

Mercedes Fuentelcésped was in her forties and had been a striking beauty; Pedro was in his fifties and had been, until well beyond his youth, what the French call a man of *bonnes fortunes*, that is to say, successful with women, one of those men who sweep them off their feet. He cut a dashing figure, which, let it be said in passing, is not essential for these conquests; he was very likable, a necessary quality, and very discreet, which is the trait that produces the best results in this field of pursuit; he was generous to a fault, something that never hurts, and a person of exceptional ability, an invaluable attribute for us men, but one that is of little use to women. Such was the couple: an aging beauty and a gallant in his twilight. But Pedro, it should be pointed out, had loved Mercedes as much as he was capable of loving, always treating her with the greatest consideration and being for her, since she had become ill, a model of tenderness and solicitude.

At the hotel where they went to stay, one of the best in Paris, they ran into the twice-widowed Pura Tablada and her stepdaughter Pepita, who was her first husband's child. Pura and

Mercedes had gone to school together as girls and were very dear friends. It is a known fact that friendship among women is a rare emotion—because they either treat each other with absolute indifference, even though the kissing and visiting may be overdone, or they love each other better than we men know how to love each other, the proof being that when women help women, they do more than we do. Pura and Mercedes were very close, and with the cooperation of the former, Fuentelcésped had arranged for the encounter at the Moscovia Hotel in Paris so that if his wife took a turn for the worse she would have company.

Pepita, Pura's stepdaughter and the protagonist of this slice of history, was eighteen and looked even younger because of her slender figure and small face, and had she worn her hair in a ponytail nobody would have believed that she was more than fifteen. Her dark complexion had a golden, almost amber, hue; her eyes and hair were jet-black; her hands and feet were tiny; her mouth, with thin lips and pretty teeth, was a bit large; and she was lithe and graceful, slim without looking scrawny, and what she lacked in weight, she made up in elegance and charm.

Although she was naturally vivacious and wily, she made a conscious effort to appear demure and diffident; by instinct she was confident and talkative, by design calculating and quiet—the epitome of hypocrisy. Her stepmother, who was very fond of her, raised or attempted to raise her unsanctimoniously, but strictly, as a real young lady. Pepita had neither governesses nor maids nor friends to corrupt her; glibness and pretense, and cunning and malice, all sprouted in her spontaneously, simultaneously. Seen in a drawing room or theater box, she resembled a young virgin conceived by an Italian painter, one of the early masters, and later modernized by a couturier of impeccable taste. Her forced primness made her seem jumpy and prudish. Always quick to look embarrassed for the slightest reason, her pale cheeks possessed the rare ability to blush whenever she wished, but every once in a while, despite so much caution, when her naturally headstrong, passionate temperament surfaced, there would be glances, smiles, attitudes and even words or phrases more typical of a consummate expert in the art of seduction than a girl whose charm should have consisted in gradually losing her innocence. In short, if, as many mystics said, woman is rope used by the devil to lasso men's souls, in this instance the rope was made of a soft, smooth material, but so tightly woven together that it sufficed to hold fast the wariest and most virtuous of men.

During the first twenty days of their stay in Paris, the three women did nothing but go to shops and dressmakers and busy themselves with purchases and orders. Mercedes was enjoying a period of remarkable relief and her husband could not do enough to please her.

While he visited businessmen, Pura accompanied her friend with the solicitude of a sister, and Pepita went with them, constantly astonished, more by the unselfishness and generosity with which Pedro consented to and even sought to satisfy his wife's costly whims than by the appeal that Paris holds for women. Dresses, coats, hats, jewelry, delicate lingerie, and the many items and odds and ends needed to complete the wardrobe and toilette of a very wealthy lady of very good taste—in other words, a whole world of temptations was passing in front of Pepita's eyes. Pura would advise and Mercedes would decide, wanting to purchase it all with unhealthy greed, as if the mere fact of acquiring something would assure her years of life to wear it. Pedro put no limits on expenditures, so that Pepita, half dazzled and half pensive, was experiencing impressions, shocks, and enticements; and the more she strove to conceal her reactions the more turmoil they caused her because those marvels of art and industry created for the delight of the fortunate—all the items that paraded before her eyes to be packed away in Mercedes' trunks—left Pepita with a bitter taste in her mouth.

Due to excessive activity or carelessness in her diet, Mercedes worsened to the point of going downhill considerably. The doctor told Pura that the patient would come out of that crisis, but that afterward it would be imperative to watch over her with the utmost care, and that in spite of it she would almost certainly die the first time she had a relapse. Pura advised Fuentelcésped to talk to the doctor, not wanting to be the one to give him such a terrible prognosis; and later, assuming that, as was natural, he had done so, she did not mention it again to avoid causing him distress. The one with whom the good woman did not stop bemoaning the approaching end of her friend was Pepita, which meant that the girl was fully aware of what would happen in the not-too-distant future. Seeing her almost always sad and self-absorbed, her stepmother attributed it to the harmful effect that Mercedes' condition could have on the girl. Pura was incapable of imagining what was stirring in Pepita's head.

After a few weeks Mercedes seemed to recover, and Pedro decided to take advantage of her improvement to return to Madrid for several days to deal with some matters of importance. He already had the trip planned when Pura received a letter from one of Pepita's aunts holding them to a certain promise that both had made to her.

During the winter the three had agreed that Pepita would accompany her aunt to a spa in Guipúzcoa because the latter disliked going alone with her maid, and afterward, as a reward for her kindness, the niece would be invited to spend the rest of the summer in San Sebastián, which was a most pleasant prospect for a young lady her age. When Mercedes read the letter, she insisted, thinking herself stronger than she really was, that they not prolong their stay in Paris. Pura refused to leave her, but anxious not to deprive her stepdaughter of the time in San Sebastián, proposed that Pedro, who was leaving soon for Madrid, take her along and hand her over to her aunt. Since they were accustomed to treating her like a young girl, it was the same as if she were going with her father. Nobody raised any objections. Pepita herself listened to the proposal and accepted it as the most natural thing in the world, but if an astute observer had studied her attentively at the moment her going with him was decided, he would have seen a gleam of joy shine in her eyes.

Several days later the experienced fifty-year-old man and the girl entrusted to his care were ready to leave Paris. Pedro had booked a compartment for two in a Pullman. The train departed. At first, since it was a delightful evening, they spent a long time leaning against the big windows in the corridor of the car, chatting about Paris, about the patient, about Pepita's aunt—about a thousand different things. Later, when it was quite late, Pedro said: "You know I don't sleep during a trip. I'll stay out here to smoke; rest if you want."

And Pepita went inside to lie down.

After a few hours and after having gone to the dining car and talked to other passengers, Pedro felt tired; when he noticed that the adjoining compartment was empty, he sat down in it now that it was possible to allow the girl to be alone. At dawn he went out again to the corridor to smoke, but as he had run out of cigarettes he decided to refill his case with the extras in his bag, and he entered his own compartment without making a sound. A useless precaution.

Pepita was not asleep; she had not even lain down. She sat in a corner, awake, her hands in her lap, holding a wet, crumpled handkerchief. Her contracted features revealed a deep sadness and she was crying silently—no sobs, no wails.

"What's this? What's wrong?" Pedro asked her, surprised, as he sat next to her and affectionately took both of her hands in his.

Pepita, without answering and without moving, continued to cry.

"But what's this? What's the matter? What has upset you?" She said nothing. "But don't you know that we all love you? Who's making you unhappy? Tell me! What is all this grief? A problem with Pura? She's not treating you well?"

And Pepita maintained her obstinate silence.

Pedro's curiosity and interest grew by the second. They sat there a long time, she persisting in weeping and not saying a word, he making an effort to gain her confidence and imploring her to speak. Never in his long life as a successful gallant, as a worldly womanizer, had he seen anyone cry like this. Finally, letting go of her hands, which he had in his, he put an arm around her waist and said in a fatherly way: "Come on, honey, tell me. Whatever it is you can trust me. Let it out. Don't you think I can help you?"

Pepita, snuggling up to Pedro as much as she could, rested her head on his shoulder and wrapped both arms around his neck like someone in search of a haven and protection; she clung to him, her tears falling on his chest, her disheveled curls tickling his face. A sensation midway between compassion and alarm had dispelled lewd thoughts, but when Pedro's body felt the heat that that other body was transmitting to his, when his face felt Pepita's breath and hair, when his neck felt the soft pressure of her gloveless hands he experienced a terrible uneasiness. He did not move her away because she might have attributed his action to indifference, and although he feared that he would look ridiculous by rejecting her, he found what was happening difficult to believe. Meanwhile, with every passing moment the sweet pressure was draining him of strength and her breath was swiftly making him immune to prudence.

"Tell me or I'll get angry with you," he bluntly exclaimed in the end.

Pepita, clasping her hands more firmly behind Pedro's neck and drawing back a little, but without letting go, looked at him through her tears, saying with heartrending sadness: "Think whatever you wish. I don't care. I know you won't understand me, but I don't care!"

"You're in love," was all he risked saying.

Pepita, without admitting it or denying it, continued bravely: "I want to enter the Daughters of Health, I want to profess, I want you to pay my dowry. I know it's a lot of money because it's the most aristocratic convent in Madrid. Will you keep my secret? Will you do me this favor?"

"You're in love!" Pedro repeated.

To which she responded with astonishing calmness: "Yes, I am—with a man who isn't free, and if he didn't come looking for me, I'd go looking for him and I don't want that to happen."

At the very moment that Pepita made this unblushing confession, she apparently recovered her sense of shame and lost her daring; she suddenly let go of Pedro and, covering her face with both hands, turned her back to him and threw herself face down on the cushioned bench seat. But he—convinced now of what that meant, unafraid of being mistaken, and spurred by vanity—felt a wave of pride wash over him. He drew her to him, separated her hands to uncover her face, and, looking at her pleadingly, said with a pronounced gentleness in his voice: "Who? Who is it? Tell me!"

With consummate skill, she lowered her eyes very slowly and once again leaned her head against his chest. Without saying a word, Pepita had answered. Pedro was gazing at her in fascination, entranced. His old conceit as a successful gallant had been reawakened, and he saw no immodesty in anything, feared no guile, suspected no duplicity; he thought neither of his wife nor the compromised future, nor did he consider his age. He took both of Pepita's hands, pulled her roughly to him, and, tilting her tousled head a little, whispered something in her ear.

She stared at him, feigning surprise, and asked: "Really? So you've known that she's seriously ill?"

"Yes," he replied. "It's a question of a few months."

"And if not," Pepita continued, "do you give me your word that you'll pay my dowry for the convent?'

"Yes, I do—but the one I'll keep is the other one."

Nothing more happened. He did not try to touch her and she did not fear an attempt.

The train was hurtling along. They sat very close to one another, without talking, as if they had nothing to say now. Later Pepita curled up in a corner, but then she slowly slid back and rested her head on Pedro's shoulder; she fell asleep—untroubled, trusting, and safe.

In the middle of the following winter Mercedes died, and after a year of mourning Pedro kept the first promise that he made to Pepita when he whispered in her ear that night of the trip.

They're married. He has taken an awful turn for the worse; she is one of the most elegant and extravagant women in Madrid.

Eva

Eve

I had a lot to write that day. I rose early, paced my room a number of times, drank a cup of black coffee, and sat down in front of the blank pages.

In a very short time I became convinced that I would produce nothing worthwhile. There are years, Murger* used to say, when one isn't up to anything. To this expression of sublime laziness might be added another of simple observation: there are days when the mind refuses to work, like a schoolboy who wakes up with the firm resolve of playing hooky.

I scribbled on several sheets of paper; I wrote; I crossed out; I wrote again; I crossed out again; and, persuaded that I would indeed accomplish nothing, I went off to Retiro Park.

It was near the end of fall. Groves and thickets were beginning to take on pale and yellowish hues. Some trees, prematurely bare, spread their empty branches across stretches of greenery. The ground was damp, and the wind, unpleasant and cool, picked up the fallen, curled leaves and swirled them around the narrow irrigation channels dug at the feet of the tree trunks. The walks were almost deserted. Occasionally you would see a solitary priest, a nursemaid holding hands with a soldier, a guard strolling leisurely with a cudgel under his arm, or a couple made up of a student and seamstress, who perhaps experienced with their books and sewing needles what I did with my sheets of paper. In the distance you could hear the quacking of the bored ducks in the ponds, the roar of a caged cat, and the singing of a carter who would now and then introduce obscene interjections and wild shouts into his song to spur his tired mules. Far off rose the muffled hum of Madrid, and the sun, setting opposite the capital, gilded with brilliant reflections the outline of small, white clouds that marbled the vivid azure of the sky.

Determined to take a good walk, I moved briskly and got away from people. I sought the most out-of-the-way places, passed by a small open space where schoolboys were playing quoits, and went into the paths of the section situated between the site of the former China Fountain and the big pond. Medium-sized pines, dead almonds, and stunted oaks form dense stands there; trails curve slightly and, after making capricious turns, lead into a long walk lined by beds of euonymus and dwarf cypresses.

When I arrived at the start of this walk, I saw a charming couple up ahead. It consisted of a lady with a graceful figure, dressed with elegant simplicity, and a happy, mischievous boy of five or six who was running back and forth picking up and throwing a huge rubber ball. If the little boy strayed too far his mother would say: "Don't run so much. Don't fall." Other times, when he lagged behind, the woman would stop and wait for him, looking toward the spot where he was scampering about in order not to lose sight of him for even a moment.

During one of those stops I managed to see her from the front. She was between twenty-five and thirty, at the height of a beauty full of promise and appeal. Her skin was white and slightly rosy like the flowers of almond trees, and her big, wide eyes were a deep, velvety black. Her hair, which spilled from her hat in loose locks and covered her neck, was a dark blond highlighted here and there by strands of a lighter blond that looked like filaments of gold. And beneath the slim figure, clad in a close-fitting skirt that revealed the lovely shape of her hips, from time to time you would see not only her small feet, but also the high instep and low-cut shoes that allowed a glimpse of pale blue stocking with each step that she took.

Her person proclaimed elegance, wealth, coquetry, and charm. She was one of those women who surprise and delight us, who pass by and cut short a conversation with a friend or intrude upon our thoughts; one of those women who make heads turn and who, when they vanish around a corner or disappear in a crowd, leave a bittersweet impression, a mixture of admiration for them and envy of the men to whom they belong.

Having to follow her little boy's games, she walked more

quickly than I did and got so far ahead of me that I nearly lost sight of her. I then turned into a tree-lined lane parallel to the one that she was following and, without being noticed, caught up with her again, to observe her more freely.

The boy, who was still running, all of a sudden picked up the ball, came back, and, giving it to her with outstretched little hands, said: "Mama, you throw it for me." The woman took the ball, rolled it on the ground, and her son chased after it. They continued playing the game, with the ball coming to a stop further and further away, until the mother, while the boy ran on ahead, shortened her step and came to a sudden stop, at which point she quickly glanced around, turning her head from side to side.

As I was hidden behind a sturdy trunk, she could not see me, and a moment later the boy appeared at the end of the walk. I remained concealed and she stood still; the boy approached his mother, and, handing her the ball again, said: "One more time, further." She tossed it one more time, with greater force, and the child ran after it until he disappeared behind one of the bushes that surround the walk on both sides.

The mother then looked around again and took three or four steps toward the side of the path. From between the clump of plants, which still retained their splendid green leaves, a young man emerged and with incredible speed caught hold of one of her hands, which she surrendered without taking her eyes off the spot where the little boy had disappeared. Putting his arm around the beautiful woman's waist, the man drew her toward him to kiss her, but she gave a start, more from fear than resistance, and the kiss, intended for her cheek or her lips, landed softly and silently on the silk of the wrap that covered her shoulders. It all happened in an instant. The man surreptitiously slipped into the woman's hand a piece of paper, which she tucked inside her muff; I heard a barely audible *"Good-bye,"* and the little boy appeared at the end of the walk—smiling, sweaty, tired, and with the ball in his hand.

"Let's go, it's late," the woman said.

"Just a little longer," the boy responded.

They continued their walk. I followed from a distance, and when they reached the Alcalá Gate, at the entrance to the Retiro, a man moved toward them—a man of dignified bearing, still young, but with a beard that was beginning to go white. When the boy saw him he ran, holding his arms out to him; the man waited with his outstretched, picked him up in the air, and planted three or four long, loud, firm kisses on the child's face.

A carriage was waiting a short distance away.

Master and mistress got in, the footman lifted the little one, seating him across from his parents, and they set off. I took the streetcar at the corner of Recoletos Street, and either because the carriage was going very slowly or because the streetcar was going very fast, both vehicles started up Alcalá Street at the same time.

Standing on the rear platform, I gazed for a long while at the figure of that strikingly elegant woman in whom every feature was bewitching, every movement enchanting. But what captivated me most was her air of noble and severe dignity.

She seemed proud to be alongside her husband who, perhaps after a day's work, had gone to meet her, while opposite them sat the little boy who embodied all the happiness and all the hopes of family life. Women eyed her with envy; men looked at her with admiration; and many people acknowledged her with respect.

As the carriage passed in front of the Calatravas church, she glanced at the door, raised an exquisitely gloved hand, and, drawing it across her beautiful face, made the sign of the cross.

* * *

The carriage faded from view. I've seen her several times about Madrid since then, but I've always refused to ask who she is, fearing that I would be told: "Her name is Eve."

El socio

The Partner

Isidoro Loranca arrived in Madrid at the age of sixteen, so poor that, not having the means to travel any other way, he came as the loader and helper of the carter from his hometown. Afterward he spent several weeks as a waiter at an inn on Segovia Street and then he became an errand boy in a haberdashery and fabric store, whose sign, in big gold letters, read: *The Fashion Place.*

Since he was intelligent, industrious, and long-suffering, they soon made him a salesman, and some time later, due to the death of a fellow employee, he rose to head salesman.

His great virtue was his love of work; his great failing, his greed. The shortcoming was so bound up with the good quality that he did not work to assure his future but for the pleasure of saving. During the summer he would have a cool drink only if someone else bought it; and during the winter, so as not to spend money on warm clothes, he would put large pieces of wrapping paper inside his shirt.

By the second year he had saved up nineteen months' salary; by the fourth he began to lend small amounts at usurious rates to portresses and servants; by the fifth he bought merchandise that he peddled on his own, using hawkers. Finally, by dint of depriving himself of everything, saving a great deal, and spending very little while continuing to earn, he was able, when payment of a draft fell due one day, to get his chief out of a tight situation by making him a small loan; as repayment he asked for a share of the business.

The employee became a partner, and from that day on he displayed all the activity and initiative of which he was capable in order to thrive and prosper.

The man who until then had been sole proprietor of the shop trusted in him and unwisely granted him excessive freedom of movement; at the second inventory that they took it turned out that two-thirds of the merchandise and credits of the business belonged to Loranca, while the former proprietor was in debt and compromised. Isidoro then offered to pay the debts, taking over as owner of the establishment; the deal was struck, and thus did the boy who came to Madrid driving mules and unloading bundles join the class of people with something to lose. He continued to say *irregardless* and *they was*, but he had his clothes tailor-made, put on a top hat, wore boots in place of white shoes, and frequented cafés without getting used to leaving a tip. As for the shop, he decided to concentrate mainly on shirts, hired a good cutter, and took on seamstresses, who some nights would come to pick up work and on others would drop it off.

Until then he had not been given to chasing or falling for women. His romances had consisted of fleeting encounters with neighborhood maids and dressmakers' apprentices, but from that point on, his constant dealings with seamstresses—and the brazenness of some, the mischief of others, the poverty of all, and the ease with which he could keep them happy by paying them in part with money and in part with work—served as an appetizer, occasioning such a hunger for love, crude love of course, that neighbors called the haberdashery the "seraglio."

It was well-known in the district that no attractive woman could go and seek work there unless she was willing to lose her virtue.

Such was his reputation when one night there came to him, recommended by the business card of another merchant, a nineteen-year-old girl who was pretty without being a paragon of beauty, apparently modest, graceful, and very proper. She did not look like a shop worker or a girl who grew up in the streets, but like a young lady fallen on hard times. As soon as Loranca saw her he decided to seduce her. It was a futile undertaking—special consideration, preferential treatment, offers, promises, flattery—nothing produced results. The attitude and answers given by Juliana, which was the new seamstress's name, could be summed up in this one phrase, sometimes spoken with a winsome coquettishness and other times with brutal firmness: "Marriage, perhaps; the other, not a chance."

Don Isidoro, accustomed to the other, paid no heed at first and waited, but after a time he became convinced that Juliana, owing to virtue or calculation, could not be seduced; he then set out to obtain what he wanted by beginning to reason with himself continuously, like the person who is determined, whatever the cost, to have his way. "A woman who resists like that is good. And how pretty! And the most refined one in the shop. As hardworking as they come. No lazy miss for me. But I can't spend my life alone like a recluse—I need a wife. Things can't go on this way. She's poor? Then she'll have to be grateful to me for everything." One morning Don Isidoro showed up at Juliana's attic room, but since she refused to open the door, he had to tell her the decision he had just made through the peephole. Not even then did she draw back the latch. She only said: "When it gets dark I'll go to the shop and we'll talk."

The result of the conversation, with the counter between them, was a marriage agreement. The husband-to-be tried to exact a foretaste of the delights that would soon be sanctioned, but until they were married she did not set foot in the back room of the shop—the graveyard of other women's virtue—and when she felt pressed she would reject his attentions half-jokingly while at the same time saying: "I'm not the kind of girl who says yes before saying I do."

Loranca got married in love, thought Juliana, who was herself dazzled by the tremendous difference that existed between her state and his. But she considered him a handsome young man, and outside of the womanizing and stinginess, he did not have a bad reputation. She would turn his fondness for skirts to her own advantage, and as for the miserliness, that would change gradually.

A year of marriage convinced Loranca that he had mistaken a passing fancy for passion, and it convinced his wife that to be happy it was not enough to be called Doña Juliana or *Miss*, wear a hat and have an elegant shop. Loranca, a rich proprietor, continued to be as coarse as when he arrived in Madrid, while Juliana was quickly becoming so polished and refined in speech, dress, and manners that nobody could guess her humble and poor origin. Her self-interest and his lust had become obstacles to happiness and also contributed to bringing about a powerful circumstance of which they were not aware.

Such was their situation when a handsome youth named Esteban Bolaño began to frequent first the shop and then their home. He was a commission agent, stylish, and wealthy besides, so wealthy that he did not care a whit about the commission, since he worked solely to please his father.

Shortly after Juliana and Bolaño met and spent time together, they were hopelessly in love with each other, with the difference that he utilized every recourse suggested by passion to be successful, while she determined to hold herself in check. The first thing that Esteban did, sacrificing his own interests, was to give Loranca impressive and exceptionally easy payment terms for receipt of goods; then whenever it could prove useful, he provided him with news about the standing of other merchants; next he advised him to advantage about the operation of his business; and lastly, he began to court him, disguising the reason behind so much generosity by expressing the false desire to form a partnership with him. "Loranca and Co.," he would usually say during after-dinner talk whenever he went to their home to eat, after first having sent flowers to the wife and cigars to the husband.

"What do you think? Whenever you want forty or fifty thousand *pesetas*, which would do it. Between the two of us, the best shop in Madrid."

The same idea had occurred to Loranca, but he wanted to be wooed.

Juliana understood that the purpose of all of Esteban's doings was to allow him to stay close and to see her more easily; and comparing the suitor with the husband, she began to feel divorced in spirit and guilty in thought. Imagination and desire triggered sin in her without the aid of her will. Finally, terrified in the face of that revolt by her senses, alone with her husband one night, she said: "I have to talk to you. Esteban's coming to eat tomorrow, isn't he?"

"Yes. What a nice guy, eh?"

"But he comes quite often."

"So what?"

"I get worn out with all the planning and preparation. And the servants end up exhausted from doing so many dishes and washing so many place settings and glasses. At midnight they're still not finished."

"Something like that occurred to me too. We have to take on more help."

"Wouldn't it be easier to take him to a restaurant whenever you wanted to invite him?"

"It's more expensive and the sauces don't agree with me."

Juliana hesitated for an instant before continuing, and then said with determination: "Perhaps it would be better if he didn't come so frequently."

"What do you mean? I don't understand you."

"I can see that, but even the servants have noticed."

"What are you trying to tell me?"

This time Juliana's hesitation lasted longer; only after a few moments did she smile mischievously, saying: "Think about it. Will you give me your word that you'll be sensible? Well, since he comes so frequently, they talk about him and about me and I want to avoid their talking about you."

Loranca burst out laughing and, putting his hands on his head, exclaimed: "What nonsense! In other words, I can't have a friend, a partner—because I've decided that he will be—without. . . . Come now! You're seeing things. Of all the stupid. . . !"

"I'm telling you he's after me."

Her husband glared at her, burst out laughing again, and finally, pretending that he was trying to calm down, said with the utmost calm: "All right, leave him be. He'll get over it."

Juliana, amazed, could not understand his attitude. Fearful of what was crossing her mind, she cut off the conversation and resolved to watch her husband.

The following day Esteban came to eat with them, and when it was time to have coffee, Juliana, without waiting for the table to be cleared as was their custom, said to the maid: "Take everything to my boudoir and put it on the pedestal table. We'll have the coffee there." And turning to Loranca she added: "You go to the study and get him a good cigar."

Following her, Esteban was both surprised and pleased, because even after having asked her repeatedly, this was the first time that he was managing to be alone with her for a few minutes. They went into her boudoir, sat down to wait for Loranca, and she poured her husband's coffee, but since he took so long she stepped over to the hall entrance and called out: "Isidoro. Isidoro."

At that moment the street door slammed shut and her maid entered the boudoir with this message: "The master says that since he's out of cigars he's gone to buy some and will return shortly."

Juliana, livid and trembling, left Esteban alone, ran to her husband's rooms, and opened the desk drawer in the study where she knew he kept his cigars, and from which he never removed the key because he was the only one in the house who smoked. She saw three boxes and raised the lids. One untouched, was of the Conchas type; another contained thirty or forty choice flat cigars; and in the biggest one there were three and a half bunches of Cazadores—huge, fresh, of the finest quality, Loranca's favorites for after dinner, and the very same ones that he had offered to Esteban other times. There were more than enough for a month.

"Did the master know that he had all of this here?" she asked the maid.

"This morning I saw him reaching in that big box and filling his cigar case."

The maid left the room and Juliana sank into the armchair, crying from anger and shame. She sat there a long while and afterward approached the balcony window. Nothing. Then, looking at herself in a mirror, she dried her tears and, without fixing her hair, whose curls had become undone, took a bunch of Cazadores, and returned to the boudoir where Esteban was savoring the last swallow of cognac. She spoke with an undefinable smile, just barely moving her lips and showing him the cigars: "The best that there is in this house is going to be for you."

El deber

Duty

We were discussing extraordinary crimes and trials famous for their grounds or circumstances, and, naturally, something was also said about the more or less proper intervention of judges and their varying degrees of honesty. Everyone of those present related an interesting or curious case, and the word *duty* came up more than once.

All of a sudden Don Cristóbal said: "Duty ... duty ... who knows what it is at certain times or what it consists of or how it's carried out? And what's even more difficult, how does one distinguish the merely legal duty, whose fulfillment is sufficient for the honorable discharge of the office, from the other more noble, more exalted one imposed by conscience? Above all, in some cases, who can guarantee us that the command, the inspiration of conscience, constitutes duty? On the other hand, I assure you that occasionally one fulfills it at the expense of the legal duty, and with no regrets."

Realizing that his comments arose from recollection of an incident in which he had intervened during his long career as a judge and magistrate, we begged him to tell it to us, and he acceded to our request.

"What I'm going to relate to you happened some time ago, when the first insurrection in Cuba during the Carlist War* was at a critical juncture. Hardly a day went by without troops departing Madrid for the north or ports of embarkation, but people scarcely took notice of them, particularly the battalions headed for Cuba, which were not seen off with the enthusiasm that you've all witnessed of late. Everywhere, in every home, there was hardship, but in general the country was accustomed to the continuous bloodshed abroad, and public attention paid more heed to the campaign in the north.

"Back then I was judge in a Madrid district. One night, in a house on . . . no reason to give the street name . . . one night two gunshots were heard, so close together that they almost seemed simultaneous, and a maid on the second floor ran out to the stairway calling for help and screaming: 'The señora is killing her husband!' The neighbors, who responded in order to lend a hand or out of mere curiosity, were terrified. Sure enough, a woman had just shot her husband twice. They notified the emergency clinic and the night court, where I was on call.

"I arrived shortly after the crime had been committed. The appearance of the rooms showed that a family down on its luck lived there, but from little details and appointments that can be appreciated by a seasoned observer, I saw that they had once enjoyed better times. In a boudoir, at the foot of a mirror-fronted wardrobe that was next to the bedroom door, a man in his forties, already dead, lay stretched out on the floor. There were two wounds, one in the chest and another in the neck. The blood flowing out of them formed two little thick-rimmed pools that rapidly spread over the carpet, reflecting on their surfaces the reduced image of the mantelpiece lamp, whose light, contained by a large shade, fully illuminated the corpse's face. The dead man's clothes showed good taste, but there were clear signs of his financial straits: frayed shirt cuffs, a frock coat shiny from too much wear, and old patent-leather boots. He had his topcoat on, so either he had been about to go out or he had just come in. He was tall and well-built, with features contorted by a sensation of pain or perhaps a grimace of anger. In the bedroom, between the bed and the wall, as if taking refuge, stood his wife, who had just killed him; she was pale, motionless, frightened at what she had done, and still holding the revolver in her right hand and clutching a small wallet in her left.

When I identified myself I overheard several people giving their impressions in brief. Things like: 'There had to be big trouble here.' 'Couldn't have been jealousy. There are no skeletons in her closet.' 'Death was instantaneous.' All of a sudden a neighbor woman from the third floor said: 'And their son? Where do you suppose Pepe is?' And a young lady, pretty to be sure, from the main floor answered: 'He's at the house next door, studying with a friend.' They went after him, and, giving no consideration to his emotional reaction, thoughtlessly and promptly told him on the way back what had happened. The boy looked less than twenty years old and was quite handsome.

"He entered the boudoir, ashen and trembling; he stared at his father, knelt at his side, and took one of his hands and kissed it with an expression of sincere filial respect, but without screaming, without despairing, without going to extremes or crying out for revenge. That quiet, reserved grief, almost dispassionate, impressed me a great deal. However, when he saw his mother, who hadn't left the bedroom, he ran over to her, took the revolver, which he tossed on the bed, and threw himself into her arms, crying and kissing her anxiously, with unmistakable signs of the most affectionate tenderness. Then, no doubt terrified in light of the terrible consequence of the crime, he said to her with acute distress: 'What have you done?' She gave him a long, loving, searching glance full of thoughts and feelings that only the two of them understood.

"I ordered the body removed to the morgue, dismissed the maids, and had the son, after he packed some clothes, go and stay with neighbors, and then I proceeded at once to take the mother's preliminary statement.

"When she came out of the bedroom, once everybody had left the apartment, she approached me and gave me the small wallet or card holder, which was surprisingly thick, and which she had been holding all that time in her hand. With the rooms cleared of onlookers, the woman, the court clerk who accompanied me, and I went to the study, while the two bailiffs and the policemen remained at the door. And at this point I should tell you that the clerk was a young man who had much to thank me for because I had saved him, no less, from going to prison. He was mine in body and soul—out of gratitude, which is very nice, and out of fear, which unfortunately is surer.

"Doña Carlota looked about forty or forty-five, and many of those years must have been hard ones, judging by her sorrowful expression and the yellowish hue, like a withered flower, of her cheeks. She was tall, slender, had black hair, and big, beautiful, jet-black eyes; her voice, despite her extreme agitation, seemed soft and sweet, one of those voices that appear to be ignorant of the changes in pitch typical of defiance and pride. As I looked and looked at that pleasant, intelligent woman, I kept wondering: what domestic drama could have prompted her to do what she did?

"The clerk sat down at the deceased's desk, where, I might add, there were no signs of work. Doña Carlota wanted to remain standing but I made her sit down too. Habit inclined me to be brusque and abrupt, to treat her without consideration; reason, and more than reason, something like a hunch, told me that although this woman was guilty, she was no criminal. Yes, the crime was a fact. But wicked, her . . . ? I found that hard to believe.

"In response to routine questions she said that her name was Carlota So-and-so, from Madrid, thirty-nine years old, and married to Don Agustín, by whom she had the son who had just left.

"Seeing that she was very excited and nervous, I tried to put her at ease; I even think that, involuntarily, instinctively, I did so with a gentleness inappropriate to the situation. 'Calm down,' I said to her, 'and tell us the truth, the whole truth concerning the motives that you believe you had for what you've done and which you must already regret.'

"'I would have given anything to avoid it,' she responded, 'but regret it—no. One regrets what one thinks out and plans and I didn't think out or plan a single thing. Two hours ago I couldn't even imagine the misfortune that was going to descend upon us.'

"'Let's hear your story, all of it, because the law discovers everything in the end anyway.'

"Little by little she did calm down, regaining her composure and expressing herself almost normally.

"'My defense, not my guilt, is in truth itself. If it weren't for my son, I wouldn't be defending myself.'

"Although her voice quavered somewhat, she spoke slowly and clearly; recollections, thoughts, and impressions seemed to flow to her lips without deception, without planning, and she made no attempt to alter any of what she was telling us.

"'I've just turned thirty-nine. My father, who was widowed as a very young man raised me at his side. I never spent twenty-four hours away from him, and the only thing I knew about convents and schools was what I heard from others. He indulged me so much, let me have my way to such an extent, that if I were going to be bad I would have shown signs of it a long time ago.

He died when I was seventeen. One of his sisters then took me in. She was considerably older than my father, a spinster with a sour temperament—selfish, accustomed to giving orders and living alone, and from the very outset I realized that I was a nuisance to her. We did not hit it off. My gentleness, my humility, and my patience, in part natural and in part exaggerated through conscious effort, ran up against her domineering and violent disposition. The following year the man who would be my husband— the one I just shot—began to pursue me. He watched me on streets, in theaters, on walks, and followed me everywhere. He was handsome, seemed intelligent, and was the first man to tell me that he loved me, and I believed him and loved him back, or imagined that I loved him, without really having gotten to know him. I took him at his word and we courted for some months, at first writing to each other, and then talking on the sly, until at last my aunt occasionally let me go out with him accompanied only by a maid. Finally, we decided to marry and my aunt raised no objections, because wanting to live alone mattered more to her than the fear of seeing me unhappy. Did my fiancé and I come to know each other as well as two people who will share a lifetime should? I'm certain that we did not, and it didn't take me long to become convinced that his qualities, or what I understood as such, were more showy than solid. As for whatever good there was in me, if there was something, he was incapable of appreciating it. My father had left me a modest inheritance with an income of approximately three thousand *duros*. Agustín also owned some bonds that yielded upwards of one thousand *duros* annually; moreover, he had just completed his law degree and on the recommendation of an uncle of his, a very influential political figure, obtained a job that paid ten thousand *reales*. Between the two of us we had more than enough to live well. Agustín managed all of it, giving me what I needed for household expenses.

"'A year later we had a son, the boy that you saw, my Pepe. Agustín, my husband, then began to change, to be someone else, or I began to learn what he was really like. His main flaw lay in his horror of work. I won't bore you with meaningless details and particulars, but as he almost never went to the ministry, he lost the job. No matter what I did I couldn't get him to take up a thing. Cafés, clubs, one diversion after another—and spend,

spend, spend, as if we had ten times more than what we did have. He seldom spoke to me of his affairs, but I would often say to him: "Work, keep busy, do something. Remember that our son is growing and that costs are getting higher and higher." But I didn't dare push too hard—and give him the wrong impression—because my income was greater than his. It all came to naught. The certainty of how little influence I exerted on him finally convinced me that he didn't love me as I had dreamed of being loved. Why, he wasn't even loving with our little boy.

"'When Pepe was ten years old the situation changed radically because Agustín became erratic about the money I needed for household expenses. Some months he wouldn't give me enough, other months he'd give it to me way behind, and as I wasn't receiving it at set times—the days on which interest was paid on our holdings—the unpredictability and irregularity played havoc with an orderly life. We were in arrears, underwent hardships, and had debts. I finally found out that he was gambling. And we went on living like that, he without working, without loving me, and I without respecting him. What could I feel for him when I even had to take Pepe out of private school because we owed five months' tuition?

"'With my hand over my heart, I assure you, Your Honor, that I've suffered a great deal. Five years ago, during one of the worst periods that I remember having gone through, I was at a friend's house one afternoon, feeling sorry for myself and complaining about my predicament when she said, apropos of the difficulties we were experiencing: "I've resisted talking to you about certain things—first, because I figured you were aware of them, second, because I didn't want to cause you grief by bringing them up, but at this point you two must be broke. Agustín has sold and gambled everything away, his assets as well as yours. My brother heard about it at the stock market—everybody in Madrid knows." Then my friend went on to say something that I'll never forget: "Just a few days ago I thought of you a great deal because my husband was very tied up coming and going from one office to another to exempt our son from conscription until he made the payment of eight thousand *reales*. And I said to myself: God only knows if poor Carlota will be able to pay to have hers exempted when the time comes."

"'Since that afternoon I haven't had a peaceful day or a restful night. Our boy was fifteen then; there was war in the north and war in Cuba, and neither showed signs of letting up. Freedom and country are all well and good, but for me my son comes first. As I watched, time went by and the months flew and they would take my Pepe away from me. I then began to do something I had never done before. Whenever Agustín gave me money, I would set a certain amount aside and save it; sometimes quite a bit, relatively speaking; other times, very little. When I could, bills, and if not five-*peseta* pieces, then single *pesetas*, even small change. I hoarded and accumulated like that with real greed, scrimping on everything, cutting down on everything, in order to exempt my son. When I had enough I would change it into large bills. Every one-hundred-*peseta* bill made me feverish with joy.'

"While Doña Carlota was telling me all this," Don Cristóbal said to us, "I had my hand in my pants pocket, fingering the wallet she had given me for safekeeping. I realized that it contained her savings, her sacrifices, her tears—what a strange corpus delicti!—and I guessed the rest of the story.

"'So I managed,' she went on, 'to put together two thousand *pesetas*, and even a little extra, just in case. Our Pepe will reach draft age at the end of this month. I had decided to exempt him without saying a word to my husband, certain that if the two thousand *pesetas* fell into his hands we wouldn't see them again. Words cannot express my anguish nor my unshakable resolve. Of late there's been no money in the house, and my husband hasn't had any, but he knew that I still had several small pieces of jewelry that belonged to my father: some garnet buttons and gold pocket-watch lids. They had survived similar situations because of how much they mean to me and how little they're worth. This afternoon Agustín asked me for them, I refused him, and he didn't insist. After we ate, Pepe went next door to study with a friend and we remained in the dining room. I had the keys to the wardrobe in my apron pocket. All of a sudden my husband jumped from his seat, and, overpowering me, snatched them and ran toward the boudoir. Imagine what must have gone through my mind! I rushed after him. He unlocked the wardrobe, ignoring my pleading, and in order to find the jewelry quickly, began to rummage through everything, throwing the clothes on the floor. The wallet came out with some old dressing gowns. In it were two five-hundred-*peseta* bills, seven one-hundred bills, and the rest in small denominations of twenty-five, along with three or four silver *duros*, which clinked together as the wallet fell. You can't imagine what took place then. It all happened so fast. He picked it up and saw the money. I told him how and for what reason I had scrimped and saved; I cried, I begged him, I dropped to my knees, clutching his legs. He lifted me, grabbed me by my arms, and threw me against one of the iron columns at the entrance to the bedroom; I didn't feel the blow, just the fear, the certainty that he was taking the money. I got up and dashed into the bedroom. From the nightstand I pulled out the revolver that he usually carried when he was out late. I shouted at him: "Give it to me. That money's Pepe's for the conscription so let go of it." He didn't believe I was capable of shooting. He began to walk away—laughing! I then closed my eyes, extended my arm, and fired twice. He fell and may God forgive me, but if he hadn't I would've fired a hundred times.'

"And as she said this, Doña Carlota's eyes were taking on a fierce expression that would have instilled fear if it hadn't inspired admiration. Her story had moved me deeply: I didn't remember having experienced such intense emotion in all my years on the bench. I had begun listening to her as a judge and ended up listening to her as a man. She was of the same mettle as my mother. And when I understood the motives that had driven her to commit the crime, because legally it was a crime, I also understood that the money she had so zealously saved to free her son was going to be impounded as evidence in the trial and was, therefore, lost. At that point it would be difficult to express the thoughts and feelings that laid hold of my spirit, and the powerful urgency that they created in me, overcoming every other kind of consideration. Besides, as I said before, the clerk with us there was mine, completely mine. 'Señora,' I said to Doña Carlota, 'in view of this statement, I see no need for you to be held incommunicado.* Prison, trial—that's unavoidable. But tomorrow you may receive a visit in jail from someone close to you and this is yours,' I said, returning the wallet to her.

"She looked at me as she would have looked at God, and for a moment I thought that my mother was in my presence.

"It was the only time," Don Cristóbal concluded by saying, "that I deliberately disregarded the law and I've yet to regret it."

El retrato

The Portrait

Dear Julia,

Seeing that you're concerned about me, I'm going to open my heart and tell you something, because if spontaneity and frankness make a friendship stronger, excessive reserve on the other hand weakens and diminishes it.

What you fear is true: I am not happy. Our brilliant position, our wealth, the peace that we enjoy in my home, and the deep feeling that both children and parents have for one another, a love returned a hundredfold like mirror images, aren't enough to dispel the sadness that has taken hold of my spirit.

You know that our fortune is very recent, and almost dates from yesterday. Do you recall how often your generosity helped me in times of need? Perhaps, like every magnanimous soul who does good, you've forgotten, but I haven't because if the person who does kindnesses needn't remember them, the one who benefits should engrave them in his or her memory.

We were poor, but happy, sustained by a resignation very similar to hope, when unexpectedly our luck changed, and our slender means, which very nearly bordered on want, all of a sudden turned into a wealth that verges on opulence.

Four years ago, during the winter, my husband suffered a strong attack of rheumatism, and the doctors advised him to take the baths of Aljama the following spring if he wanted to guard against the effects of the illness the next winter; you, as you well know, lent me the four thousand *reales* that we needed. Our wealth dates from that trip. In Aljama Juan ran across an old friend and fellow student of his named Mateo Resmilla. Mateo had been utterly destitute when they were students together, but now he was very wealthy and as happy as he could be in the face of the persistent pain that brought him to the same spa as my Juan.

Mateo Resmilla was a small, dark, and thickset man with a ruddy complexion and a short neck; boring, given to falling asleep in any position, and easily irritated, he showed all the symptoms of hypertension—the kind of person who seems to be constantly threatened by a stroke. He and Juan reminisced about their youth, the mornings they went to the university together, their worries on nights before exams, the awful beds and even worse food given to them by their landlady, the jams they got into over a lack of money—and I suspect that in all likelihood they even relived one or another of the escapades experienced by all men as youths and which we women rarely hear about. During those few days they renewed their friendship so solidly that the pro forma questions were soon followed by others motivated by genuine fondness, and then they both learned that they had reached very different stations in life. My Juan was poor: to support himself and his family he had only the eight thousand *reales* earned on the job that he had landed after finishing his studies; Resmilla, on the other hand, desperate when he went off to Cuba, had made a great fortune.

He started out as do many of those who go there with only a dream and the will to succeed—that is, by sweeping a shop in which he began as a servant, in which he then worked as a clerk, in which he was later made a partner, and of which he finally became the owner, transforming into a rich banking establishment the wretched little shop at whose door he had knocked, helpless and miserable. Resmilla explained all of this to Juan in great detail, but did not tell him his net worth, nor was it easy to guess it because he lived modestly. His only luxuries consisted of smoking select cigars and wearing a magnificent diamond on the little finger of his left hand.

Nine days later, at the end of their stay at the spa, the two of them decided to return to Madrid together, and, in order to travel comfortably, they booked the three seats in the closed compartment of the diligence that was to take them from the town to the nearest train station.

It was around the end of May and very hot; the coach moved

slowly, enveloped in a thick, suffocating cloud of dust; the sun bore down on the parched fields; not a breath of air stirred; and dirty, thirsty, withered branches drooped on the wilted trees seen at intervals on either side of the road. As the hours passed the heat grew worse—an intense, suffocating heat that baked the body of the coach, made the poor mules who pulled it under the whip sweat profusely, and occasionally elicited expressions of bad humor and impatience from the two unhappy travelers. My husband, frailer in appearance, but actually stronger than Resmilla, withstood all that discomfort, but the latter began to feel ill, became nauseous, suffered two or three dizzy spells, and ended up losing consciousness, which alarmed Juan who tried futilely to bring him to.

Shortly before nightfall the diligence arrived at a fairly large town where the passengers were to have dinner while the coachman and his helper changed the team of mules to continue the journey. But Juan, seeing what a bad state Resmilla was in, refused to accept responsibility for getting his friend back inside the coach in that condition, nor could he leave him alone and among strangers. Therefore, he ordered their luggage brought down from the rack, asked for a room with two beds, put the sick Resmilla in one of them with the help of a servant, and got ready to spend the night in that awful inn, first arranging for the town doctor to be called.

When the latter arrived, Resmilla had regained consciousness.

"Don't be alarmed," Juan said to him. "This is nothing. We packed ourselves into that damn coach right after eating, you felt faint and had indigestion. I'm telling you, it's nothing. We'll continue on tomorrow's diligence."

The doctor examined Resmilla carefully, wrote a prescription, ordered that he be kept quiet, and left the room, signaling Juan to follow him. Outside he asked: "Are you a relative of this gentleman?"

"No, sir. I'm only his friend, but I didn't think it wise to leave him here alone and in that condition."

"Well, you did the right thing because he's gravely ill. What you see is an instance of out-and-out apoplexy, the kind that comes suddenly, without warning, and that we're helpless to combat. If he has family, notify them; if he's a believer, tell him to make his peace with God, because he's going very fast. And unless it's something extremely important keep him quiet: the priest, the notary, and you—but very, very little talking."

Imagine Juan's quandary. He hesitated a long time before deciding, but who would accept responsibility for letting a man die like that, without warning him of the risk he was running, without thinking that he might have family he wished to see or important affairs to arrange? Juan had the innkeeper summon the mayor, who was in a nearby café playing dominoes, and having the good fortune to encounter a quick-witted official, spoke to him for several moments; then, taking advantage of a moment when Resmilla was lucid and in possession of all his faculties, he went in to see him.

"I thought you were sleeping. That's why I didn't come in."

"I'm ill, very ill. Come close, I want to talk to you. I'm done for. Two years ago I had another attack, and I was told, or rather, I found out that the doctors had stated if there was a repeat—in short, I know I'm dying. Have them bring a notary and witnesses."

Juan left the room, not without having attempted to console his unfortunate friend, and ordered a notary brought in. The mayor and a brother of his acted as witnesses, and a moment later Resmilla dictated his will in a clear voice, in simple terms, and signed it with a steady hand. But just imagine Juan's surprise when, on naming his inheritor, Resmilla declared that he had no family and was leaving his entire fortune, close to a million *duros*, to his friend Don Juan de Alerce. My husband!

In vain did Juan, astonished at what he was hearing, try to dissuade him and ask him if he didn't have other obligations to fulfill or instructions to give him. Resmilla stood by his decision and requested that the mayor approach his bed; he repeated his will clearly and decisively, declared again that he had no family, and added a final note: "Give me a modest burial, and you, Juan, have a school built in my hometown. You'll have money left over for that and a lot more."

In a matter of two hours, Resmilla was a corpse and we were rich. Three days later Juan left for Madrid, and four months afterwards we were in possession of that man's fortune, a fortune that, in such a strange way, had made us powerful.

What a transformation occurred in our home, and even in us, the people in it! Juan quit his job; we rented a much better apartment than the one we had; we replaced our own furnishings, which had been accumulated little by little, with new ones ordered in a hurry and paid for on the spot; we took out a season ticket to the opera; I had magnificent dresses made; and I engaged a French governess for the children. Our tastes changed radically and our values almost became distorted, as if through contact with money and excused by wealth, defects could be put on display, but we continued loving and treasuring one another as if we were poor. I am certain that Juan does not spend one duro without my knowing on what and I don't make a move that he's not aware of.

And nevertheless, I no longer enjoy that calm, quiet happiness of earlier days. For some months now sorrow has been stirring in the depths of my heart, a sorrow like an air bubble on the bottom of a glass—not sufficient to shake it up but enough to disturb it.

You already know that my father was obsessed with ancestry and heraldry. For that reason when I got married he gave me, among many other things, two small pictures on which he himself had drawn our coat of arms, a very peculiar hieroglyphic that only he could decipher. It consisted of two big ugly birds, a mace that looked like a fire shovel, two cauldrons, and one dog. Now then. Not long ago my husband wanted to redo a room, so a decorator came. He took measurements, drew lines, made plans, and, lastly, asked us how we wanted the drapes, advising us to make them very wide, of red plush and with our coat of arms superimposed, embroidered in silk in the middle. I was going to say that we didn't have a coat of arms when Juan replied: "Fine. Come back in a few days and we'll give you the design."

My husband had remembered the two pictures that I received from my father when we got married.

Sure enough, and as I had suspected, no sooner did the decorator leave than Juan asked about the two escutcheons in order to choose the "better one."

"They're in the attic," I answered.

"Well, have them brought down."

I instructed a servant to do so, but he couldn't find them; I then entrusted the task to my maid and she couldn't find them either. In the end, I decided to go up and look for them myself, because even though Juan's pretentiousness struck me as ridiculous and I didn't feel like making the climb, I agreed to everything rather than have a falling-out over such a trivial matter.

The next morning I went up to the attic, where, to be sure, I hadn't been since we'd moved, and where, besides all our old junk, some of poor Resmilla's things had been stored, things like the rickety furniture from his boardinghouse room. I spent two long hours searching for the escutcheons of my nobility. I finally found them in a corner with the frames undone, the glass broken, and the color faded.

I was about to leave that dark, dirty attic when, at the other end, I saw Resmilla's haphazardly placed furniture: a broken-down filing cabinet with the contents of the drawers emptied out in a large esparto basket; a wobbly easy chair with a greasy back and leather ripped by cats' claws; a wardrobe of painted pine; and a small, worthless mahogany nightstand full of ink stains that had drops of candle wax built up on them. What dirty, old furniture! What sweet, intense emotion! Nobody will be able to explain to me how the sensation I experienced welled forth. Nobody will be able to tell me by what mysterious means that grimy, worm-eaten woodwork awakened such a powerful and profound feeling in my spirit. My eyes filled with tears and I dropped the two small pictures of the coat of arms.

I tried to calm down before leaving, and was about to put the key in the lock when I saw, propped against a wall, a painting whose size and shape I didn't recognize. I thought that perhaps it too had belonged to Resmilla, and I went over and managed, even though it was heavy, to turn it toward the scanty light that came in through a narrow little window covered by a natural curtain of dust and cobwebs. It was a portrait of a young man—dark, small, thickset, ruddy, and short-necked. I thought I knew who it was, but I wanted to be certain, so that very afternoon I asked Juan.

"In the attic there's a portrait of a man I don't know. Who is it?"

"Stocky, a flushed face, common and ordinary-looking, short-necked?"

"That's the one."

"You don't know? That's Resmilla's portrait."

Yes, Julia, yes! It was the man to whom we owe our fortune; the one who assured our children's future; the one who changed the humble employee who earned eight thousand *reales* into a man of means; the one who covered my fingers, blackened from needle pricks, with diamonds. That picture, as ridiculous as it might seem, should have been sacred to us and hung in the best room of our home, in the very same room where Juan wanted to, and indeed did, put my father's coat of arms.

I admit that since then, although I haven't stopped loving him, my respect for Juan has gone down because he's one of those people who ignore the fact that there's something more beautiful in the world than doing good, and that's being grateful. Good-bye.

Affectionately yours,

Notes

Page references in this volume precede each note.

(29) *War of Independence:* 1808–14; the struggle against the Napoleonic invasion and Joseph Bonaparte, who assumed the Spanish throne as Joseph I.

(30) *Alonso Berruguete:* 1488–1561; Spanish sculptor influenced by Michelangelo and noted for his altar screens in Valladolid and choir stalls in Toledo's cathedral.

(30) *Alonso Cano:* 1601–67; Spanish baroque sculptor, painter, and architect especially known for his work on the cathedral of Granada (the façade and statues of saints).

(50) *sub conditione:* conditionally (Roman Catholic doctrine, in case the soul is lingering in the body).

(55) *if the bishop . . . it:* literally, if Prester John says it [*aunque lo diga Preste Juan*]. Prester John: a legendary priest and king of the Middle Ages reputed to have had a kingdom in the Far East.

(57) *Teresa . . . room:* a slip on Picón's part; they are already in Teresa's room.

(57) *twenty . . . prettier:* if Juana and Luisa are both twenty years old, Don Diego could not have (met and) had relations with the former's mother several years *after* becoming a widower. Picón clearly forgot that Don Agustín had told Luisa and Teresa that Juana was nineteen.

(64) *Salamanca:* José de Salamanca y Mayol, Marquis of Salamanca (1806–83); Spanish banker, lawyer, and politician. He made a fortune in the railroad business and built the district in Madrid named after him.

(64) *Salustiano Olózaga:* 1805–73; Spanish politician and orator.

(64) *Godoy:* Manuel de Godoy y Alvarez de Faria (1767–1851); a Spanish army officer who won the favor of Queen María Luisa and became her lover. Godoy's tenure as chief minister of the Spanish government—to which he was appointed by Carlos IV in 1792—was rife with corruption and he barely managed to escape mob justice when the king abdicated.

(64) *Don Alvaro* [*Don Alvaro o la fuerza del sino*]: Spanish Romantic play by the Duke of Rivas, 1791–1865.

Notes 219

(64) *The Goth's Dagger* [*El puñal del godo*]: Spanish Romantic play by José Zorrilla, 1817–93.

(69) *But . . . fortunate:* Florambel and Amadís are the titular protagonists of two books of chivalry (*Florambel de Lucea* [1532] and *Amadís de Gaula* [ca. 1508]); the former's fair lady is Braselinda (not Groselinda) and the latter's is Oriana. Leander [Leandro] loved Hero [Cupídea?] and swam the Hellespont nightly to see her. He was guided by a torch that she set on a tower, but one night a storm kicked up and he drowned; when his body washed ashore, Hero committed suicide by jumping from the tower.

(152) *Baldomero Espartero:* 1793–1879; Spanish general, statesman, and politician.

(168) *As a . . . scoundrel:* Don Quijote, I, 28.

(193) *Henri Murger:* (1822–61); French novelist known for his autobiographical novel *Scènes de la vie de Bohème* (the basis of Puccini's opera *La Bohème* [1896] and Leoncavallo's *La Bohème* [1897]).

(203) *The Carlist War:* The Salic Law introduced in Spain in 1713 by Felipe V of the Bourbon line excluded females from the throne. Although it was abrogated as the Pragmatic Sanction by the Cortes [Parliament] in 1789 at the request of Carlos IV, the change was never published nor printed in the collection of laws. The tyrannical Fernando VII, eldest son of Carlos IV, was childless after the death of his first three wives; he married his fourth, María Cristina, 12 December 1829. Several months later, in March of 1830, he decreed the royal Pragmatic Sanction so that Cristina's children, even if female, could succeed to the throne. After his death on 29 September 1833, his brother Carlos (to become known as the Pretender) contested Fernando's will, which provided for Cristina to rule as regent for their two-year-old daughter Isabel. The civil wars that ensued bore his name; the first Carlist War was from 1833 to 1840, the second from 1846 to 1848, and the third (and last) from 1872 to 1876.

(210) *incommunicado:* which would ordinarily have been the case, due to the seriousness of the crime.

Select Bibliography

[Short story collections are marked with an *]

First Editions of Picón's Short Stories and Novels

Lázaro: Casi novela. Madrid: Fernando Fe, 1882.
La hijastra del amor. Madrid: Est. Tip. de El Correo, 1884.
Juan Vulgar. Madrid: Est. Tip. de El Correo, 1885.
El enemigo. Madrid: Est. Tip. de El Correo, 1887.
La honrada. Barcelona: Henrich y Cía., 1890.
Dulce y sabrosa. Madrid: La España Editorial, 1891.
*Novelitas.** Madrid: La España Editorial, 1892.
*Cuentos de mi tiempo.** Madrid: Imprenta de Fortanet, 1895.
*La Vistosa.** Madrid: M. Poveda, 1901.
*Drama de familia.** Valencia: F. Sempere, 1906.
Juanita Tenorio. Madrid: V. Suárez, 1910.
*Mujeres.** Madrid: V. Prieto, 1911.
Sacramento. Madrid: V. Prieto, 1914.
*Desencanto.** Madrid: Renacimiento, 1925.

English Translations of Picón's Short Stories

"After the Battle" ["Después de la batalla"], "The Menace" ["La amenaza"], and "Souls in Contrast" ["Almas distintas"]. Translated by Charles B. MacMichael. In *Short Stories from the Spanish*. New York: Boni and Liveright, 1920.

"A Moral Divorce" ["Divorcio Moral"] and "Tarsila's Ideal" ["El ideal de Trasila"]. Anonymous translation. In *Tales from the Italian and Spanish*. New York: Review of Reviews, 1920.

"Sacrifice" ["Sacrificio"]. Translated by Robert M. Fedorchek. In *Connecticut Review* 13, 1 (1991): 19–23.

Original Spanish Texts of Picón's Short Stories

Cuentos de mi tiempo. Madrid: Imprenta de Fortanet, 1895.
La Vistosa. Madrid: M. Poveda, 1901.
Drama de familia. Valencia: F. Sempere, 1906.
Mujeres. Madrid: Renacimiento, 1916.

Desencanto. Madrid: Renacimiento, 1925.
Novelitas. Madrid: Renacimiento, 1928.

SECONDARY SOURCES

Amezúa y Mayo, Agustín G. de. "Apuntes biográficos de don Jacinto Octavio Picón," en *Obras completas* [*Vida y obras de don Diego Velázquez*] de Jacinto Octavio Picón, pp. vii–xliv. T.X. Madrid: Renacimiento, 1925.

Baquero Goyanes, Mariano. *El cuento español del siglo XIX*, pp. 177–79; 342–43; 385; 422; 614–16; 646–47. Madrid: Consejo Superior de Investigaciones Científicas, 1949. A listing by categories: religious stories, social stories, psychological stories, etc.

Clemessy, Nelly. "Roman et feminisme au XIXème siècle: Le thème de la mal mariée chez Jacinto Octavio Picón." In *Hommage des hispanistes français à Noël Salomon*, pp. 185–98. Barcelona: LAIA, 1979. A perceptive presentation of Picón's views on love, courtship, marriage, and divorce as seen in *La honrada* and *Sacramento*, views that are carried over into his short stories ("The Prudent Woman," "Moral Divorce," "The Overdressed Woman," "Sacrifice").

Gold, Hazel. "Jacinto Octavio Picón: El liberalismo y la novela del siglo XIX." Ph.D. diss., University of Pennsylvania, 1980. *Dissertation Abstracts International* 41, 10 (1981); 4412A.

———. "'Ni soltera, ni viuda, ni casada': Negación y exclusión en las novelas femeninas de Jacinto Octavio Picón." *Ideologies and Literature* 4 (1983): 63–77.

Gutiérrez Díaz-Bernardo, Esteban. "Los cuentos de Jacinto Octavio Picón." Unpublished *Memoria de licenciatura*. Madrid: Universidad Complutense, 1977.

———. "Jacinto Octavio Picón en la crítica coetánea. Aproximación a un narrador olvidado." *Anales del Instituto de Estudios Madrileños* 19 (1982): 253–68.

Mandrell, James. "Forbidden Fruit and the Lessons of Picón's *Dulce y sabrosa*." *Letras peninsulares* 1990; 3, no. 2–3 (1990): 371–87. Revised as "The Psychology of Forbidden Fruit in *Dulce y sabrosa*" in Mandrell's *Don Juan and the Point of Honor*, (University Park: The Pennsylvania State University Press, 1992), pp. 170–93.

Ortiz Picón, Juan Manuel. *Una vida y su entorno (1903–1978). Memorias de un médico con vocación de biólogo*. Granada: Universidad de Granada, 1980. (Memoirs of Don Jacinto Octavio Picón's grandson; discusses his grandfather's ideas, character, and literary and artistic interests.)

Peseux-Richard, Henri. "Un romancier espagnol: Jacinto Octavio Picón." *Revue Hispanique* 30 (1914): 515–85 (especially pp. 525–27 and 530–34).

Rosa, William. "Estudio temático y formal de los cuentos de Jacinto Octavio Picón." Ph.D. diss., Ohio State University, 1984. *Dissertation Abstracts International*, 46, 1 (1985): 165A.

Sáinz de Robles, Federico Carlos. "Aniversario de un gran novelista madrileño: Jacinto Octavio Picón (1852–1923)." *ABC* (Madrid), 18 June 1952.

Sobejano, Gonzalo. Introduction to *Dulce y sabrosa* by Jacinto Octavio Picón. Madrid: Cátedra, 1976.

Valis, Noël M. "Una primera bibliografía de y sobre Jacinto Octavio Picón." *Cuadernos bibliográficos* 40 (1980): 171–209. Annotated—primary and secondary sources—with 715 entries.

———. "Adiciones a una bibliografía de y sobre Jacinto Octavio Picón." *Revista de Literatura* Jan.–June 1985; 47 (93): 165–71.

———. *The Novels of Jacinto Octavio Picón*. Lewisburg, Pa.: Bucknell University Press, 1986. An analysis of Picón's eight novels with copious (and very useful) notes and select bibliography.

———. "The Female Figure and Writing in *Fin de siglo* Spain." *Romance Quarterly*, 36 (1989): 369–81.

———. Introduction to *La hijastra del amor* by Jacinto Octavio Picón. Barcelona: Promociones y Publicaciones Universitarias, 1990.

———. "Más datos biobibliográficos sobre Jacinto Octavio Picón." *Revista de Literatura* 1991 Jan.–June; 53 (105); 213–44.

Zorita, C. Angel. "Lázaro y sus parientes literarios." *Kentucky Romance Quarterly* 35 (1988): 289–98.